Acclaim for Betsy St. Amant

"I'm a Betsy St. Amant fan! Writing with smooth prose and clever metaphors, St. Amant blends truth with swoon-worthy romance. Her characters are vivid and real. *Love Arrives in Pieces* explores the reality of how love and faith fill the cracks of human brokenness, creating a beautiful mosaic worth viewing. Don't miss this book!"

—RACHEL HAUCK, AWARD-WINNING, BESTSELLING AUTHOR
OF *THE WEDDING DRESS* AND THE ROYAL WEDDING SERIES

"With the maturity of someone well beyond her years, Betsy St. Amant pens yet another amazingly sweet story about falling in love. *Love Arrives in Pieces* starts out with a bitter, broken young woman and ends with a strong heroine who literally regains her faith and her life piece by piece. I loved how Stella and Chase found each other again and worked toward the life God had intended for them all along. This story shows that we don't have to wear a tiara in order to find the crown that heals all of us. We are all broken and abstract but with God's help, we can be put back together. I loved *Love Arrives in Pieces*. An indulgence that will hold you captive, page by page!"

—LENORA WORTH, AUTHOR OF *AN APRIL BRIDE*

"St. Amant (*A February Bride*) has written a convincing tale of hope, love, and faith that readers of her popular books and fans of Melody Carlson will enjoy. Those coming to her work for the first time will appreciate the realistic characterizations and the inspirational romance that springs from a longtime friendship."

—*LIBRARY JOURNAL* FOR *ALL'S FAIR IN LOVE AND CUPCAKES*

"Packed full of fun, flavor, and the perfect amount of sassy humor, *All's Fair in Love and Cupcakes* will keep readers turning those pages as quick as can be, and maybe craving a cupcake or two (or three) along the way! Betsy St. Amant's latest is sure to be a favorite among fans of inspirational romance."

—KATIE GANSHERT, AWARD-WINNING AUTHOR
OF *A BROKEN KIND OF BEAUTIFUL*

"Betsy St. Amant has whipped up a romance as yummy as her heroine's cupcakes. A wonderfully fun read from a talented author."

—LIZ JOHNSON, *NEW YORK TIMES* BESTSELLING
AUTHOR ON *ALL'S FAIR IN LOVE AND CUPCAKES*

Other Books by Betsy St. Amant

Love Arrives in Pieces

Betsy St. Amant

ZONDERVAN

Love Arrives in Pieces
Copyright © 2015 by Betsy St. Amant

This title is also available as a Zondervan e-book. Visit www.zondervan.com.

Requests for information should be addressed to:
Zondervan, Grand Rapids, Michigan 49546

Library of Congress Cataloging-in-Publication Data

St. Amant, Betsy.
 Love arrives in pieces / Betsy St. Amant.
  pages ; cm
 ISBN 978-0-310-33847-5 (softcover)
 1. Single men--Fiction. 2. Divorced women--Fiction. 3. Man-woman relationships--
Fiction. I. Title.
 PS3619.T213L69 2015
 813'.6--dc23

                                         2014048149

Interior design: Lori Lynch

Printed in the United States of America

15 16 17 18 19 20 / RRD / 20 19 18 17 16 15 14 13 12 11 10 9 8 7 6 5 4 3 2 1

To Lori, Katie, Anne, Sarah, and Angela—you warred on your knees with me for my marriage. And when it ended anyway, you stood up and helped me gather the broken pieces of my heart. Never has anyone demonstrated being the hands and feet of Jesus like you. From the depths of my heart—thank you.

one

*F*airy tales lied.

Plink. Stella Varland plucked another edible pearl off the glittery periwinkle icing in front of her and let it slip from her fingers onto the counter beside the others. Her cupcake might look like Cinderella's dress, but there was no Prince Charming anywhere in sight. *Plink.*

Nope. He'd straight up turned into a frog.

Plink.

Didn't they all?

"Kat! She's doing it again!" A gravelly voice barked from the other side of the homeless shelter's serving counter, rising above the low din of big band music blasting from an ancient jukebox.

Stella looked up just in time to see Dixie, the shelter's longest-served and arguably favorite patron, leave her conversation with the shelter's director and rush toward her like a linebacker. The throng that had gathered for the Wednesday catered fellowship parted like the Red Sea.

Definitely not her fairy godmother.

"Your sister's wasting the good stuff." Dixie snatched the cupcake from the counter in front of Stella, clutched it like a Louboutin bag on clearance, and deftly stuck her tongue in the center of the peaked icing. Officially claimed.

Stella held up both hands in surrender. "It's all yours, Dixie." The sixty-something-year-old woman was there every time Stella volunteered with Kat, yet for all of the older woman's roughness, she probably had one of the softest hearts in Bayou Bend.

Until it came to sharing anything sugar-coated.

And somehow, the woman always managed to smell like cinnamon.

Stella's older sister, Kat Brannen, sidled up to the counter with a tray of fresh cupcakes from the kitchen. "Stella, I know you've always been one to count calories, but if you're going to just play with my cupcakes, I'd rather you not choose my new fairy tale line."

She set down the tray and adjusted the ties of the pale pink apron cinched around her expectant belly. "I can give you a plain ol' vanilla cupcake to destroy."

Dixie nodded her adamant agreement and licked at the baby blue frosting smeared across her chapped lips.

This wasn't about calories. Once upon a time, it definitely would have been. No, this ran a little deeper. And besides, easy for Kat to say. Her sister had found the proverbial fairy tale. Married her best friend, had a cozy house in the country, and now, after winning a popular reality show called *Cupcake Combat*, was living her dream of owning a cupcake shop—all with a bun in her own oven.

Her sister's success should give her hope, really. And yet . . .

Stella pulled in her lower lip and watched as Dixie picked up a few of the discarded candy pearls and smashed them back onto the cupcake. Life hadn't exactly been a fairy tale for Dixie. So what did that mean? Maybe one shot at love was all anyone really got.

And Stella had apparently chosen very, very wrong.

More than once, actually.

"Is it the pearls? Would you rather try the Snow White one?" Kat pointed at the tray she'd just set down. Red velvet cupcakes perched in dainty rows, topped with fondant apples nestled inside faux crowns. Another masterpiece. When it came to baking, Kat was capable of nothing less.

She really was proud of her sister.

Jealous, maybe, but proud.

"No thanks. Not really hungry." Hadn't been for a few days now, and it wasn't because of the anniversary date on the calendar. Well, maybe a little bit because of that. But she was past the grieving stage.

Some scars just still pinched a little, regardless of the hands ticking away on a clock. Time healed wounds, sure. Maybe not all of them.

Or maybe just not all the way.

Kat frowned. "If you're not hungry, then why'd you ask for a cupcake?"

Stella hadn't asked. Kat had just handed it to her the minute Stella sat down at the serving counter of the shelter, sort of like a bartender sliding a drink to an old regular. But she didn't have to remind her sister of the truth. Pregnancy brain lasted only so long, and from the glimmer in her sister's eye, the pieces were slowly sliding into place.

"Wait a minute." Kat looked at a watch she wasn't wearing, then hiked up her apron and reached into her pocket for her cell.

Yep. Here it came. Stella waited, glancing at the smudged glass door leading out to the street, then sighed. Escape was pointless. Kat might be pregnant, but when on a mission, the girl could haul it. She'd catch her before Stella could even make it to the parking lot.

Which would be pointless, since Stella had left her car at the bakery and ridden with Kat to the shelter across town.

Sigh.

She defaulted instead to dropping the remainder of the edible pearls one by one into the big sugar-cookie candle on the serving counter. The one the homeless shelter director had lit for "ambiance."

It was gonna take a lot more than a candle to light up this place.

"Hold on." Kat tapped the screen and began scrolling through her phone. She was looking for her calendar—Stella knew it as surely as she knew Vaseline on one's teeth made it easier to hold a pageant smile. The whole thing would be humorous, really, if that stupid scar didn't still pull so tight on days like this one.

Stella sucked in a deep breath and released it, slowly, as her counselor had taught her. The room wasn't *actually* getting smaller. Or darker. Emotions were funny things. Powerful things.

Annoying things.

She wanted a hug.

"Today is . . ." Kat scrolled faster, her brow puckered. Dixie peered over her shoulder, smacking.

Three.

Scroll, scroll.

Two.

Kat's fingers stilled.

One.

"Ah." Kat's lips twisted to the side as she slid her phone back into her pocket. "One year since your divorce was final."

The music stopped in unison with her words. Silence fell over the shelter, the kind of quiet that smothers instead of warms. Like a scratchy wool blanket you'd rather just shuck off in the middle of the night.

The silence began to hurt her ears. Stella shifted on her chair, wishing she'd stayed home instead of taking the "stay busy by volunteering and helping others" route her counselor had drilled into her. Hence her involvement with the shelter in general.

But tonight . . . she should have passed. Should have hidden herself in her art studio or maybe gotten back to the long-ignored punching bag in the gym, the one she used to totally own when getting in shape for pageants. *Something*, be it physical or creative, to release this tension that had been building for days.

Yet, as her late Aunt Maggie used to say, wishes weren't horses, and nobody was riding away today. Time to deal.

"It's okay. I'm fine." Really, she was. She avoided Dixie's steady stare, the one that sprang up from some deep place where angels visited and prophecies were revealed. The older woman might be homeless, though many rumored it was by choice. And she might be half off her rocker, as Aunt Maggie would say. But the woman *knew* things.

Some called it insight. Some called it a gift.

Stella just called it mind-your-own-business.

She dared to meet the woman's gaze, partly because of the manners her southern mama had embedded in both her and Kat, and partly out of morbid curiosity. What if Dixie really did have a prophetic word for her? What if somehow God did reveal His plan for Stella through the mouth of a half-crazy old lady? At this point, she should probably take what she could get, because she'd been frozen in the in-between long enough. Fairy tales might lie, but the facts didn't, and the simple truth remained that if Stella didn't land another interior decorating job soon, she'd be scrubbing her mother's kitchen floors without a single mouse or bird to help.

Some princesses had all the luck.

Needless to say, she could stand some direction at the moment.

Frustration whittled down to a sliver of hope. Dixie's eyes drilled hard back into hers, as if dissecting Stella's soul, as if she could see straight through the past few years riddled with wedding albums and smeared mascara and cell phones lighting up with other women's phone numbers. Of pageant smiles and sweaty gym clothes and unacceptable numbers flashing on a scale's digital screen.

Of voices hoarse from yelling and court gavels slamming and canvases laced with angry red paint.

As if maybe she had an answer.

"HOWARD!"

Stella jumped, nearly sliding off her chair, as Dixie bellowed full-steam without even remotely shifting her gaze away from her.

"We need another song. This place is like a cemetery." Dixie finally looked away, over the shoulder of the thin blazer she wore year round, the one with the hole in the elbow and the patchwork floral print that had long since faded from crimson to blush pink. "I ain't dead yet."

Dixie's buddy, the man she swore she wasn't involved with but who was the first to jump to her every command, hitched his fingers in the straps of his overalls and grinned through his gray speckled beard. "What's your pleasure, darlin'?" He nudged the bottom of the jukebox that a well-meaning local business had donated to the shelter four months ago. Didn't even require quarters.

Stella turned pleading eyes to Kat, who just shrugged and grinned as she continued setting out her gourmet cupcakes on napkins for the line starting to form behind Dixie. At least once the music started, everyone could quit staring at her. And quit whispering.

Isn't that Kat's sister? That pageant queen that got divorced a while back?

Such a shame. So much beauty and yet . . .

Bet Pastor Varland never saw that one coming. PKs aren't supposed to get divorced.

She'd heard it all.

Dixie clasped her hands against her chest, her expression nearly reverent as she flitted toward Howard. "Elvis. 'Heartbreak Hotel.'"

Oh, for the love . . .

Stella buried her face in her hands. Why hadn't she driven her own car? She'd volunteered these last few months with Kat, and this kind of drama had never been an issue before now.

What was *in* those cupcakes?

"Stella." Kat's whisper in her ear made her grunt but not look up. She wasn't coming out. No way. Denial was her only chance. She sank lower on the counter and shoved her face into her elbows. Was the room spinning again?

She wanted to paint. Wanted to slap acrylic across a canvas and watch the bare become beautiful. See white morph into color. Get proof that something could still be made from nothing. God had done that once, with creation.

She wanted it for her heart.

The shelter door squeaked open, and a warm breeze drifted across Stella's neck. She hadn't even bothered to dry her hair completely before meeting Kat, just thrown it up in a forget-about-it clip. Getting ready sure did take a lot less time when you didn't worry about hair or makeup anymore. She used to waste so much energy on that stuff. On clothes. On tanning creams and waxing and all things appearance-related.

Pretty was a moot point now. Hence her plain thermal top and baggy jeans.

Pretty wasn't enough.

Pretty played her for a fool.

"Stella." Kat's whisper turned urgent. "I hate to say this. But what would be one way to make this evening even more terrible for you?"

"Tornado?" She kept her head down, mumbling the words into her folded arms.

"Worse."

"Land shark?"

"You're getting warmer."

Perfect. Stella looked up with resignation. "Hi, Mom." She smiled wide, showing all her teeth, a skill she'd perfected on stage at pageants when waiting for the judge's decision. Cool detachment.

Had perfected it even further after Dillon left.

"Why were you lying on the counter, Stella?" Disapproval flew before Claire Varland like a banner over royalty. She ran a manicured finger over the scratched wooden surface and made a show of checking it. "Pageant queens don't—"

"I'm not a pageant queen, Mother." Same argument, different day. Stella had left that lifestyle behind years ago, after Dillon had proposed, choosing to pursue interior design instead. It'd been a way to experiment with art from behind the safety of a degree—a smokescreen, really, since her heart pulsed with the need to paint. Sketch. Draw.

With interior design, she could play around with color and texture while keeping her personal projects out of the spotlight—safe.

Mom twisted her lips to the side in the way that Kat did. "Once a queen, always a queen."

No. Those sashes were long since retired. Stella looked to Kat for help, but Kat just peeled the wrapper off another cupcake and rested an elbow on the counter as if gearing up for a show. Some big sister.

Mom never knew when to quit. "You don't compete in pageants anymore, but you're still a winner, Stella. It still happened."

True. She had the tiaras and the dried bouquets to prove it. But maybe Stella didn't want to remember. Maybe she'd rather forget all of it.

But then she'd disappear in her mother's sight completely.

Mama pointedly wiped her hands with a napkin and blessedly changed the subject. "Still no job offers yet?"

Well. Not a *better* subject.

"What are you doing here, Mom?" Kat jumped straight to the point, a new trait that Stella still had trouble getting used to. Marrying Lucas had definitely brought out her sister's sense of confidence and independence.

The pregnancy hormones probably took care of the rest.

No doubt about it, Kat had come a long way since her insecure days with her ex, Chase. The guy who'd broken her heart years ago before Lucas claimed it for his own.

The one who'd broken a piece of Stella's too.

That secret still weighed heavy. She shifted in her seat, focusing back on her mother. One crisis at a time.

"Yeah, Mama, you didn't come down to the shelter to find me and ask about a job. What's going on?" Not that her parents didn't have legit reason to be overly interested in Stella's career, seeing how if something didn't change soon, Stella would be right back living with them. As if she wasn't twenty-five years old and divorced. As if she didn't already have enough labels to fight.

"Regardless of whether I did or not, you still need a job." Her mother looked for a place to discard the tainted napkin. "But you know you're welcome to stay with us if nothing turns up."

More like, *You're welcome to stay with us and let us control the rest of your life since you've messed it up doing it on your own so far.* Mom meant well, but she didn't have to actually say the words for them to linger in the air.

No thanks. Stella would rather stay at the shelter. Besides, Daddy had already handled her legal fees. She was done depending on her parents like a college kid. "I know, Mama. It's okay, rent is just a little late. Apparently Louisiana isn't interested in color swatches and throw pillows right now."

"Come on, you do more than decorate people's living rooms. You did that big job for that office complex over in Texas last summer." Kat finally spoke up, swatting at Stella's arm. "You have a great portfolio. Something will turn up."

But what if it didn't? What if she really ran out of options? Stella's stomach twisted. Her parents hadn't saved years' worth of a preacher's salary to finally get their forever house and then be expected to support their grown daughter. Dillon had promised before God and Daddy to do that, instead. It wasn't their fault he had commitment issues.

And a penchant for redheads.

Besides, she couldn't bring herself to ask Mama for anything after coming across that file the other day in their home office when scrounging for a pen, the file that held a copy of her divorce papers. She'd left them there when she'd come home after the divorce, then couldn't bring herself to take them into her new apartment— her sanctuary, that was all hers, with no shadowy reminders of the past.

The part that galled her the most was that the file was simply labeled STELLA. It looked funny, minus the last name she'd had for the past two years. Incomplete. Like she was nothing more now than a tidy label, something else for her mom to organize and keep straight.

Too bad a glossy sticker couldn't package up the turmoil of the past two years—much as her mother had tried.

Mom crossed her arms over her chest, then thought better of it and smoothed out the wrinkles she'd created in the material. "Kat's right. Something will turn up."

The repetition of the vague sentiment didn't do much to lift her hopes. How many times had she said the same things to Dillon in an attempt to convince him to stay?

First, the initial round of questions. *What do you need? What can I change? What can I do?*

Nothing.

Not. A. Thing.

Then came the desperate bribes and promises. *Go ahead and buy that new truck you've been wanting. I've cooked your favorite dinner tonight. Why don't you go out with the guys later, blow off some steam . . .*

He'd blown off steam, all right. But not with the guys.

"Anyway, of course I didn't come down here to quiz you on your job options. I just got out of a meeting with the Junior League committee, and I've brought you something." Mama dug in the oversized purse on her arm, the one that could house a litter of Chihuahuas but instead carried her mother's entire life. Right down to the day planner penciled in perfect cursive. Stella used to joke that Claire Varland didn't organize, rather, organization Claire *Varlanded.*

She handed over the creased papers she'd pulled from her purse, which Stella recognized from the heading as the court documents finalizing the divorce. Ones she'd seen a hundred times. It was a thicker stack than usual, though. She thumbed through to the back pages.

The initial filings, when she was served.

That arrow found its mark. She let out a sharp breath.

"Mom! Why would you bring those?" Kat tried to tug them away, but Stella clenched them tight.

"No, it's okay. I'm fine." *Lies.* Pageant smile fixed firmly in place, Stella set the papers on the counter, knowing her sister wouldn't see through the mask. Sort of like when Stella was trained to give the right answer on stage for the judges.

"What do you most long for, Stella Varland?"

Shoulders back. Eye contact. Show all your teeth. "World peace, of course."

Man, she'd have a different answer today.

Mama shrugged. "I thought these needed some attention. You've been mopey lately."

"Attention?" Stella raised her eyebrows, a hundred snarky comments begging to leave her tongue. Those papers didn't need *any* more attention—the words were already forever burned in her memory. Kat had always been the smart one in the family when it came to school and memorizing, yet Stella could quote the legal documents line for line. Probably because of how many times she'd pored over the text, searching for answers that now she realized even Dillon didn't have.

"Wait a minute. She didn't say positive attention." Kat picked up the top page and held the corner close to the dancing flame of the candle between them. Dangerously close.

Totally not close enough.

Stella grinned, snatched the sheet from her sister's grip, and dipped the corner into the hungry flame. It quickly devoured the corner, spreading black ash up the page, the text smearing and burning and disappearing before the flicker snuffed out.

"Girls." Their mother's disapproval was sharp and so expected it felt cliché. She pinned her stare—the same one she used to get her way with various committees, church teams, and even the mayor—on Stella and Kat. "That's not what I meant. You're a grown woman, Stella. And a pageant queen. Pageant queens don't play with fire."

Actually, that was about all Stella had ever done; she just hadn't realized it until this moment. A flash of memory—of

Chase—suddenly jabbed into her, and she shook herself free of the image. Not here. Not now.

Definitely not in front of her sister.

Kat handed a cupcake to a man in ripped jeans who smelled like a car's pine air freshener, then took a big bite of a Snow White cake. "Then what exactly *did* you mean, Mama?"

Great question. Stella waited, papers dangling from her fingers.

Claire reached for a cupcake, too, then apparently changed her mind. Stella got her calorie-counting practice honest. "It's high time Stella realizes the past is the past. This is an anniversary worth noting but not worth grieving over."

She still hated that word. Probably because the voices still hadn't died completely. *You have to grieve, Stella. Don't fight the grief, Stella. Grieve it out, Stella.*

Grieve. Right. In the immediate months after Dillon left, everyone in her narrow circle of friends and family had encouraged her to vent. Process. Feel. But then it got old. They never said so, of course, they didn't have to. It was in their eyes. No, her family was much too proper and polite to ever say something so honest and raw. "Chin up, Princess," her daddy said instead. "Don't let the frogs get you down."

But then one day, their gazes turned from compassionate to frustrated. As if they wanted to shout, "Aren't you over this by now?"

Maybe if they *had* said what they were thinking . . . maybe if just *one* time Mama had actually said what she was thinking instead of constantly running her magic vacuum cleaner over the messiness of life, they all could have felt a little better.

Some things couldn't be organized or cleaned up.

Sometimes a princess just needed to sit in the dirt.

"We should celebrate, really." Mama looked back at the cupcake she'd rejected and picked it up, raising it in Stella's direction like a toast. "To fresh starts."

Kat nudged another frosted dessert closer toward Stella. "Not a bad idea, sis. You're one year free and clear. Think of it that way."

The room shrank another a few inches. No, she wasn't grieving anymore. Yet she wasn't ready to celebrate, either. Celebrate what? The fact that her marriage had failed? That she had failed?

Everyone knew Dillon had failed.

But what category did that leave her in? A marriage took two.

No, she was trapped in the barren land between grief and celebration. Mourning and joy. This vast emotional wasteland was perhaps even darker than the initial shock of separation. This was numbing and indefinite.

"Celebrate with us." Mama took a bite of cupcake, wiping crumbs from her lip and somehow miraculously managing to keep her lipstick intact. As if even the cake knew its proper place in her presence.

Celebrate?

Maybe.

But not with cake.

Slowly, Stella sucked in a deep breath and fingered the edge of the papers. She held them a little closer to the flame, wishing she had it in her to just let them burn.

Maybe destroying them would finish healing her.

Only one way to know.

She unfolded the papers and held a corner steadily in the flame, until the entire stack ignited.

"Stella!" Mama gasped and jerked away from the counter as smoke billowed from the pile, now rapidly turning to ash and dust. Kat shrieked and grabbed the cupcakes, moving them away from the flames.

Mama flapped her hands like a bird attempting flight. "Water! We need water over here!"

Stella stared at the flames licking higher, devouring her past, orange and yellow light swallowing the memories whole. Forget cupcakes. *This* was a celebration.

The director rushed to the counter just as Kat filled a pitcher with water from the sink and doused the black charred papers. A whiff of burned sugar cookie aroma wafted in their direction, and then it was over.

They all looked at each other in relief.

Until the smoke alarms blared, and the automatic sprinkler system turned on.

Water sprayed like a shower from above, seeping into Stella's skin. Chaos erupted, shouts mingling with laughter and cries of outrage.

She tilted her face to the makeshift rain, letting it wash the rest of the last year away. Fresh start, wasn't that what Mama had said? *Cheers.*

"Stella Varland!" Claire shouted over the din of the water and the raucous response of the shelter's patrons. She held her giant purse over her head and tottered toward the door in her high heels. "That was completely unnecessary!"

Probably. But seeing her mother dripping in her best pantsuit made it a little worth it.

The man who'd just gotten his cupcake from Kat shoved the

entire thing in his mouth with a wide smile and extended his arms wide. "Free showers, everyone!"

A mob descended on the counter, snatching the leftover cupcakes before they completely soaked through.

"Everyone out!" The shelter's director began waving her arms, directing everyone to the door. "Single file. No one panic, the fire is out."

One by one, the crowd shuffled through the front doors after Claire, Kat bringing up the rear, her apron clinging to her drenched basketball belly. "Stella, come on. We can't stay here."

Stella caught the door behind her sister and looked back once more into the dripping chaos she'd created. The last thing she saw before the door silently closed behind her was Dixie and Howard.

Dancing to "Heartbreak Hotel" as water rained around them.

two

Stella Varland had made the newspaper again.

Except this time, the headline didn't announce yet another pageant win.

Chase Taylor couldn't help but grin at the grainy image spread across his cousin's kitchen table. It didn't take a lot to land the front page in Bayou Bend, but setting fire to a homeless shelter would definitely do the trick.

Stella stared back at him from the newspaper, mouth open as she protested—what? The photo?—adamantly to the camera. She looked good. But what did he expect? She couldn't help it.

Beside her in the picture, her sister Kat stood beside a woman who the caption identified as the shelter's director, Nancy Martin. And one Kat Varland had apparently become Kat Brannen.

Chase set the paper down, mind racing. And his heartbeat, too, if he was honest. Brannen . . . wasn't that Kat's BFF from back in the day? Luke—no, Lucas. That's right. The football coach. Wow, times changed. He shook his head. Good for Kat.

That would make his homecoming to Bayou Bend slightly less complicated.

A familiar pang of regret over the way he treated Kat rose unbidden in his stomach. It had been years ago, another lifetime, practically, since their relationship, but still. He'd done her wrong.

It was just that Stella . . .

No. No more regrets. He was done with all of that. He'd buried a giant regret in that polished oak coffin with his fiancée last fall, and that would be the last regret he ever had.

He tried to drown the rush of memory with a swallow of black coffee, and nearly spit it out. "Dude, did this even brew? It's like a solid."

His cousin, firefighter Ethan Ryland, joined him at the kitchen table, crunching a piece of bacon. "Hey, I just make it the way Chap makes it."

He narrowed his eyes. "Chap?"

"Chaplain. Darren Phillips, at the station."

Chase peered into his mug at the sludge posing as liquid caffeine. "Tell him his methods could use some prayer coverage."

"Watch it, now. Are you really complaining about staying somewhere for free?" Ethan slid into the chair across from Chase, grinning around his bacon. "I can turn all the cooking over to you, man. Or better yet, just let you go hang out with your folks." He wiggled his eyebrows at the threat.

"Think I'd rather bathe in that coffee." Chase stood and took his mug to the sink, briefly debating pouring it down the drain or into the garbage disposal. He opted for the disposal and flipped the switch. He raised his voice over the sudden gargle of the machine. "And I told you I'd pay you half the rent after my first check."

"I'm messing with you." Ethan rocked his chair back on two legs and reached up to adjust the brim of his navy department cap. "I'm only here every other twenty-four hours, anyway. Could stand a roomie for a while."

The two-bedroom apartment with his buddy beat crashing indefinitely at his parents' place, anytime. He'd find his own place, eventually—assuming he decided to put down roots in Bayou Bend again. That was still undecided. Chase loved his family—they were half the reason he'd moved back to Bayou Bend from Houston after Leah's death. The job being the other half. He'd been torn for months over what to do and where to go after her passing, so when the job opened up for a contractor to renovate Bayou Bend's old run-down theater, well, he decided that was sign enough.

He'd wrangled a lease-to-own deal on his house in Texas, packed up, and moved back home within three days. He started work tomorrow.

"I'm glad I'm back." Mostly. No—completely. He squared his shoulders. He needed to own his decisions. Life was wasted on the indecisive. If Leah's untimely death had taught him anything, it was that life was too short to do anything halfway or half-hearted.

Go big or go home.

In his case, it happened to be both. Literally.

"And just in time for our ten-year reunion next year." Ethan made a show of checking his watch. "Who knows. Maybe we'll actually find dates by then."

Chase cringed before he could hide it, and Ethan threw both hands in the air, bacon skittering across the table. "Whoa, sorry, dude. I forgot. I mean, I didn't forget. I just wasn't—you know. I mean, I haven't ever—"

"Don't worry about it." Honest mistake. The reminder of his singleness and loss didn't sting quite as bad as it had last month. Or the month before that. What was the saying about time healing wounds? He had always figured it was a bunch of garbage, but maybe it had its merits.

In Chase's case, time didn't necessarily heal so much as motivate. Since Leah's death, he'd run his first mud 10k, mountain climbed in Arizona, tried his hand at surfing the Pacific, and mailed his nephews custom-made paintball guns. Time was of the essence—not to heal, but to fulfill. He had to move, and move quickly, because time was always running out.

And there'd be no more regrets.

Ethan stared at him, the familiar angst-filled expression of a guy with his foot stuck permanently in his mouth. "Dude."

It was almost comical at this point. "Seriously, it's okay."

Besides, it wasn't the first time someone spoke before they thought, and it wouldn't be the last. Chase didn't want people censoring themselves around him, anyway. Part of the beauty of moving to Bayou Bend was leaving Houston and all of his and Leah's mutual friends behind—the ones who brought him homemade lasagna and unidentifiable casseroles after the accident, and put him on their church prayer lists, and couldn't look him in the eyes without glancing away.

He was done with the label of "Leah's fiancé" and "the guy who was engaged to that girl on the news." Even now, the memories persisted. Flames roiling from the hood of her car. Pavement smeared with smoke and ash. The clank of the gurney being lifted into the ambulance . . .

No, he couldn't walk in that identity anymore, not if he wanted a glimpse of a future. Yet staying in Houston left him little room to skirt the shadows.

Besides, he'd missed enough of his nephews' young lives. And his dad could stand to go fishing with him . . . it was time. Time for a new chapter. Time to move forward and not look back.

Leah wouldn't stand for him living in the past, anyway. She'd kick his tail and tell him to man up and get a move on, already.

He forced a smile at Ethan. The only way around the awkward was straight through. "Can't guarantee either of us having a date, buddy. But I can guarantee I'll look sharper than you."

"In your dreams." Relief flooded Ethan's face, the same relief that always came over those who blundered in some way about Leah's death. He'd gotten used to giving that grace. It was almost second nature now.

Almost.

"If you want a date, you better start shopping now. You only have ten months." Chase nabbed the last piece of bacon, hating the way Stella's picture in the newspaper kept popping into his thoughts every time either of them said the word *date*. Like that would ever happen, again, for about thirty different reasons. She was probably married, anyway.

Though her name in the photo caption had read, Varland.

He shoved the entire piece of bacon in his mouth. It didn't matter. That chapter, however short-lived it had been, was closed, and Chase had no interest in rereading old pages. His vision was cast forward, and at this point?

He doubted any woman could keep up, anyway.

 celes

Stella dabbed a touch of baby blue paint carefully on her canvas, already smeared with streaks of aqua and cerulean, and wondered if she should give up on the attempted sky and just call the thing abstract art instead.

She swirled her brush in the water, cleansing the bristles and watching the water tint blue, and snorted. If her former pageant friends could see her now: Living in a rented duplex that would have technically been a studio apartment, except for the small room at the back corner of the living area that happened to boast a tiny window and an interior door. Painting, of all things. Painting as if she actually had talent, at that. As if she believed she was something more than she was.

Fantasy.

The nook had just enough room for an easel, a stool, and a skinny end table she used as a workbench for her more adventurous artistic attempts. Stella had claimed it for her own studio—an art studio.

And just shut the door when anyone stopped by.

Which, to be honest, wasn't all that often.

The sky on the canvas seemed to mirror her irritation. Frustration built the longer she studied the painting. It didn't look like the beautiful, clear sky that had initially inspired her this morning when she'd stepped outside with her coffee to get the mail. It didn't look like anything.

A big, fat nothing.

Stella stabbed her brush into the jar of red paint and smeared it across the entire canvas. There. Failure complete. She dropped the dripping brush into a plastic cup of water, stood, and shoved away from her stool. Some days she wondered why she tried.

Then other days . . .

Her eye caught the one canvas she'd actually deemed decent enough to hang on her studio wall, and shook her head. Irony at its finest. A portrait of a princess, pastel ball gown swirling around her legs, one lean arm curled up over her heart as if caught by surprise. Her expression was concealed by blonde ringlets as she spun toward a faceless figure in a white suit.

The fairy tale.

Why was it so stuffy in here? She wrestled open the window and let in a wave of sticky, humid summer air. Sun streamed through the leaf-dotted limbs across the street and played across her cheeks. She closed her eyes against the afternoon light and breathed in the warmth. Breathed in peace.

Joy?

No. That was asking too much.

She'd be happy with peace.

Well, on second thought, she'd just be happy if she *hadn't* made the newspaper. That would have been fun to wake up to. She rubbed the pinched space between her eyebrows and bit back a groan. Rested her head against the warm window pane . . .

And watched her mother slam her car door from a parking spot on the street.

Mama stepped carefully across the grass, a folded newspaper under her arm. The emerald stalks appeared to salute as she passed, as if even they knew better than to slouch in Claire Varland's presence, even in the humid Louisiana heat. Had she really come all this way just to show Stella the newspaper?

She'd seen it all right—and received about a dozen texts about it in the past six hours too. Including those from her sister, who had started cracking herself up.

Hey sis. What's black, white & red all over? U in the newspaper!

Can I have ur autograph?

If U were ready to leave that night, u could have just said so.

Guess smokey the bear forgot to mention u as a disclaimer.

Mama disappeared from view as she rounded the corner to the front door. Yeah, so not in the mood for this. What would happen if she just didn't answer the door? Did Mama still have the key Stella had given her in the early days after her separation?

Probably. Knowing her, she'd made a dozen copies and had them stashed in various convenient places.

No one escaped Mama.

The doorbell rang, followed by a knock.

No one ignored Mama.

Stella checked her fingers for signs of paint, then shut the studio door and headed for the front door, trying not to look over her shoulder at her secret. She wasn't ready for anyone to know it. Not now.

Maybe not ever.

It was one of the only things left that was truly and completely hers.

Mama bustled inside the second she twisted the deadbolt. "I have good news."

Definitely wasn't talking about the newspaper headline, then. Stella stepped aside, not in invitation but simply to avoid getting run over. "Define *good*."

This should be interesting. But whatever distracted her mom away from the topic of the fire worked for her. She couldn't handle the lecture. Could hear it now in her head. *Pageant queens don't set fire to homeless shelters, Stella.*

Maybe she could avoid the inevitable a little longer. Get some sanity back first. "Want some coffee?"

"It's three in the afternoon!" Claire said with the same disdain and shock as if Stella had offered her hard liquor at 9:00 a.m.

"Fine. Coffee for one, then." Too much caffeine was a concept she had never understood. Stella made her way to the tiny kitchen area and fumbled around for a Keurig cup. One of the only things she'd insisted on keeping after the divorce. It'd been her companion for more than one sleepless night after Dillon left.

And more than one sleepless night, fighting away dreams of Chase.

Or maybe those had been nightmares.

Her mom settled onto a bar stool Stella had recovered in coral fabric, smoothing the pleats of her dress pants. "The mayor and I had lunch yesterday."

"That's the good news?" Stella grabbed a mug from the cabinet, her favorite one with turquoise polka dots, and stuck it under the drip as the coffeemaker bubbled to life.

Her mother ignored her, as Stella expected. "We were discussing some of the events I intended to bring up at the Junior League committee meeting." She sniffed. "You know, the one I went to right before coming to the homeless shelter last night."

Here came the fire comment. She knew her mom would be unable to dodge it completely. After all, Kat and Stella got their sarcasm honestly. They just owned theirs, while their mom tried to hide it under the pressed and pleated façade. Daddy missed sarcasm completely. Flew right over his balding head.

"Thankfully we had this discussion yesterday, before the incident."

Incident? She turned her back so her mom wouldn't see her roll her eyes. Smoke detectors went off and turned on a sprinkler system. It wasn't as if the building had become engulfed in flames.

Though the shelter would be down for a few days while they dried it out.

She bit her lip as the coffee dripped into her cup. Where would everyone go? That part still made Stella sick. She was never impulsive these days. What had possessed her to do that? Flighty and self-oriented was her MO of the past. She wasn't the same woman she'd been onstage at pageants. That tiara only fit a big head.

Hers had shrunk right down to where it belonged.

"Anyway, the mayor mentioned he had granted the Downtown Development Committee the budget to finally restore the old theater."

Stella turned back around. "The Downtown Development Committee? Bayou Bend has one of those?"

"It's new. Formed about six months ago."

She picked up her warm mug from the Keurig and smirked. "Wait—there's a committee in Bayou Bend that you're not on?"

Now it was her mom's turn to roll her eyes. "Very funny, Stella. What's wrong with getting involved, anyway? It might do you some good these days."

"You do recall that the last time I volunteered I made the front page of the paper?" She blew on her coffee as steam spiraled into her face. Maybe the "incident" could work in her favor for once. She had no desire to follow in her mother's shadow and flit from committee to committee. She loved Bayou Bend, but that didn't mean she wanted to control it.

That was her mom's specialty.

"Stop interrupting. I'm trying to get to the good news." Claire shifted on her bar stool, her expression not nearly as annoyed as her words sounded. In fact, she almost looked the way Kat did when she knew a secret and wasn't ready to tell.

Did she even want to know?

"Go ahead, Mom." She braced herself for the unknown and took a sip of coffee. Maybe the mayor had asked her mother to head yet another team. Maybe she was about to take over downtown. Or the world at large.

Maybe Mom was about to run for mayor herself.

"I got you a job."

Stella sprayed coffee on the counter.

"Stella Varland." Now the annoyance in her tone matched her features. "Pageant queens do *not*—"

"What job?" She grabbed a napkin from the dispenser by the sink. How had they gone from talking about the mayor and some random committee to Stella having a job? A job her mother secured for her . . . through the mayor? Was she about to become a committee hopper after all?

She tried to clean up the spill as her mom rambled on.

"I told you. The Downtown Development Committee has a budget now to restore the old theater on Ninth Street. They've been campaigning for the cause since they formed, and before that, Marcie Jenkins went on a yearlong tangent to get it done but couldn't get the funding."

The Ninth Cameo Theater had been shut down most of Stella's life. She remembered vaguely going to see a few plays as a young child, sitting on the end of the aisle next to Kat, swinging her Sunday-shoe-clad feet and hating the way the wooden seats bit into the back of her knees.

"They've hired some contractor from Texas. I didn't get his name." Mom waved her hand, as if the actual reconstruction of the theater wasn't of any importance. "But three guesses who the interior designer will be?"

And the first two didn't count. "Me?"

"Exactly." Mom folded her hands on the countertop, leaning forward and practically beaming over her good deed.

Mixed feelings roiled in Stella's stomach. Was she such a charity case now she couldn't even find her own jobs? But this would be a good one . . . and it'd be fun. Definitely a change from the typical residential designing she could do with her eyes closed. Maybe a challenge was what she needed to get inspired again for her own artwork. Not to mention it would build her portfolio toward future jobs.

Claire took the napkin Stella had abandoned and finished wiping the coffee drips from the Formica. "They've gotten approval to pay for the whole works. It'll be like new again."

Like new again . . . now that was a concept. If only.

But Stella wasn't getting anywhere hiding in her apartment, waiting to get evicted and creating unsightly works of art. Something had to change.

And this would be it. She took a deep breath. "Okay. I'll do it."

Her mom raised a perfectly groomed eyebrow. "Of course you will. I already accepted for you. You meet with the contractor tomorrow."

three

The Ninth Cameo loomed over Stella's head like a ghost—a ghost who didn't particularly care to come back to life. Shutters, once painted gold, slumped on their tired hinges. Every window had broken panes, while the giant marquee sign, once sparkling white, couldn't muster more than a dingy tan sigh. The ripped awning leading to the gilded front doors flapped in the early morning wind.

A warning? A cry for help?

The entire structure seemed to shudder.

She had her work cut out for her. Yet a tiny spark of inspiration ignited inside, and she closed her eyes against the breeze, letting the summer sun warm her bare arms. She hitched her purse higher on her shoulder and breathed in the potential of the building, picturing gold and black décor, maybe with subtle red accents. Something classic, vintage. Something to restore the Ninth Cameo to its original glory.

That too-familiar, bittersweet ache tugged in her heart, and she quickly opened her eyes. This was about the theater. Not her past. And definitely not her future.

Some things couldn't be restored.

She carefully made her way up the cracked sidewalk to the front doors and slipped inside. She struggled to take a full breath of the humid air and winced as the silence of the theater confirmed her earlier feelings of ghosts at rest. Where was the contractor? He was supposed to meet her—and the Downtown Development Director—at eight o'clock. It was now ten after. Her daydreaming outside might have cost her a good first impression.

Unless they weren't here yet. But the door had been unlocked, so surely . . .

She resisted the urge to tiptoe across the stained, tattered burgundy carpet of the lobby. Ridiculous. Either she was the only one here, or the men were nearby, ready to get to business. Either way, there was no need for hiding. It was just . . . something was different here. She'd been in vacant buildings before, buildings long deserted and forgotten. Buildings like this one.

Except this one still had a voice.

She just couldn't hear it yet.

She paused at the concession stand, running her fingers along the dusty wood. The high counter seemed in good enough shape. Wouldn't take more than a quick sand and finish job.

She turned a slow circle. Giant frames, empty of their movie posters, hung bare on the lobby walls. Sagging velvet ropes on golden stands still lined the hallway, eager to form crowds waiting for quality entertainment.

Maybe this ghost of a place was a little more eager to live again than she'd first thought.

"Hello?" Stella called out as loudly as she dared. Raising her voice in such a tomb felt irreverent. The hairs on her arm prickled, and in spite of the heat she fought back a shiver. "Anyone here?"

"There she is!" A loud, twangy male voice echoed across the lobby.

Stella jumped, clutching one hand to her heart and nearly dropping her purse on the carpet. She spun around, purse swinging wildly from her arm—until it connected with a solid thump.

"Oomph." The second figure bent over double, holding his stomach. Sandy brown hair filled her peripheral vision.

"You okay there, little lady?" The owner of the booming voice, wearing cowboy boots and a studded belt, let out a laugh as big as his waistline, startling her again. She spun the other direction, her purse once again slamming into the second man. He ducked a moment too late.

"I am *so* sorry." Was this really happening? A rush of heat flared up her neck. Apparently being a few minutes late wasn't the sum of her negative first impression today. "You scared me." She struggled to get her purse under control as her poor victim stood and her adrenaline slowed.

And then spiked.

"Chase?" Chase Taylor. In living flesh.

What?

How?

"Stella?" His blue eyes widened. Either he was still an expert at hiding the truth, or he really was just as shocked to see her as she was him. Talk about ghosts from the past.

She blinked, but the man before her didn't fade away. He was still there, still right there before her in faded jeans and a black

T-shirt stretched tight against toned muscles. The fact that he hadn't gotten any less handsome over the years only made her angrier. "What are you doing here?" She wasn't nearly as sorry about her purse now.

Make that not even a little sorry.

Make that she wished she had put some bricks in her purse this morning.

"Well, now. It looks like you two don't need an introduction." The paunchy middle-aged cowboy held out his hand to Stella. "But I believe we do. Ma'am, I'm the newly appointed Downtown Development Director, Bob Erickson." He grinned. "I know your mama."

Didn't everyone.

Stella glanced at Chase. His eyebrows lifted at Bob's comment, but to his credit, he didn't say anything. Maybe just overwhelmed by the sheer number of sarcastic responses he had to choose from. She tried to put a confidence she didn't feel into her handshake. "Stella Varland."

"Right. Our interior designer on the project." He released her palm and clapped a beefy hand on her shoulder instead as he turned to include Chase in the conversation. "This gal comes highly recommended."

Like that would impress Chase. Like she even cared if it did.

Why was he here, again?

"And so does Chase. All the way from Texas." Bob hitched his thumbs in his belt and rocked back on the heels of his boots.

"Texas. Wait. *You're* the contractor on the project?" Understanding dawned, followed by a shockwave of protest.

He nodded. "Contractor and foreman, actually."

"But—"

"But what?" Chase turned those lifted brows on her now, and she swallowed back everything she longed to say. Had wanted to say for years.

Not in front of Cowboy Bob.

She tried again, praying the truth wouldn't erupt from her lips unbidden. "I was just going to say that's quite the commute."

"Nonsense!" Stella jerked again. Bob's voice could have scared a pretzel straight. "He's done up and moved back home to Bayou Bend."

Moved. Back.

An instant headache began throbbing. Stella reached up automatically, as if she could touch it. As if she could make any of this madness just go away. How could this day have started out so normal? If the sun rose and birds chirped, Chase Taylor was not supposed to be living back in Bayou Bend. That would have called for a hurricane. Tornado. Some form of natural disaster.

Bob's beaming smile morphed slowly into one of slight confusion. "So how do you two know each other, exactly?"

The panic in Chase's eyes mirrored the panic in Stella's racing heart. The truth was definitely not called for right now. At least not the entire truth. Her mouth dried and her palms grew slick.

"Old family friend."

"He dated my sister."

They spoke at the same time, looked at each other, and then back at Bob.

"He meant we were friends."

"She meant I'm old friends with her sister."

Bob's bushy eyebrows furrowed into a caterpillar of gray. "Right, then."

Cue crickets.

Chase broke the awkward silence by gesturing toward the double doors leading from the lobby into the theater. "Have you seen the inside of the theater yet?"

Stella shook her head. The fact that she needed this job was the only thing keeping her feet on the floor at the moment instead of racing out of the place in midair like some cartoon character.

And the vision of her mother's face when she learned Chase Taylor was the contractor she hadn't bothered to learn about. That would be priceless.

"Come on, then." Bob led the way, and Stella fell in line behind him, feeling Chase's gaze burning into her back with every step. Those eyes had always had the ability to see right through her.

Good thing there wasn't much to look at anymore.

Bob pulled open the doors, the theater significantly cooler than the lobby. "Here she is." He stepped out of the way by the top step so Stella could get a clear view. "Still a beauty."

Behind her, Chase murmured an agreement in the back of his throat, and Stella's ears burned. The theater. He was talking about the theater.

The aisle sloped slightly downward, stairs guiding the way past rows and rows of worn seats toward the stage. Stella moved slowly down as if drawn by a magnet, taking the stairs one at a time in the near dark. The hushed space around her hovered tight with expectation, of dreams unfulfilled, of potential to shine.

This theater wasn't a ghost. It still had plenty of life yet.

She finally reached the stage, dropped her purse on the floor, and hoisted herself up. She stood and reverently walked the space, forgetting about Chase and Cowboy Bob and all the scandals of the past. Closing her eyes, she pictured the rows of seats once again full of people—of couples on first dates and children on field trips and middle-aged parents holding hands.

Yes. Plenty of life to be had.

The building hadn't shuddered or sighed earlier.

It just needed a hug too.

"What's she doing?" Cowboy Bob couldn't whisper if his life depended on it.

Chase answered, softer, but his voice carried in the stillness. "Listening."

Ignoring them, Stella opened her eyes and looked up. A giant projection screen was rolled up tight above the massive wooden platform. If it was still in working order, it would save a lot of money not to have to replace it. The stage lights, from this distance anyway, still seemed whole too. They wouldn't know for sure until the electricity was turned back on, but at least there was hope.

Plenty of hope.

Bob pulled a flashlight from his back pocket, and he and Chase began making their way down the stairs. "We'll see about getting the power on as soon as possible for you guys to get started. When is your crew coming?" They reached the floor by the stage under Stella.

"I've got a few guys supposed to meet with me this afternoon, so we can draw up a game plan. I wanted to see the space first, and of course get the designer's ideas before we moved forward." Chase ran a hand through his hair and shot a glance at Stella. "It's important we're all on the same page at this stage—pardon the pun—or else it'll stalemate real quick."

"Oh, I'm not worried about that. You guys already know each other. I'm sure it'll be easier than pie to agree on the remodel." Bob dismissed the concern with a snort. "Now look at that. I've got a hankering for some apple pie now. Anyone want to finish this little meeting over at the diner?"

Pie? At eight thirty in the morning? Now she knew how her mom must have felt when she offered her coffee in the afternoon. Stella quickly shook her head from her position atop the stage. The only thing worse than playing nice with Chase in this giant theater would be playing nice in close quarters across a breakfast table.

"I'd just as soon get started if it's all the same to you, Bob." Chase smiled what Stella had always secretly dubbed his own pageant smile—the one containing nothing genuine other than well-placed manners. "We're burning daylight."

Stella nodded. "And clearly we have a lot to discuss."

Chase shot her a bewildered glance, and she smiled sweetly. Now who was sweating? "About the construction, of course."

"Of course." His eyes narrowed. He didn't believe her.

Good.

"That's what I like to hear." Bob hitched up his jeans and gave Chase a firm nod. "I knew we made the right choice hiring the likes of you." He turned to include Stella. "And you, little lady. I know your vision for this theater will knock us right out of our boots."

Only those who chose to wear them.

"Well, I won't hold you kids up any longer. We'll get together for an update meeting in a few days." Bob saluted them both before flicking his flashlight back on. "You two have fun."

"Yes sir."

"Will do."

They waited silently until Bob disappeared back up the stairs into the dimness of the lobby, his flashlight bouncing and then fading completely away.

"Of all the contractors in all the world—"

"Of all the designers in all the world—"

They stopped at the same time they'd started. Stella crossed her arms over her chest and glared down at her ex. "Get out of my head."

"Tried that years ago." Chase stepped up onto the stage with minimal effort. Now she had to look up at him. She wished she had a stool.

She lifted her chin instead. "You tried a lot of things years ago."

"And how far did that get me?"

"Great question. Why don't we ask Kat?"

They scowled at each other again, arms crossed, chests heaving.

Then Chase slumped, arms slack at his side. "I'm not going to fight with you, Stella. We're both adults. Different people than . . . before."

"Before what, exactly?" She couldn't turn off the need to challenge him, to make him face everything head-on the way she'd had to. The way she still had to when he sneaked uninvited into her dreams. But that wasn't her anymore. She'd gotten downright mellow. No one had sparked that kind of emotion in her in years.

What was going on?

"You know what." His voice held a warning now, and a maturity she wouldn't have recognized. Maybe he had changed. She had no idea what he'd been up to these past . . . how many years now? Four? Five?

And how much did he know of *her* past? Oh, man. The room blurred around the edges and she fought to inhale.

Definitely time to change the subject. "You're right. Let's just talk about the theater." She tucked her hair behind her ears and released a sigh. Regroup. Refocus. This was a job, not a couples-counseling session. The room wasn't shrinking—only her tolerance. She breathed again, deeper.

"It's a little dark in here. Let's go talk in the lobby." Chase climbed off the stage, and held up a hand to assist her down.

Oh no. No way was she touching him. If their former chemistry was anywhere near as alive as it had been a few years ago, the entire theater would combust.

And wouldn't that make for a great follow-up headline?

She slid her hands into her back pockets. "Let's stay in here. I can envision things better when I'm actually in the space." It was true. But she had another reason for suggesting it.

"Arguing already, are we?" He said it lightly, as if joking, but she sensed the undercurrent. It moved between them in a relentless wave.

"Hand me my notepad?" She pointed to the legal tablet sticking out of her purse. "Please?"

He hesitated, blue eyes calculating the cost as they stared up at her.

This was about so much more than location. This was setting the stage—great, now *she* was thinking in puns—for the rest of their working relationship. This was setting a precedent of who exactly was going to take how much.

The Chase she knew wouldn't stand for it for long at all. In fact, Alpha Male Chase from her past would have already been barreling his way up the stairs, leaving her to follow—or not.

But the Chase before her hesitated a moment longer, then bent down and plucked the tablet from her purse. "As you wish."

The room immediately shrank four sizes.

⨍

When Chase left Ethan's apartment for work that morning, he imagined meeting with the Downtown Director, shooting the bull a bit, and then chatting vision with the interior designer on the project, all before grabbing his hastily hired crew together for donuts and some seriously hard labor. It was time to move—to go, to create. He'd been stagnant for four days in his transition from Houston, and it was almost his undoing.

Today, the plan was to be productive at all costs.

Nothing in his morning plan included fanning a lifeless ex-girlfriend back to consciousness on a deserted stage.

"Stella." He knelt beside her and gently tapped one cheek, then the other, unable to help but notice the way her golden hair spilled around the deep wood of the stage like a halo. He nudged harder, then shook her shoulder.

Nothing.

He really didn't think mouth-to-mouth would be appreciated at this point, and she was breathing, anyway, so it'd be pointless.

Unfortunately.

"Stella!" He shouted now, his voice reverberating around the theater, hinting at the panic beginning to build in his gut. Had she hit her head when she collapsed? What had happened, anyway? Delayed shock at their being thrown back together after all these

40

years—or did she have some kind of illness he wasn't aware of? It was hot in here, but she'd been fine earlier.

Either way, she needed to open those fiery eyes of hers. *Now.* Those eyes that had always put him in his place. The ones that he never could completely get out of his head, even after proposing to Leah and determining to move forward from the past once and for all.

What a joke. His past kept relentlessly tapping his shoulder, forcing him to look back in one form or another. And if Stella had gotten hurt . . . hurt like Leah . . .

She stirred slightly, then, just enough to curb the tightness consuming his chest. He sank into a sitting position beside her and exhaled a year's worth of stress. Okay. She was okay. He tried to relax, tried to force calm through the adrenaline burning his veins. Another minute, and if she didn't come all the way to, he'd call 911.

And then Stella could make the papers two days in a row.

She sat upright so fast it made *his* head swim.

"Whoa, slow down. You all right?" He held both hands toward her, wanting to touch her but knowing better. Knowing she'd probably punch him in the face and knowing he probably deserved it.

"What happened?" She rubbed the back of her head and flinched, pulling her fingers away as if checking for blood. Thankfully, there wasn't any.

"Great question." He pulled his legs up to his chest and looped his arms casually around his knees. "We were talking, and I handed you the notepad, and you peaced."

"I *what*?" She squinted at him, whether in pain or confusion he couldn't be sure.

"You know. Like peace out?" He held up two fingers in the

universal sign. "Never mind. You fainted, Stella." He dropped the jokes. "Seriously, are you okay? I almost called an ambulance, but I figured you'd kill me later."

"You figured right. There was this incident yesterday . . . never mind." It was her turn to stop short. A hint of red began flushing her pale cheeks.

He couldn't resist. "I was meaning to ask you how you found time for interior design in the middle of a career as an arsonist."

She reached over and slapped his bicep—before she thought it through, apparently, by the way she quickly pulled her hand back to her lap. The momentary spark that had lit, the spark that reminded him of the real Stella, quickly extinguished.

He missed it already.

"So you saw the newspaper." A statement, not a question.

He nodded.

She sighed. "Welcome back to Bayou Bend." A slight grin turned up one corner of her mouth, at least. There she was. Still in there.

There was more relief with that than there should have been.

He stood and reached down to help her. "Slowly, now."

She paused, biting down on her bottom lip the way she always had done when debating something, and finally slid her hand into his. The contact of their palms was at once familiar and different, half memory, half dream. He let go as soon as she steadied on her feet, unable to bear her touch without a full assault on his mind.

"Thank you." Mellow Stella was back now, this stranger he didn't recognize, and he found himself wishing he could make her smile again.

"Do you do that often?"

"What? Say thanks?" She held her yellow notepad against her chest like a shield, and he almost envied the form of tangible protection. Could stand some armor himself right now.

"No, drop cold on the floor."

"Oh. That." She looked at the stage where she'd landed, as if it held an answer she didn't have. "Sometimes."

There was a lot more she wasn't saying, and the lack of invitation to probe further was more than evident. Point received. "Can you drive?"

She nodded, certain.

Certain enough to make him think this wasn't that rare for her, after all.

He frowned. "Then why don't you go home and rest for a little while, take some medicine for that headache that's sure to be on its way. I'll meet with my crew here in a bit and you can join us this afternoon. We can talk vision then. There's plenty of demolition I can get them started on that won't interfere with our plans."

He waited, fully expecting an argument—Stella Varland never took orders from anyone. Not even when hurt.

"Yeah, okay." She nodded slowly and immediately sat down to slide off the edge of the stage. "I'll see you later."

The disappointment that lingered at her agreement was more tangible than that yellow tablet in her hand.

And the girl he used to know as Stella Varland walked out of the theater.

four

Passed out.

One look at Chase Taylor, and she had passed out cold.

Stella's counselor told her the anxiety attacks were to be expected now and then, when circumstances triggered her memories of the past. Shaking, hyperventilating, lack of oxygen to the brain. As she healed and dealt with the pain and trauma, they would pass.

Well, they weren't passing fast enough.

She needed a cupcake. And a hug.

But she couldn't get either one without telling Kat the whole story.

And she wasn't sure if she was ready to tell Kat the whole story. Or if Kat was even ready for the whole story.

Yet Chase was in Bayou Bend, and for all appearances, it seemed he was here for good, so Kat was bound to find out through the small town gossip mill any day now. And from all the connections their mother had, more like any minute. Would it be better to hear the news from Stella, or from their mom?

Stella had to bite this bullet, and the only way it was going to go down was with a heaping spoonful of sugar. Besides, her head throbbed a rhythm that would have made Aerosmith jealous. She needed a sugar fix, stat. And maybe an emergency round on a punching bag.

She pushed open the door of Sweetie Pies, the bakery her sister had bought from their late Aunt Maggie, and immediately missed the feisty older woman. Even though the shop had been Kat's for several years now, it still reminded Stella of Maggie and the months they spent together after her cancer diagnosis. If Aunt Maggie were here, she'd know what to say. And would probably crack them all up in saying it.

The bell over the door chimed her arrival. Kat poked her head out from the kitchen, then planted one hand on her rounded hip. "If you're going to start a fire or play with your food, you can turn right back around." The sass was broken by her grin.

"Hilarious."

"Just joking. What kind do you want?"

"Vanilla." She pulled a chair out from the table nearest the display counter, the iron legs squeaking against the black-and-white checkered floor.

Kat glared, hand still on her hip. "You've got to be kidding."

"Duh. I know better than to order that to your face. Give me one of your raspberry lemonade torte thingies."

Kat pulled a cupcake from the display tray, plopped it on a serving plate atop a red doily, and set it on the counter. "Come get it. You're not pregnant, you can walk farther."

Stella got up and met her sister at the counter. "We need to talk."

"Mom again? I told her to leave you alone about that stupid newspaper article." Kat whiffed at a strand of hair that had escaped her ponytail.

"What'd she do this time?" Lucas suddenly appeared from the kitchen doorway, flour streaked across the front of his hunter green T-shirt.

"Where'd you come from? Who else do you have stashed back there?" Stella peered over her sister's shoulder toward the industrial kitchen.

Lucas slipped one arm around Kat's widening waist and winked. "Love begins in the kitchen, Stella."

"Gag me."

He slid a wooden spoon across the counter to her.

"Very funny."

Kat shook her head at them both. "He's helping me today since my part-timer is on vacation."

"That, and I don't want her to pop." Lucas poked Kat in the side. "Not while she's here by herself, anyway."

"Hush. I still have two months to go and you know it. Now, what did Mom do?" Kat leaned into Lucas's side and Stella bit back a pang of longing at their closeness. No time for any of that. Not that Dillon had been all that affectionate, anyway.

Chase had, though . . .

Don't go there. Just say it and get it over with.

"That bad?" Kat frowned, and even Lucas's joking demeanor turned stoic. "Was it about the shelter?"

"No, it's not Mom. She actually tried to help." Stella unwrapped her cupcake with trembling fingers, pausing to lick lemonade-flavored icing off her thumb. It did little to ease the sting of what

46

was to come. Her sister was going to flip. Hopefully not faint, as Stella had done onstage. Of all the times for her anxiety to get the best of her.

Chase better not have tried mouth-to-mouth.

"Really?" Kat closed the display case and then leaned forward against the glass countertop, propping on her elbows. "Mom trying to help usually ends up in disaster."

"Well, yeah, there's that."

"What happened, Stella?" Lucas's calm voice steadied her nerves as he mimicked Kat's position and leaned over the counter, focusing his full attention on her. Best brother-in-law ever. Kat had done good.

And she deserved it, after what Chase had done to her. To both of them. The way he played them against each other.

Then bailed.

She drew a ragged breath and blew it out. Then took a bite of cupcake. "I got a job." She mumbled around the cake. Kat squinted and figured it out.

"You got a job."

Stella nodded.

"It was either that, or 'I bought a Bob.' I went with the most likely."

She almost choked on her cupcake. "There is a Bob, actually. The Downtown Development Director."

Lucas tilted his head. "Bayou Bend has one of those?"

"Apparently. And he wears cowboy boots."

"There's a committee your mother isn't on?"

"See!" Stella accidentally sprayed crumbs across the counter with the outburst, and hastily swiped them onto the floor with her sleeve. "That's what I said."

"*This* is what you needed to talk about?" Kat raised one eyebrow at Stella in that intimidating way she always had growing up. Her favorite party trick that Stella could never match. "I'm so confused."

"No. I mean, partially, yes." She tried again. "I got a job as the interior designer on the renovation of the Ninth Cameo Theater."

Kat brightened. "That's great! I always loved that old theater. Congrats. And hooray for Mom doing something helpful."

"Well . . ." Her voice trailed off. How to even say this? "Sort of."

"Sort of helpful?"

"More like she didn't know all the details before getting me hired." To put it mildly. Claire Varland would never have allowed Stella anywhere near Chase. In fact, she might even try to put a kink in the entire gig once she found out about it. Looked like Stella had a second stop to make before meeting Chase back at the theater later that afternoon.

If she didn't need this job so badly . . .

Kat shook her head as if trying to catch on. "Wait. Mom missed details? That's odd."

Even Lucas murmured his agreement on that one.

Stella pinched a piece of cake off the wrapper with her fingers, wishing the sugar had numbing powers. "You know how I said there's a Bob?"

They both nodded at her.

"There's someone else too."

"You're not making sense, Stella. Just spit it out." Kat held up both hands. "Without spraying cupcake on me, ideally."

Stella took a bigger bite than before, stalling, her mumble unintelligible even to her own ears.

"You've been invited to a foot race?"

She tried again, wincing.

"Someone sprayed you with mace?"

Oh, for crying out loud. Stella swallowed her cake. "I said . . . there's also a Chase."

"Chase." Kat's voice was so monotone, Stella was tempted to look behind her for a robot. "As in, Chase."

"Chase-Chase?" Lucas's eyes widened. "You mean, *the* Chase?" He looked torn between wanting to punch a wall and hug Kat.

"The one and only." Stella shoved her cupcake away from her, any remnant of appetite or sugar craving long evaporated.

"Where is he?" Violence won the battle, apparently. Lucas started around the counter.

"Stop." Kat's voice, only slightly more lively than before, halted Lucas in his tracks. Probably the only thing that could have, judging by the lightning storm of anger in his eyes.

"Stay."

Lucas turned a half circle at the end of the counter, chest heaving.

"Let's hear the rest of the story." Kat patted the glass top, and Lucas released a large breath before sidling back up next to her.

"I don't know the story," Stella said. "He just turned up as the contractor on the job." She wiped her fingers with her napkin, digging the bits of cake from her nails and wishing she could rid herself of Chase's memory as neatly. But those were embedded much deeper. "And apparently the foreman, as well."

She stumbled over the word. Great. That hadn't fully sunk in before. That meant she'd be in contact with Chase even more closely than with a typical contractor, because as foreman, he'd

49

actually be on-scene managing the construction around the clock. "I'm working with him on the project."

"You have to work with Chase?" Now Kat's tone held more sympathy than shock. "Stella. How are you going—"

"I don't know. Okay? I don't know. I've already had one anxiety attack." Stella slapped the counter with both hands. "But I need the job."

Lucas bowed up again. "I'll pay your rent before I'll let any sister of mine work with that—"

"Yeah, Mr. I-Have-a-Mortgage and Mrs. Baby-on-the-Way, thanks but no thanks." Stella shook her head. "There's no way you guys can afford that, and there's no way I'm letting you." She could do this. It would help if they would stop freaking out. Then she could convince herself this wasn't nearly as big a deal as it clearly was.

"But it's Chase." Kat rolled in her lower lip, leaving the rest of her sentence unspoken. *Isn't being homeless better than dealing with him?*

Maybe.

Well, no, not after Stella rendered the shelter useless.

She'd managed to forget about that for all of two hours. She buried her face in her hands.

"Maybe we're overreacting?" Her sister was trying, bless her heart.

Stella peered up at her. "I passed out, Kat. In front of him. On the middle of the theater stage. I think we're past overreaction."

"Don't give him that power over you." Lucas looked even more ticked than before, though it seemed to be carefully under control for the moment. Probably because of Kat's condition. Not much else would keep him inside the bakery right now. Chase's betrayal to Kat hit Lucas almost as personally as it did her sister, because he'd had to pick up Kat's pieces over the years. The memories had almost destroyed *their* budding relationship.

Needless to say, Chase knew how to leave a mark. "No one *gives* Chase anything." Stella leveled her gaze at her brother-in-law. "He takes it." Takes it, to the point where you didn't even realize it was gone until you looked up and suddenly wondered why there was a hole in your heart.

"That's ridiculous. What kind of superpower does this guy have?" Lucas picked up Stella's discarded cupcake and tossed it into the trash. What was he doing? Trying to channel his frust—

Yep. He went for the rag next and began wiping the already clean counter.

"It's not a superpower, really." Stella looked at Kat for help explaining the enigma that was Chase. "More like . . ." Where to even begin? How did one even start to describe the effect one guy—one jerk—could have on not just women, but sisters?

Kat chimed in. "More like a cancer than a superpower. He does damage in one area and the effects take over. Consume."

Cancer. Aunt Maggie. Stella couldn't hear that word without instantly going back to her great aunt's death in hospice. She squeezed her eyes shut. What would Maggie advise her to do in this situation? Her head thrummed too loudly, with too many voices. She couldn't hear her aunt's voice as clearly as she did a few months ago. The voice that always pointed Stella in the right direction. Away from the façade. Away from striving. And always toward Jesus.

The voice was fading.

Stella opened her eyes. She couldn't depend on anyone else— not even family—to do this for her. She had to go it alone.

And maybe proving to herself she could handle it was just what she'd been needing this past year. She'd survived divorce. An ex-boyfriend should be a piece of . . . well, cake.

Except Chase wasn't just an ex. An ex was someone you dated and broke up with and moved on from. Someone you occasionally sent a Christmas card to or avoided eye contact with in a small-town grocery store or searched on various social media sites in secret hopes they'd gotten really unattractive. Exes were about as confusing as the maze on the back of the kid's meal menu at the local diner.

Chase was a labyrinth.

Lucas set his jaw. "Maybe one day someone can teach him to use his powers for good instead of evil." His fist clenched as if he was itching to be the one to invoke such a lesson.

Kat snorted. "How was he this morning? You know, during the parts of your interaction where you were conscious."

Ha ha. "He was . . . professional." Until they got into that near fight on the stage, before she dropped dead away. But for some reason, she didn't want to tell her sister everything. Harping on Chase didn't feel productive. She had to hitch up her big-girl trousers and do this thing, and really, she should do it with as much grace as possible. Her livelihood depended on it.

And besides, wasn't living well the best revenge?

It'd be a lot easier to do if he didn't bring out the most annoying childish instincts in her. The kind that still wanted to wear Disney Princess panties under said big-girl trousers. The kind of instincts she had battled, against all odds, and stuffed into a box much like Pandora's, and buried the key.

Instincts that needed to stay far beneath the surface.

That wasn't her anymore.

Dillon had seen to that. And it was too dangerous—far, far too dangerous—to go anywhere near that box.

Enough. "I need to go." Stella grabbed her purse from the table where she'd abandoned it earlier, and scooted the chair back into place. "I have to meet with him and the construction crew for some pre-demolition planning."

"You're really going to do this?" Kat crossed her arms over her chest, her apron pulled tight across her belly. "You're really going to work with him?"

"I don't have a choice, Kat. As bad as it is, it beats living with Mom and Dad." Stella hiked her purse on her shoulder and turned at the door. "Maybe. Guess I'll find out."

Her sister started to respond, then stopped, lips pressed into a thin line. When she finally opened her mouth again, her tone was final. Resigned. "Just—just be careful."

There was so much more she obviously wanted to say, and didn't even need to. Stella knew.

She was headed straight into the labyrinth.

∽

Twenty bucks she wasn't coming back.

Chase sat around a card table in the middle of the Ninth Cameo lobby and its long-forgotten mess, surrounded by three men in various degrees of holey T-shirts. All of them were drinking some form of energy drink except for Lyle, who spit dip into a crumpled Sprite bottle.

This was his crew.

And he really hated to think who would be their interior designer if Stella didn't show up. The choices weren't promising: Middle-aged, scruffy-faced Lyle, whose quality building skills and experience with Sheetrock were the only reasons Chase put up with the constant spitting. Jack, an upper-middle-aged man recommended by Lyle for his hard work ethic and "mad skills with painting." And Tim, whose college-aged enthusiasm for his first "real" job made him perfect for grunt work, clean up, and errand running.

Stella had to come back.

Did he want her to?

He felt as if he were watching a tennis tournament. Back and forth, left and right.

Left. Sure, Bob would hire someone else if Stella bailed, but Stella's eye for color and design would do the theater a huge favor. The theater needed her.

Right. Yet at the same time, his and Stella's history—as messy and clouded as it was—could easily get in the way of progress and actually hinder the project.

Left. But only if they let it.

"So what's first, Boss?" Tim leaned back on his chair, balancing on two legs, and drummed his fingers on the edge of the card table. Nothing but energy. Chase had half a mind to nudge the chair with his boot, just to see what substance the kid was actually made of.

Lyle beat him to it. "Feet on the floor, Junior." He kicked harder than Chase would have, and Tim fell backward in a heap. "See how dangerous that is? If you're gonna play in a construction site, boy, you better play by the rules. Safety first." He spit in his bottle and shot Chase a wink as a red-faced Tim clambered back into his chair.

"Got anything I can beat with a sledgehammer?" Tim directed the question to Chase, but glared at Lyle. He grinned back and toasted him with his spit cup.

Chase bit back a laugh. Good. The boy had some spark. He was going to need it to survive Lyle—and probably Jack, too, though the older man so far had been a lot more reserved in comparison. It appeared respect would be hard-earned around the Cameo.

"We're waiting on our designer to get here." Chase checked his watch, trying to remember if he'd ever told Stella an exact time or just implied vaguely about meeting after lunch. Maybe she was still resting from whatever had come over her that morning.

Hopefully she hadn't hit her head harder than he'd realized. In fact, wasn't sleeping after a head injury a bad idea? Had he just sent her off into a coma? What if—

"What's wrong?" Tim frowned at him and Chase groaned. It figured the college punk would have intuition.

"Nothing. She'll be here." He shrugged as if it didn't matter.

Because it didn't.

Or maybe it'd be for the best if she didn't show, anyway.

He had to quit doing that.

Tim stared as if he couldn't believe him less. Fair enough. Chase didn't believe himself. He cracked his neck, the sudden snap yanking Jack away from a near-snoring state at the table, and stood to his feet. "Okay, guys, listen up." He needed to get them on the right track, here, with or without Stella. With or without a designer. There were plenty of things to do.

Then Stella walked in, and for the life of him, he couldn't remember what any of those things were.

"Who. Is. That?" Tim's eyes bugged out of his head and he caught himself before slipping out of his chair a second time. Even Jack sat up straight and Lyle set his dip bottle on the ground, out of sight, as Stella made her way toward the group across the sun-streaked theater lobby, her wind-tangled blonde hair streaming behind her.

Thank the Lord she didn't have on makeup, or Tim might not have lived to see twenty-one.

Which was a little odd, now that Chase thought about it. And funny he didn't notice that morning. Because the Stella he remembered wore full makeup even to get the mail. The pageant queen couldn't go anywhere without personifying perfection—which in her case, wasn't that difficult to obtain.

Stella hesitated near the table, her uncertainty also brand new to Chase. What happened to the confident girl who could easily wow a room full of strangers with a smile, and had no trouble making small talk with anyone—and he meant *anyone*, ranging from a homeless woman to the CEO of a thriving business?

"Guys, this is our interior designer on the project, Stella Varland." He kept his tone intentionally professional, as a reminder to the men to keep it business, and as a reminder for his own heart to do the same. He couldn't afford to let Stella's accident earlier or their history together jade his mindset and conjure up some sort of ill-advised compassion. They had a deadline to meet and a theater to renovate, and it wasn't going to happen if he kept trying to psychoanalyze Stella.

Stella tucked a thick file under one arm and held out her hand

56

to first Lyle, then Jack. "Nice to meet you all." Chase recognized the voice then, the pageant voice, the one that used to speak of world peace, Americana, and sugar and spice and everything nice.

That fake voice he never could stand to hear. It was how he'd always imagined Barbie would talk. And when he realized his own name wasn't Ken, well . . .

He hadn't been good enough for Stella. Not what she deserved. And the way he treated her sister after realizing Stella had nabbed his heart, well . . .

Neither of them deserved the likes of him.

Chase shook away the memory. No time for that. Business only.

When she got to Tim, the kid stood so fast his chair clattered to the floor behind him. He then proceeded to hang on to her hand about ten seconds longer than necessary. "A pleasure to work with you, ma'am."

"Thank you." Stella finally used her other hand to tug her captured one free, and shot Chase a glance, one reminiscent of the spark she'd had earlier with him onstage. One that threatened to take them all down with her leftover kickboxing skills if they didn't acknowledge and own their place.

Feeling as if the world made a tiny bit more sense now, Chase sat down, relieved. Stella was fine. She was in this. They could carry on.

He pulled out the empty chair between him and Lyle, narrowly missing knocking over the spit bottle. Lyle rescued it just in time. "Tim, you've got to quit leaving this nasty thing sitting around."

The boy sputtered, shooting a nervous glance at Stella. "What? That's not even my—"

"As I was saying before . . ." Chase raised his voice over Tim's high-pitched protests and ignored Lyle's responding chuckle. "We've got a lot of work to do, and there's plenty of it to go around. So let's focus on business."

His tone, the one he'd perfected on various crews over the past several years, left no room for argument. "First, a little bit of house-keeping. Tim, you can wield that sledgehammer, but don't you dare pick it up without permission first as to what you're about to destroy. Just because something looks ruined doesn't mean it needs to be pulverized. Almost anything in here can be rebuilt with some effort."

Stella shot him a look then, one he couldn't decipher, and one that seemed to pack a punch much harder than any he'd seen her land on a bag. In fact, it made him pause long enough to drink a swig of energy drink. One that was doing nothing but making him nervous and unfocused.

Or was that Stella's effect, rather than the sugar and caffeine's?

Tim fist-pumped the air in victory. "Yes! The sledgehammer is mine." Then he caught Stella's eye and shifted in his seat, slowly lowering his hand to his lap. "I mean, that's cool, Boss."

Jack snorted, shaking his head, his grin nearly covered by his salt-and-pepper beard. "I'll supervise Junior on that one."

"Thanks, Jack." Chase continued before Tim could argue. "Right now, I'd like for you three to spread out, look over the theater and lobby areas, and get familiar with the place. Take some industrial trash bags with you, and let's start clearing out what we know can be tossed. Lyle, you get final say over what's deemed trash. If it looks remotely valuable or vintage, make a pile and I can go through it later. Stella and I will start going over some design ideas here."

"Aw, man."

Chase had to give Tim props for the softer-voiced complaint, but he heard it, nonetheless. From the way Stella tucked her hair behind her ears and looked away, he could tell she probably had too. But she didn't seem to bask in the compliment, the way she used to. In fact, she looked downright . . . embarrassed? Awkward?

The men started to stand, and Chase tossed Jack the roll of trash bags. "Remember, guys, the goal here is to start clearing stuff out so we can see what we're working with. Think big picture."

He waited until they began to fan out through the lobby space, bags dragging the ground behind them, and turned to Stella with a deep breath. "That's the crew."

She nodded, lips pursed. "Eclectic mix."

He felt an odd compulsion to defend them. Or maybe defend himself, since he technically hired them. "They're hard workers. You'll see."

She squinted after them. "I don't doubt that."

So what *did* she doubt?

Man, he had to quit getting so deep. The inner workings of Stella Varland were no longer his territory. She'd made that crystal clear, and he'd moved on years ago. No sense in rereading an old chapter in his life. Not when there was too much to do going forward.

He tapped her folder. "What'd you bring?"

"Some design ideas I put together last night, color schemes and stuff." She slowly slid it across the table to him. "I based the drawings off old images of the Cameo from the Internet, to get an idea of the layout since I hadn't seen the theater in person since I was a child."

He took the proffered file and flipped it open. Various sketches filled several pages, rough drawings of the theater and even more of the lobby, shaded in colored pencil with what he supposed were vintage movie posters hanging on the walls. Black, red.

And not much else.

He glanced at Stella, confused. Where was the vibrancy, the way she used to nearly assault things with life and color? These sketches felt stale. Half-hearted, at best. He cleared his throat. "I take it you favor a . . . classic style."

Stella nodded. "Simple. Subdued."

Since when? And besides, these weren't simple or subdued. More like boring and cliché.

He shut the file. "Well, now that you've actually seen the theater, you can go back and work on a new design that fits."

"What do you mean, fits? This still fits." She gestured around the lobby. "In fact, I'm even more certain of it now that I've seen it in person again. A classic black and white theme would be perfect. Bob said vintage."

"He did. But vintage doesn't have to mean boring."

Her eyes widened. "Excuse me?"

He hadn't been particularly *trying* to bring back her fire, but apparently crossing her was still the way to do it. Note taken. "Stella, this design isn't going to work. Just head back to the drawing board, pardon the pun, and try again. You'll get it."

"I don't need to be patronized, here." She grasped the file with both hands, knuckles squeezing white.

"I'm not patronizing. I'm just saying, there's no need to be embarrassed. I Googled some of your work—you know what you're doing." He pointed to the file. "So, you know. Go do it."

Her eyes narrowed to slits, and he was suddenly grateful that looks couldn't actually kill. "There's nothing *wrong* with classic."

Chase leaned back in his chair, rocking back on two legs as Tim had, and offered a casual shrug, hoping his noncombative stance would slow her roll. "Maybe. But that doesn't mean it's *right*, either." She'd said she'd done the drawings the night before, before she'd even seen the theater up close. How could she still be convinced it was the best choice?

"*I'm* the designer for the theater." She leaned forward as he rocked, her blue eyes angry, and lowered her voice to a harsh whisper. "I was hired to make these decisions."

"And I'm the contractor and foreman on the job." Chase met her gaze, half admiring that familiar spark of hers that always got what she wanted, and half wishing she'd go back to Stranger Stella who seemed too distant to fight. "I'm hired as final say in everything that happens here at the Cameo, and I'm saying that this classic style isn't going to cut it."

"We'll see about that." Stella stood, tucked her file under her arm, and strode past the table.

"Where are you going?" He craned his head over his shoulder at her retreating figure, watching as she made an about-face and doubled back, lips pursed.

She smiled, the pageant queen smile, the one that made him

want to strangle every Barbie doll in existence. "Oh, I'll be back, don't worry."

A sudden thump on the legs of his chair registered much too late. He landed hard on his back.

"Oops." She pressed her fingers over her mouth, eyes full of mock concern. "Don't worry. There's no need to be embarrassed."

And the Stella Varland he knew all too well walked out of the theater.

five

She hadn't meant to do that.

Well, maybe a little.

Stella yanked open the doors to the Chamber of Commerce building, where her mom told her the Downtown Development offices were temporarily located, and welcomed the rush of air conditioning on her flushed face. Chase had just looked so smug, rocking in that chair, arrogant and know-it-all. It was such a flashback to when he used to hit on her.

While still dating Kat.

Tangling her heart up. Knowing it was all off-limits. Was that the only appeal the whole time? That she was forbidden?

She landed at the receptionist's desk, trying to find a pleasant expression that hid the turmoil raging inside. "Hi, there. I need to speak to Cow—I mean, Bob." She couldn't even remember the Director's last name, now that she'd ingrained Cowboy Bob in her head as his title. Great. That was one way to be professional.

The brunette receptionist grinned knowingly from behind the tidy desk. "And your name?"

"Stella Varland. I'm working on the Cameo Theater." She hesitated a little, a bit of the fire that had driven her here slowly extinguishing. Had she made the right decision in coming? Maybe her emotions had taken over. It wouldn't be the first time—though it would be the first time in ages.

Except for the other night at the shelter, of course, when she ignited her divorce papers.

What was *wrong* with her lately?

She just couldn't let Chase get away with the . . . the what? Bullying? No, that was probably a little strong, especially for someone who had no idea of their history together. It was that condescending, almost insulting way he'd addressed her work that gnawed on her so badly. What had he said, exactly? *You know what you're doing. So go do it.*

As if all her work on the Cameo so far had been a tease, a mere shadow of what she'd once done. As if it hadn't even counted or had been some kind of joke.

She gritted her teeth. Dillon might have taken a lot from her, but he'd not stolen her ability in the design field.

Now her *art* ability—that was a different story. But that had nothing to do with Dillon. Or the theater. Or Chase.

And it never would.

"Right." The younger girl punched a few buttons on her phone. "Mr. Erickson, Stella Varland is here for you."

She heard him coming before the receptionist could even hang up the receiver. Was he wearing spurs? Something jangled as he came down the carpeted hallway. "Stella! Trouble in paradise already, little lady?" He adjusted his hat and peered down at her.

She squared her shoulders. Chase had gone too far, and they needed to clear up this little matter of who was in charge right away. Before it went any further. Before the negative chemistry between her and Chase mixed into some kind of explosion.

She cleared her throat. "Not exactly. Just have a few questions for you."

"Of course. Come have a sit-down." Bob led the way to his office, which gave the impression of being a renovated janitor's closet. If Stella had doubted the newness of the development committee, their allotted space certainly confirmed it.

Maybe that was why her mother had dodged this one.

Bob squeezed behind the rickety wooden desk and gestured to a single folding chair across from it. "How can I help you?"

"I know you're a busy man, Bob, so I won't waste your time with small talk."

"Well that's mighty considerate of you, ma'am." He smiled, and a rush of hope for the Cameo flooded Stella. Maybe he'd take her side and they could settle this a lot quicker than she'd originally hoped. "What's your question?"

Chase Taylor could stand to be taken down a peg or two, last she remembered.

And after she had fainted in front of him, she was way behind on the scorecard.

"Theoretically speaking, if two people working on a project—say, an interior designer and a foreman—had different visions for said project . . ." Stella nibbled on her lower lip, suddenly feeling a lot like a four-year-old tattling in preschool rather than an established businesswoman working on a city's beloved old theater.

"Yes? Go on?" Bob scooted to the edge of his seat, face lit as he waited for her to continue.

Ten bucks said he watched soap operas in his spare time.

"Well, *if* an unfortunate situation like that were to occur . . . who would get the final say?" She shifted in her chair, hoping the flush working up her neck didn't show as strongly as she feared.

Bob leaned slowly back in his chair, steepling his fingers and raising his chin as he appeared to stare her down over his mustache. "I would imagine the most important part is that the project wouldn't suffer in the scuffle."

"There's no scuffle." *Yet.* She tried to put on a reassuring face but figured it probably came off more as a wince. This meeting was not going as planned. But what had she expected? This is why she stopped doing things full speed and spur of the moment. It always got her in trouble. Like accepting Dillon's offer of a first date. Like accepting that diamond ring a few months after their second.

And like agreeing to work her rear off to help put him through school so he could achieve his dreams, while she stared at the shattered remains of hers that he left in his wake.

"I would hope not." Bob jerked her back to reality, back to the present, where she remembered all too quickly she wasn't fireball Stella anymore. She wasn't light 'em up and burn 'em down Stella, the one who could get anything she wanted with a wink or a smile. The one who flirted her way out of traffic tickets and couldn't walk into a room without giving at least one poor guy whiplash.

Her days of Vaseline teeth and tiaras and world peace had

long since faded in the rearview mirror, despite her mother's desperate attempts to keep those particular objects closer than they appeared.

She didn't use her beauty anymore. In fact, she didn't want anything to do with it at all. If she hadn't been so gorgeous, she would never have caught Dillon's eye in the first place.

Even worse was knowing that if she'd somehow managed to be *more* than just a face, she'd have kept his eye a lot longer.

And now Chase was back, Trouble with a capital T. And he made Dillon come off as amateur.

Because if Chase hadn't broken her heart first, she might not have been so quick to trust Dillon with all the crumbling pieces.

"Is there a problem, Stella? Honestly, now." Bob's chair squeaked under his weight, and she tilted her head, appraising, calculating, trying to figure out how much of her vulnerable, bleeding heart to bare. How much did Bob really want an answer to that question?

He had no idea how many problems she had.

But the real Stella was done reacting. Her last reactions had ended in a soggy shelter and a headline, while this one was possibly about to end in the unemployment office. The old Stella kept trying to raise her perfectly coiffed blonde head and escape the box she'd locked her in. But she couldn't afford to let that happen. No, she had to remember who she was now.

No more spotlight. It was time for backstage Stella to learn how to blend in.

Because shining equaled heartbreak.

"No problem at all, Bob." Offering one last beaming pageant smile, she quickly stood and hoisted her purse on her shoulder. "We'll get it figured out. Like I said—theoretical question." She turned for the door as Bob stood and tried to get around the edge of his desk to open it first, spurs jangling.

"Was a pleasure, ma'am."

"Likewise." Stella shook Bob's hand and headed down the hall, swallowing hard. What a bust. She'd either have to go toe-to-toe with Chase and fight for her original scheme, or just rework the entire design and eat a giant helping of crow in the process.

She somehow doubted even crazy-craving pregnant Kat had a cupcake recipe for that one.

~

Chase Taylor had lost a lot of things when he left town years ago. Stella's respect and admiration, to name a few.

Unfortunately, he had not lost a single ounce of muscle.

Stella stood in the shadows of the theater entryway, watching Chase show the youngest guy on the crew—the one who'd all but drooled over her earlier—how to use a sledgehammer. The muscles in Chase's shoulders and upper back bunched and released through the thin fabric of his gray T-shirt, spotted damp with sweat down the middle as he raised the tool and swung it with the authority of a man who knew exactly what he was doing. Even the young guy looked impressed.

"You've got it, Tim." Chase clapped him on the shoulder as he handed over the sledgehammer. "Finish taking out that portion of the wall."

Tim eagerly accepted the task and went to work, fumbling only once before swinging with confidence. So Chase was still a good teacher too.

But her respect and admiration were safely tucked away out of reach. No way was she going there again. Just the memory of Kat's tear-stained face was enough to keep that wall up. And it was one no sledgehammer could crack.

She took a few steps into the light of the theater—

Wait a minute. They had lights now. A few, anyway. She squinted up toward the canned lights above the stage and then noticed an electrician perched atop a tall ladder. Chase certainly didn't waste any time.

The ache that had been building in her gut all afternoon intensified. Wasting time was turning into *her* specialty. First with the passing out and extended break today, and then with her running off to Bob like a child who'd gotten her hair pulled on the playground.

"Look who's back." Chase started climbing the stairs toward her, stopping a few feet away and hooking his fingers in his back pockets. "Is it safe to come closer? Don't want to get pushed down these stairs."

She briefly closed her eyes against the two very different and simultaneous waves that flooded her senses. Regret that she could be capable of such an immature reaction as to shove him out of a chair . . .

And frustration that she hadn't been able to catch it on video to enjoy over and over and over.

"I'm back. Ready to work." She dropped her purse into one of the upholstered theater chairs.

"You sure about that?" He took a cautious step closer. Four steps away.

She crossed her arms, half tripping over her own foot as

she shifted her weight anxiously. Her defenses rose as he edged nearer. What was it about this guy that threw her so completely off balance—both emotionally and, apparently, physically? Any remaining chemistry between them was a joke. A really awful, world's-worst-pun type of joke. One that would make chickens crossing roads seem downright hilarious.

Three stairs away.

Her heart thudded in her chest.

Two stairs.

Her crossed arms grew prickly with goose bumps.

Who said God didn't have a sense of humor?

She made an about-face on the stair, grabbing her purse. "I'll be in the lobby with my sketch pad. There's better lighting." Only because she wouldn't be at risk of the world going pitch black due to unconsciousness like the last time she'd been in Chase's extended presence.

He followed her. "The electrician is here."

"I saw that." She kept walking, and he kept following. Another plan foiled.

"He's seeing what needs to be replaced to be brought up to code, and what we can keep as is. This could be a huge factor for our budget, hopefully in the positive." They stepped into the lobby, and Stella dropped into a seat at the card table they'd abandoned earlier.

"Fingers crossed, then." If she didn't look at him, she wouldn't get angry.

Or want to kiss him.

Whoa. That was one memory she wouldn't—couldn't—let get the best of her. Talk about unproductive. Chase had very nearly ruined her life—and her sister's. She wouldn't fraternize with the enemy any more than absolutely necessary. This was work. Business. This was a roof over her head so her parents' roof wouldn't be. The end.

Chase stood beside her, almost over her, tapping her sketch pad with one finger. "So where did we leave off?"

Did he really want *that* particular instant replay? She opened her mouth to bite off the sarcastic retort rising in her throat, then stopped. Backstage Stella. Subtle Stella. She swallowed, then tried again. "It's back to the drawing board, I guess."

"You guess? You don't agree with what you're saying?"

Oh, why did he always have to push it? He'd asked her out when dating Kat. She'd said no. He'd backpedaled, playing it off as a mere coffee date between friends, then asked again a few days later. She'd said no. Again. Then a few weeks later, he was back. Wanted to talk about Kat, needed someone's advice who understood her better than most.

So she'd gone. For her sister.

And fallen in love over a nonfat, white-chocolate mocha.

"I—"

He tapped the notebook again. "What do *you* want, Stella?"

"What does it matter, anyway? You didn't like my idea." She snatched the sketch pad away from his hand, resisting the childish instinct to yell at him not to touch her stuff. He didn't have the right. He'd lost all those rights.

Shouldn't have ever had them in the first place. If her sister ever knew, really knew . . .

"This isn't Chase versus Stella, you know." He pulled out the chair across from her and sat down, bracing his elbows on the table as he leaned toward her, pulling her in as he always had. "I'm not trying to run a dictatorship, here. We just need to get on the same page and don't have any time to waste, because—well, we've already wasted some."

Her fault. He didn't have to say it out loud to make it true. She gripped the sketch pad tighter. "I agree." Why did that almost literally burn her lips to say? She didn't want to agree with Chase on anything. If she had learned how to argue with him sooner, maybe she wouldn't have gotten hurt so badly.

Or hurt others so badly.

Then the truth hit her. *She didn't want to agree with Chase.*

On anything.

Not even designs for the Cameo.

A sinking feeling filled her stomach, like a thousand rocks raining from a cliff edge. She hadn't even given consideration to his suggestions earlier. Maybe he had a point she could learn from, if she could just hush her bias and jadedness long enough. If she could give Backstage Stella a pass to take over and calmly, rationally, hear him out.

The Cameo deserved that much—and so did her landlords when rent came due again. She had to make this happen, somehow.

Just hopefully without unearthing the contents of that Pandora's box she'd locked away.

"What does Stella Varland want?" Chase repeated his question. Then he grinned. "Still working on that world peace thing?"

"Haha. You're hilarious." She gave in to the eye roll, and then took a deep breath. "Seriously—I'm willing to go back to the drawing board. If you thought the classic movie posters weren't a good fit, or the black and white theme, then I can start over."

Maybe it was a little cliché, but sometimes, clichés became that way for good reason—they were grounded in truth. They were safe.

Still . . . maybe he was right.

She *could* do better.

Recognizing that fact grated on her nerves even worse than his initial insult.

"Wait a minute. Are you saying I'm right?" Chase grinned, a slow one that started at the corners of his lips and revealed a dimple in his left cheek she'd never fully forgotten.

She looked away, then back. "I would never do that."

"Out loud, anyway." His grinned stretched even wider.

She started to stretch across the table to slap his arm, then thought better of it and played it off as reaching for her pencil. "Whatever. Go back in there and play with power tools while I do some real work out here." *And more importantly, get away from wreaking havoc on my five senses.*

Her heart skipped at the banter between them, but she kept her focus on her paper, absently resketching the basic lines of the lobby and pretending not to notice the way his eyes lingered on her before he slowly—reluctantly?—acquiesced.

❦

Stella wandered slowly around the lobby with her sketch pad, her creativity more stifled than a stopped-up drainpipe. She had doodled on her notepad at the card table for a while, until the memories of the past eventually gave up tapping her on the shoulder. From there she'd moved to aimlessly strolling the lobby, seeking inspiration and hoping Chase would keep his distance long enough for her to find it.

But her muse wasn't hiding behind the refreshment counter or between the rope-stand poles or in the faded wallpaper in the bathroom. Apparently, it had decided to run away completely.

And with Chase having looked at her like that, who could blame it? She sort of wished she could hit the highway, too, where all she had to think about was her next stop for gas.

But you had to have money to travel, and a job to make money, and so here she was.

Besides, not even a souped-up V-8 could outrun these memories.

She headed back into the theater, where she'd originally come before Chase interrupted earlier, and set her bag in a vacant chair. Thankfully the crew working near the stage hadn't noticed her there on the back row.

Something shiny glinted on the floor, reflective against the dark stairs. She bent down and picked it up. It was a piece of metal, broken off of something unidentifiable. The sides were smooth, nearly polished, the ends blunt instead of sharp. She started to drop it back on the ground, but the cool weight of it in her hand convinced her otherwise.

She slipped the piece into her pocket, then picked a seat a few down from the aisle where she could hopefully stay hidden from Chase. Until she had something productive to show him, she'd rather not see him.

Honestly, would rather not see him at all, period.

She slumped into her seat, propped her sketch pad on her knees and tilted her head back, drawing a deep breath to inhale the sounds and scent of the room. What did she see when she closed her eyes? That was the missing piece of her design puzzle. She just hadn't *seen* it yet.

So Chase didn't want black and white and red, didn't want classic or old movie posters or anything she'd previously come up with. What, then? The opposite? Instead of neutrals, bold colors? Instead of subtle and classy, bright and obnoxious? How was that better?

There had to be a middle ground she hadn't discovered yet.

With the design, of course. Not with Chase in general.

"I'd offer a penny for your thoughts, but ya know."

Stella jumped, her heart clawing its way into her throat. Her notepad slipped off her knees and landed with a thwack on the floor under her feet.

Dixie laughed from the chair beside her, her familiar cinnamon scent wafting toward Stella. "I ain't got one! Get it?"

No. Yes. Stella never knew what to say when Dixie, or anyone homeless for that matter, joked about their poverty. She pressed her hands against her chest, willing her heart back into place.

"Sorry there, Honey Bunny. Didn't mean to scare ya." Dixie bent down and picked up the book, then slapped it back into Stella's lap. "Why you so jumpy?" Her all-too-seeing eyes narrowed to slits. "Jumpy people usually have secrets. Or guilt. Or maybe guilty secrets."

"No secrets, Dixie." Stella slowly lowered her hands away from her heart, then felt for her pencil where it'd dropped into the seat by her leg. None she was willing to share, anyway. "I was just trying to focus." She really loved the older woman—in some ways, she reminded her of her late Aunt Maggie.

Except for the crazy part.

Which made her wonder, not for the first time, if the rumors were true—that Dixie didn't have to be homeless. But why in the world would anyone fake that? There might be scammers who threw on scruffy jackets and stood with cardboard signs on the corners of the highways, but there was no hiding the smell that lingered deep under Dixie's cinnamon surface. Or the dust that constantly coated her calloused hands and worn shoes. Or the rumbling she often heard from the woman's hungry stomach.

"No secrets? Not even one?" Dixie squinted, as if narrowing her eyes might let her see between the slats of Stella's brain.

Nope. She had a theater to design, and didn't have time for cryptic small talk. She had wasted enough time as it was. She pointed to the sketch pad. "Focusing, Dixie. I'm focusing."

"I'll help. What are we focusing on?" Dixie leaned over, hogging the armrest between them, and peered down at the sketch pad.

Stella quickly flipped the page. "What are you doing here, anyway, Dixie?" Then she remembered: the shelter wouldn't be up and running for a few more days, at best. Probably weren't a lot of other places for the woman to go.

"I come here all the time." Dixie finally took the personal-space hint and leaned back against her seat, settling in and propping worn shoes with a hole in the pinky toe up on the seat in front of her. "I can hear better."

"All the time?" Stella repeated. As in, before the city had decided to renovate the theater? Wasn't that dangerous, in the dark, with all the broken glass and—

Wait a minute. "What do you mean, you hear better?" A shiver crept over the back of her neck, like a dozen tiny moths fluttering at the base of her hair.

Dixie leaned her head back and closed her eyes. "You hear it too. Or you will."

Stella wasn't entirely sure she wanted to. Her mind replayed those eerie feelings from her first moments alone in the theater, before Chase, before Cowboy Bob, before this entire nightmare of a day had begun. What exactly did Dixie hear?

Or rather, *who*?

Whatever or whoever it was apparently wasn't terrifying, judging by the slight smile on Dixie's relaxed face. Hmm.

Stella glanced back at her sketch pad, uncertain how to proceed. How did Dixie sneak in like that, and why did she come to the abandoned theater frequently? It was peaceful here, of course. Quiet. When it wasn't crowded with ex-boyfriends and unseen voices, at least.

"You should go for the gold, dear."

She cut a look at Dixie, but the woman was still laid back, eyes closed, hands folded primly in her lap, fingers wrapped around the edges of that same patched blazer she was never seen without. Go for the gold? As in the Olympics? She opened her mouth to ask but Dixie wasn't done.

"Golden. Gold dust."

Now she was rambling. Crazy Dixie had taken back over. The woman always seemed to go in spurts. Stella smiled, shook her head, and opened her sketch pad.

"Gold nuggets."

Stella started tracing back over old lines of her drawing, trying to find her groove again.

"Golden man." Dixie's voice was softer now, as if she was drifting into sleep.

Golden. Her pencil stilled. What if they used a gold color scheme inside the theater, instead of the black and white and red? More European, almost. Her pencil flew beneath her fingers. Gold . . . and burgundy? No, too old-fashioned, like the red crushed velvet ropes in the lobby. Too done. Gold and . . . black? Nope. Too Hollywood, which was back to cliché and would just earn her another lecture from Chase.

Gold and silver?

Maybe. Now *that* idea had potential. She began sketching faster, filling in the white spaces with Gs and Ss to come back and shade later with her colored pencils as Dixie snored softly beside. Her muse was back—yet from the looks of it, sound asleep.

Stella worked quickly, rapidly flipping pages as more ideas flooded her mind and begged to be released onto the page. Time flew and she filled page after page with more ideas to flesh out and compare later.

She didn't stop until Dixie shifted beside her, stirring awake.

"See? Told you you'd hear 'em."

six

He hadn't had Mom's meatloaf in years.

About four bites in, he remembered why.

Chase rotated his half-full plate to go to work on the mac-n-cheese instead. Across his parents' fenced backyard, his cousin Ethan threw a football to twelve-year-old Memphis, Chase's nephew, as the rest of the immediate family scraped paper plates clean and stood gossiping, trading recipes, and joking along the landscaped patio. Enjoying the weekend. Enjoying life.

He was home.

So why was he already itching to go?

Chase pushed his plate away, no longer content to just sit and eat. He wanted to move. Play. Do.

"Hey, look at that. He caught it this time." Chase's older brother, Jimmy, sat down in the empty chair across from Chase and gestured toward his son. "Who'd have thought it?"

Chase followed his pointing finger toward Memphis. "I thought he made the junior high football team last year." Or so the Christmas card letter had stated.

"He did." Jimmy scooped a heaping spoonful of banana pudding into his mouth and shrugged, mumbling around his mouthful. "Benched the whole season."

And Chase hadn't made it to a single game. He pushed away the regret. This year, once school started back, things would be different. Uncle Chase was here, and he would make up for all of it.

Starting now.

He shoved his chair back. "Hey, let me in on that." He cupped his hands for the ball, and Ethan smoothly tossed it straight into his grasp.

"I want to play." His other nephew, Jimmy's youngest son Aaron, tried to tug the ball from his hands.

"Watch it, now, Freckles." He poked eight-year-old Aaron in the side and dodged the kid's giggling attempts to make him fumble the ball. "Your Uncle Chase hasn't lost his game completely." Not yet anyway, though every minute he inched toward thirty he got a little closer.

"Over here, Uncle Chase!" Memphis waved his arms, and Chase faked out Aaron in exaggerated slow motion before chunking the ball to Memphis. Aaron chased after it, protesting, and after slight encouragement from Ethan, the game quickly turned into keep-away.

"It's like you never left."

Bent over, hands braced on his knees, Chase looked up from his stance in the yard and shook his head at his mom. "I wish that was true." He'd missed so much, and for what? Memories from an abruptly ended relationship that still gnawed at his heart. A pink slip from a job he probably shouldn't have pursued in the first place.

And a trail of regrets he swore he'd never repeat.

Mom took a sip from her plastic cup—he'd bet money it was sweet tea; some things never changed. She mock-frowned at him. "I've never lied to you, Chase Taylor."

No—not entirely true. She'd never liked Leah. Neither had Jimmy, for that matter. The one time she'd met his family, it'd been so awkward they'd all been relieved when that particular brunch was over. He never thought he'd see the day when he'd be happy to abandon a half-full plate of cinnamon rolls. Even Leah had commented on the tension from his mom on the drive home, but for the life of him, Chase couldn't figure out why she hadn't taken to Leah.

Didn't matter now.

He exhaled sharply to release the lingering pain in his heart, a trick he'd learned in the thick of his grief. Breathe out the negative, force it out from the inside. Fill the left-behind space with something positive. In his case, it was usually prayer.

When he slowed down long enough to remember.

He easily jumped up and snagged the ball from thin air. His mom ducked out of the way as he tossed it neatly to Aaron, who paraded his victory in front of his brother.

"You've still got it, you know."

His mom didn't mean his football-throwing skills. He shot her an appreciative smile. "Thanks."

"You ready to put down roots again?"

He knew that was coming. Had prepared for it, sort of. But he still didn't have an answer. "I haven't been back that long, Mom."

She shrugged. "Some things the heart knows right away."

Yeah. Some things.

Others . . .

Did he want to stay in Bayou Bend for good? He watched his nephews playing, watched their smiles and cackles of laughter, and felt a little piece of the old grief knock off and roll away. "We'll see, Mom." It'd be good to be back here permanently. Good for everyone.

As long as Mom found a new meatloaf recipe.

"Might not hurt to keep an eye on the local real estate for me."

She smiled, the slow smile that always ended up straight in her eyes, and nodded calmly though he knew she was dying to jump up and down. But she knew—as she'd realized quickly enough when he was a teenager—that overreacting would make him about-face.

Chase really owed his mom a lot. He gave her an impromptu hug, which she returned while complaining about his sweaty T-shirt.

She dodged away, laughing, pausing to take a sip from her cup. "So what's next at the theater? All you said at lunch today was that you have a crew at work, and an interior designer you've been debating some ideas with."

Chase winced, his good mood slowly ebbing. Mom didn't know the designer was Stella. The two families didn't exactly have a Montague and Capulet thing going, but she had gotten enough of the gist of his and Kat's breakup to know that any kind of relationship with anyone from the Varland family—platonic, business, or otherwise—would be a potentially explosive situation.

The niggling feeling he'd had since first laying eyes on Stella at the theater flooded back in full force. He needed to make a truce with her. If the Cameo was going to be a success—if his job, his reputation, his career were going to be a success—then he and Stella needed to clear the air and find a way around all the awkwardness between them.

Maybe then she'd stop taking offense at everything he suggested.

He looked back at his mom, grateful she couldn't actually read minds the way he and his brother had always joked she could when they were kids. "That's about it." He tried to keep his tone casual. Just another job. Nothing interesting about it. "The electrician was able to give us a good quote, thankfully, which will keep us on budget. We've about finished the demolition stage, and a plumber is coming to evaluate tomorrow."

"So much to do. I can't even imagine keeping up with it all." Mom shook her head as she watched the boys play. "What did the designer decide to do on the inside?"

"It's not nailed down yet." He avoided eye contact, knowing if Mom's eagle-eyes landed straight on him, she'd sense his uneasiness and be on him like a dog with a new squeaky toy. Mom's subtlety was about as good as her meatloaf.

Better to play it cool. Detached.

"She pretty?"

Worse than the meatloaf, really. Chase groaned. "Mom, come on."

"I'm just asking!" Her voice pitched in protest, and she laughed. "Forgive a mother for wanting her son happy."

He had been happy—with Leah. *She* just hadn't been happy with Leah.

He shook away the lingering melancholy. It wasn't about Leah, not this time. This wave of grief was over something totally different, something he couldn't quite identify. And to be honest, he was terrified even to try. It felt dishonoring to his late fiancée to put words to it.

Because deep down, he didn't need to. The feeling didn't require words.

It already had a face.

⁂

Stella tossed a hot pink bib into Kat's already brimming grocery cart. "I told you we should have gotten two carts." Or three. And her sister hadn't even had a baby shower yet. This kid would be beyond spoiled.

"Stella." Kat scolded as she plucked the pink bib from where it'd landed on a package of newborn-size diapers. "You know we aren't finding out the gender of the baby until she or he gets here."

"Hey, real men can wear pink." Stella tossed it back in. "Besides, it's the only one that has a cupcake on it."

"Ohhh, you're right. And look at this one. It says *I get my looks from my mommy.*" Kat held up a onesie from a different bin, also in pale pink. "Oh, man, Lucas is going to kill me." She set it down, left both bibs inside the cart, and pushed it farther down the row, away from temptation. "That's what he gets for skipping shopping for a pick-up football game with the guys."

"Is he hoping for a boy?"

"He hasn't said so outright, but I think he has visions of a future quarterback." Kat stopped to examine the price on a package of crib sheets.

Stella tugged her away from the overpriced bedding. "Hey, if guys can wear pink, then girls can play football."

"Said the pageant queen." Kat winked.

"Enough with that already." Stella groaned. "I get plenty of it from Mom." How long did it take after a girl abandoned the stage and the tiaras to lose the title?

And how had she let that title define her life to the point that it was all anyone ever remembered?

"It's all about redirection. I've been reading parenting books." Kat leaned over the buggy to shift the contents into a more orderly pile. "And I think it'll work on Lucas too."

Oh, good grief. "That can't be good."

"No, hear me out." Kat held up the pink bibs. "Like with these. He'll see them. Might or might not have a tantrum. If he does, I'm prepared with the TV remote and a bunch of fantasy football stats I've looked up online." She snapped her fingers. "Redirection."

"It can't be that easy."

"Sure it is. He goes to the TV, bibs go in the drawer, marriage saved."

The words slipped effortlessly from Kat's mouth as she continued down the aisle with the cart, still jabbering about what she'd learned from the book, completely clueless to the dart she'd just unintentionally launched at her sister.

Marriage saved.

No. Definitely not that easy.

Stella hesitated in front of the rows of tiny newborn shoes as Kat meandered away. Miniature loafers and white patent sandals. Her gut twisted from her sister's flippant words. Would *she* ever get past it? Would she ever have reason to register for baby items?

She ran her finger across the tiny shoes and drew a shaky breath. She could have been pregnant now, the same time as Kat, sisters expecting babies together. Or maybe she and Dillon would have waited a few more years, had a bit more marriage time under their belts first. Either way, at her age, the dream should be alive and vivid, a heartbeat of hope in her chest.

Not a fading, dying ember of a dream turned to ash.

"Stella, you coming?" Kat twisted around at the end of the aisle, her full belly even more prominent in her favorite cupcake T-shirt she refused to stop wearing.

Yes. Nothing for her on this row.

She joined her sister, finding her pageant smile to hide the lingering emotion. No way was she going to put a damper on Kat's fun. "What's next?"

"Mom said to price the cribs here and let them know how much they are. They're on the next row." She turned the cart, then immediately got distracted by an end-cap display of baby monitors. "To video, or not to video?"

"Video. Might come in handy when he or she is a toddler. Or a teenager for that matter." Stella snorted. "If it is a girl, has Lucas started polishing up any shotguns yet?"

"He's already said she can't date until she's thirty." Kat pushed the cart around the corner toward the cribs. "Or a mature twenty-five."

Sounded like Lucas. Mr. Protector. Whatever their child was, boy or girl, it was going to be in great hands. Kat and Lucas would be some of the best—and probably craziest—parents the baby could ever have.

Maybe it was better Stella wasn't getting a chance to follow suit. Maybe she was still too selfish to be a mom. Too distracted, too inward focused. There'd been progress in that area since she'd gotten divorced, but was her heart truly in it? Did she actually *want* to be less selfish? Or was she just following through with the suggestions from her counselor by volunteering and doing things in the community?

God looked at the heart. What would He see?

Maybe she should keep working toward that. If nothing else, serving someone else again would distract her from Chase.

As long as she didn't set anything else on fire during said serving, of course.

"When are you doing cupcakes for the shelter next?"

Kat set the monitor back on the display and picked up a cheaper one, scanning the description on the back. "Funny you ask. I was just talking to Nancy today about a fund-raiser. She called me at the bakery earlier, wanted to know if I'd be interested in helping cater. They're about to do a big event to raise money for rebuilding."

"Rebuilding? From the sprinkler flood?" Stella's heart thudded hard in her chest. Had she really messed things up that bad with her impulsive, immature decision?

"No." Kat laughed. "You're so paranoid."

She'd flooded a homeless shelter. Paranoia sort of fit here.

Kat gave up on the monitors and turned her full attention to Stella. "They've been planning an expansion and update for a while, and the timing finally came together. No relation to your little candle experiment."

"What kind of fund-raiser?" Maybe she could help somehow, be more involved than usual. She could be Kat's assistant with the desserts, and help during the actual event. Paranoid or not, she sort of owed them—all of them.

And owed herself.

"It's going to be kind of like a big garage sale, but inside the shelter since it's so hot right now. They're asking everyone in the city to donate items for the sale, and the residents are supposed to make things to contribute too." Kat grinned. "Should be pretty fun, actually. I can finally get rid of some of that bachelor-stuff Lucas keeps insisting we hang on to."

Stella nodded slowly, mind racing. Donations. What did she have to give away that would raise money for the shelter to add on? Did she have anything of value?

An image of her art flitted through her mind, like a wayward butterfly. She swatted it away. Hardly. She'd be lucky to get fifty cents for someone to buy her amateur efforts. But surely she had something . . . jewelry?

Her wedding rings.

She swallowed, heart knotting. That was a decision for another day.

Kat squinted at her, lips pursed like she was trying to hold back a grin and failing miserably. "You do know the shelter still isn't open though, right?"

"Yes, I know." *Thanks for rubbing it in, sis.* "Dixie actually came and hung out at the Cameo yesterday while we were working, so I sort of figured."

Kat stopped pushing her cart and raised one eyebrow. "How'd *that* go?"

"Which part? Us working, or Dixie dropping by?"

"Both."

Obviously, Kat wanted to know about Chase. But what was there to say? *Yeah, we fought, and I tattled on him to the Downtown Director, then realized maybe he was right about my designs after all?*

No. It was one thing to admit Chase had a point. It was another thing entirely to say it out loud.

Especially to her sister.

Stella stalled, flipping over the tag dangling off a beautiful oak crib. "Dixie was her usual self. Entertaining and cryptic, and then fell asleep. After popping up out of nowhere and scaring me half to death."

"And Chase?"

Great. Kat wasn't even pretending to beat around the bush at this point. If there was a bush, she was more like barreling right through the middle of it—thorns and all.

"We're making it work. For the sake of the Cameo." Stella pointed to a cherry changing table next to the crib. "Hey, that one's pretty."

"Making it work—what do you mean? Have ya'll talked things out?" Kat crossed her arms over her chest, a slight frown nestled on her brow.

Well, that attempt at redirection didn't work. Probably wouldn't on Lucas, either. *Or* on their baby, if the poor thing had even half the stubborn streak that his or her parents possessed.

Suddenly, Stella wasn't nearly as jealous over not being pregnant.

"No. Definitely not. I don't think it's necessary." Or desirable. In fact, that was the last thing she and Chase needed—some kind of truce. The past was the past and should stay exactly that. They could be mature and work together without having to dredge up skeletons.

"You're being careful, right?"

Stella laughed, the sound awkward to her own ears. "Kat. He's not a serial killer."

She didn't laugh back. "Some hurts are worse than death."

Preaching to the choir. Time for another attempt at redirection, and this time, she wouldn't play fair. "Hey, look. Baby's first baking set."

"What? Where?!" Kat nearly shoved her cart into an elderly woman toting a basket full of oranges before grabbing the wooden set off the shelf. "Real men bake, too, right?"

Stella smiled sweetly. "Absolutely."

Maybe their kid had a chance after all.

⚬⚬⚬

Stella crossed an angry X with a pencil over her latest design failure and flipped her sketchbook to another page, letting out a frustrated huff as she adjusted her position on her living room couch. She'd gotten confident in the gold and silver color scheme, but there was a piece of the design puzzle still missing. The Cameo deserved something . . . something extra. Some focal point in the lobby, something to grab attention, to welcome the guests pouring through the front doors, to set the mood and tone of the evening.

What that focal point was, she had no idea.

Though Chase had certainly made it clear it wasn't classic movie posters.

Hopefully he'd like the color scheme she'd chosen, because right now she had no idea what else to do if not. Everything she'd researched online lent to the same "been there, done that" ideas Chase was tired of.

Yet wasn't there something to be said for classic? For timeless? For glamorous? Why fix what wasn't broken? Cliché became that way because people expected it. Wouldn't those enjoying a night out in Bayou Bend appreciate an old-fashioned look to the stage and screen? She'd been flashy for years, and flashy definitely wasn't all it was cracked up to be. So why was Chase so bent on something outside the box?

There was nothing wrong with the box.

She was supposed to meet him Monday morning at the theater to finalize the design and get a timeline projection of when she could start shopping and implementing her design around their construction. He had said his plan was to finish the theater first and work their way out to the lobby. Except for the bathrooms, which would get updated based on the plumber's schedule.

Which reminded her. She needed to tie the overall theme into the restrooms, as well—subtly, of course, but it was all still part of the experience. She wanted more than wire baskets with flowers on the counters and a few framed photos on the wall. No, she wanted the women primping in front of the mirror to feel like they were still out on the town. Still in a different world.

Still someone.

Or maybe that was just what *she* wanted when she looked in the mirror.

A sudden knock sounded on her front door. Stella frowned as she moved her sketch pad and pillow from her lap and headed toward the door, hitching up her baggy sweatpants. Seven o'clock on a Saturday evening . . . wouldn't be Mom. She always stayed in on Saturday nights to cook a hearty meal while Dad finalized his sermon for church the next morning. Some nights he'd breeze out of his home office, relaxed, completed sermon in hand and all ready for pork chops or beef stew. Other nights he'd stumble out of the office, a Bible tucked under one arm and a notepad under the other, muttering prayers mixed with frustration as he gulped down half his dinner standing up and returned to work.

Hopefully tomorrow's sermon would be a relaxed, God-sent, pork-chop version. She could use the encouragement. And any advice God wanted to share on how to deal with Chase was plenty welcome.

She opened the door.

Chase.

She shut the door.

He knocked again. "Stella. Stella? Seriously?"

She sagged against the frame, back pressed against the painted wood, wishing she had a metal arm to barricade it like the castles she saw in movies. Chase, in her house. Her gaze frantically caught the open door to her art studio, and she flew across the living area and slammed it shut.

Chase kept knocking. "Stella, we need to talk."

She hesitated. Maybe she was being a little immature. She glanced back at the shut door to her art studio. But Chase, within mere feet of her deepest and best-kept secret? It felt so wrong. As if by allowing it, she was a traitor to her own heart.

He knocked harder. "Stella. Come on, it's about work."

He wasn't going away. Figures he'd turned persistent. Oh no, he couldn't have fought for her half a dozen years ago. Yet now . . .

Men.

She opened the door, shaking back her hair and attempting a calm expression, as if she hadn't just reacted like an insulted toddler. "What's up?"

He stared at her. Maybe she suddenly resembled an insulted toddler too. "Can I come in?"

No. Never. "Sure." She flattened her stomach, stepped sideways so he could pass, and forced herself to avoid looking at her studio door. She could feel it, though, the tell-tale heart thumping from the corner of the living area. Her art, her heartbeat, her private sanctuary in danger of discovery.

Which meant *she* was in danger of being discovered.

Stella drew a deep breath to rid herself of the melodrama. "How'd you find me?"

"Find you? I didn't realize you were hiding." Chase crossed his arms over his chest. The sleeves of his shirt pulled tight across his biceps, and he studied her cautiously, the way a man might view a threatened tigress in the wild.

"I'm not hiding. Just wondering how you got my address." In other words, wondering who had betrayed her and ratted out where she lived. Not Kat. Never in a million years would she help Chase. Nor did Stella think Chase dumb enough to seek Kat out. And it wouldn't have been her mom, meddling as she was. Not this time. Not with Chase.

"It's Bayou Bend. Not really tricky to find someone's address."

What did he mean? That was no answer.

And why did Chase keep scanning the room, as if he was mentally taking a snapshot of her living quarters? She felt exposed, and he wasn't even looking at her. She crossed her arms, too, wishing she could pull a curtain to shade off her entire apartment the way the teal curtain in the corner sectioned off her bed. Thankfully she'd tugged it into place earlier that day in an effort to tidy up and not distract herself from work.

Hard to feel professional when your office was four feet from your bed pillows.

"I know it's Bayou Bend." She frowned at him, but he wasn't looking at her. He was avoiding her question. Who was he protecting? Had he gotten her address from Cowboy Bob, somehow? Was it on a form the Downtown Development office had on her after hiring her? But it was Saturday. How could Chase have gotten in touch with—

He finally stopped his visual scan of their surroundings and met her eyes. "The phone book, Stella. You're listed."

Oops. Maybe Kat was right. She *was* turning paranoid these days.

She turned to hide her embarrassment, heading back to the couch and her sketch pad. "Well, since you're here, you might as well see what I've come up with for the design. That way if there are any changes, I don't have to start over Monday at the theater." Not that there'd be any. This time, he had to like it.

He took the pad she offered and sank down on the edge of the couch, resting his elbows on his knees, glancing back and forth from the sketches to her. "This wasn't why I came."

There didn't need to be any other reason. She pointed to the notepad, a desperate effort to keep his attention and effort directed only toward what mattered. Toward the only thing that *could* be between them. "Gold and silver. What do you think?" She'd shaded in with colored pencils all the spaces she'd outlined at the theater the day before, while Dixie had napped half on her shoulder.

It had turned out pretty, in her opinion. Regal, almost. Once he approved it, she'd plug the ideas into the computer programs she always used to experiment with color and find the perfect shade, and then finalize her designs and print them.

"Stella . . ." Chase's voice trailed off as he flipped the pages.

He sighed, then shook his head as he shut the book and handed it back. "It's still not right."

She sat down hard on the couch, not even worrying about the proximity she'd tried so far to avoid. "How could gold and silver be wrong? It's not overly done, but it's elegant. No red, no black. What else do you want?"

"It's elegant, yes." He pushed his hands through his hair, frustration evident. "But where's the color? Where's the life?"

Her own frustration boiled. That was Chase. Always unable to be pleased. Always rushing off toward the next thing, the next idea.

The next girl.

With no regard or consideration for anyone's feelings around him.

She was sick of it. Briefly she visualized what might happen if she slapped him across the head with her notepad. "That's not fair. There was plenty of color in the design you originally shot down."

"The red?"

Yes, the color she was currently seeing. "The red and black and white. You hated that idea."

"Red isn't a color."

Huh? "Excuse me? Have you ever seen a rainbow? You know, the big pretty promise God gave Noah and the rest of the world?" Her sarcasm was taking over by now, but she couldn't stop it, couldn't stop the broken dam of words pouring from her mouth. She ticked the colors off on her fingers. "Red, orange, yellow, green—"

He covered her fingers with his hand and gently lowered it to the couch between them. "I know red is technically a color, but you know what I mean, Stella. Black and white and red? That's done.

That's dark." His voice trailed, lowered. "That's . . . morbid. Red is blood."

Stella frowned. "But blood *is* life."

"No. No. Not always." A dark shadow crossed his face, and he abruptly pulled his hand away from hers. "What I'm trying to say is that the Cameo deserves color. A color that's hope and beauty and—"

"Why do *you* get to decide what's considered beautiful?" She jumped off the couch, away from him, away from his misplaced logic. Why were there always men in her life telling her the definition of beauty? The pageant judges. Dillon. Chase. Pluck this. Plump that. Enhance here, minimize there.

This wasn't about the Cameo anymore, or colors, or design schemes. It was something much more. But she didn't know how to stop.

She glared down at him, fury beating a rhythm in her chest. "Trust me, Chase. Beauty is beyond overrated."

He stood to face her, inches away. "And what—you think you can hide from it because you throw on sweatpants and don't slap on any makeup? You think that saves you from beauty? You think that changes anything?"

He was almost yelling now, the pain shooting from his eyes proof that he was also fighting a private battle she knew nothing about. They were engaged in two different wars, sharing a battleground and catching each other in their own crossfire.

It had to stop.

Stella released a long breath, deflating both her anger and the hot air rising within. "Why did you come, Chase?" She snorted a laugh. "Pretty sure it wasn't to yell at me about the color wheel."

"I was yelling, wasn't I?" Chase ran a hand down the length of his face, fingers scratching against the five o'clock shadow claiming his lower jaw. "Oh, man. I'm sorry, Stella."

"I yelled too. And probably yelled first." She sat back on the couch and motioned for him to do the same.

He sat down, cautiously, farther away than before. "I actually came because I want a truce."

"Ironic."

"Tell me about it." He laughed a little, the heavy shadow that had consumed his features moments before lifting slightly. "I just . . . I don't want to work with all this awkwardness, you know?"

"I know." She didn't, either. But where was he going with this? Did he want them to pretend as if nothing had happened, or was he actually implying being friends?

Or more?

Her traitorous heart skipped a beat and a rush of memories flooded her senses. She felt her neck flush at the memory of his arm tight around her waist. The roughness of that five o'clock shadow under her chin. His lips pressing a kiss on her forehead.

"So I think it's best if we call a truce."

She stumbled off Memory Lane. "A truce?" So he wasn't suggesting them getting back together. Duh. Of course not, she'd never agree to that in a million years anyway.

Well, maybe never in a thousand.

"An agreement. To forget the past and just move forward." Chase gestured with both hands, as if pointing them toward some unknown, drama-free future. "A fresh start."

A fresh start. Was that even possible with Chase? Yet the Cameo—and her career—deserved her best effort. And he would probably be able to focus a lot better on his own work and on the crew if he wasn't worried about offending her every two seconds or starting a fight.

It was just that . . . well, letting go of the past meant letting go of her guard, her wall, her defense. If she forgave Chase once and for all and treated him as she would any new stranger in her life, she had nothing left to hide behind.

She glanced at the door to her right, the one hiding her secret. She was still Stella. Dillon, and Chase, for that matter, hadn't taken all of her away. She could hide behind her art. Deal with Chase at work, do what needed to be done, and then pour out her passion and aggression into her art. Maybe channeling her efforts and emotion like that into one place would help her find the breakthrough she needed in her creations.

She'd do it. For the Cameo, for Chase.

And for herself.

She nodded. "Agreed. Truce."

"So no more screaming at me about rainbows?" Chase grinned, and she shook her head with a smile.

"No more screaming about rainbows." They stood at the same time, and she reluctantly picked up her sketch pad. "And I'll keep working on this."

As if pleasing him would ever be possible.

"You're getting there." His teasing grin dissipated as they walked toward the front door. "You're talented, Stella. You're just holding yourself back."

A spark of indignation flared, then quickly extinguished. He was being serious, not condescending. Not patronizing. He meant it. And it seemed as if he cared. A little, anyway.

Maybe more than was required for the project.

Or maybe he was just still really good at hiding the truth. She couldn't quite tell—never had been able to. She nodded, instead, choosing silence, and opened the door for him. But he wasn't done.

"Let down the guard, okay?" He gently touched her shoulder. "I think you already know, deep down, what to do."

Not really.

Well, maybe.

"And Stella?"

She licked her lips, not trusting her voice, not wanting to yell or question or, worse—cry. She raised her eyebrows instead, the touch of his fingers burning a hole through her T-shirt. The memory assaulted her—his arms around her, holding her, hugging her. She wanted that hug so badly, but feared the effects of it. She met his gaze, then avoided it, not trusting her response to that either.

"Don't be afraid of color." His hand slid from her shoulder down the length of her arm and briefly squeezed her hand. "Don't be afraid of beauty."

Then he was gone.

seven

The look in Stella's eyes from Saturday night's impromptu visit to her apartment played on repeat in Chase's mind as he went through the motions at the Cameo. Tell Tim to sweep and bag up that pile of trash from the wall demo they'd just completed. Ask Lyle what he'd heard from the plumber on his time frame estimate. Then send Tim to the store for materials. It was time to sand the stage, choose a stain.

That would probably involve input from Stella.

Man, that look in her eyes—it had stuck with him all night, whether he had his own eyes open or shut. That look that begged for a hug. She'd always needed hugs. Nobody else knew it; she kept the stoic façade up so well that nobody knew she needed anything.

He wished now he'd given her more of them.

He'd finally given up on sleep after tossing and turning for three hours, and sat up in the living room with the Sports Channel on low. Thank goodness, Ethan had slept through his fitfulness. No way could he explain to his cousin he was up because of a woman.

But it wasn't like *that*. He just couldn't shake the sensation there was something Stella was hiding from him, something she was holding back. Not that he blamed her, with the history between them. And wasn't he holding back from her too? She had no idea about Leah, about the wreck, that he'd been engaged to someone else . . .

Man.

How was this truce ever going to work if they had so many secrets? It would be one thing if they were strangers, thrown together on a project. Then they could duke out their conflict about the work involved and just go home each night and put it behind them as professional differences. He'd fought with interior designers before, more than once. It was the nature of the industry.

But it wasn't that simple, because of their past and their history . . . their once tangled hearts . . .

Because he still cared about Stella.

The miles had made that a little easier to deny, but now that they were back in the same city—in the same room, for that matter—denial was a luxury he no longer had. He wanted her to be okay.

And something about that look in her eyes last night was absolutely not okay.

He pinched the bridge of his nose, fighting back the tension headache that'd been building all morning despite three cups of coffee. Maybe a truce was impossible, anyway. So much water under that particular bridge . . . with his luck, he'd just end up causing a flash flood.

He looked up and barked another order to Tim, softening the unintentional sharpness of the comment with a quick follow-up "please." Wasn't the boy's fault he was tired and stressed. He just really hadn't meant for that conversation with Stella to go anything like the way it had. How had he turned an attempt to form a truce into a yelling match about colors?

This wasn't the Stella he knew. The Stella he knew would have been slapping bright colors on every square inch of surface in the theater. The Stella he knew would need to be held back, not pushed and prodded to let her ability shine.

Speaking of Stella . . .

He stiffened as she came down the theater aisle toward him, wearing jeans that looked a size too big and a simple navy V-neck top, a bulging bag slung over one arm. Her high ponytail swung as she neared. "Mornin'. How's it going in here today?" Her pageant smile was in place, the one he hated. He'd rather her mope and frown than be fake with him.

That. That was what he meant when he told her the other night to let down her guard. Why did she hold back from being real? In both her interactions with people *and* with her work?

What in the world had happened to Stella Varland?

"Pretty good, actually." He didn't smile back, wasn't going to match her fakeness and be a hypocrite. "The inspector was here an hour ago and confirmed the ceiling doesn't need as much work as I feared."

"That's good." She set her bag in a theater seat and glanced up at the roof, even though she: a) couldn't begin to see the details of the structure high above their heads, and b) wouldn't know what to look for if she could.

"Yeah, the grid is still good, just need to replace the tile."

She nodded as if she had a clue what that meant, and he

suppressed a laugh. She was trying, which was more than he could say for some of the past designers he'd worked with.

"After church yesterday, I drove to the Bayou." Stella pulled her sketch pad from her purse and clutched it against her chest. It was noticeably thinner than it'd been the first time he'd seen it. "Started the design from scratch, and . . . I used color."

Her nervous laugh punctuated the tension between them, highlighting the fact that she was trying hard, so very hard, to make this a no-big-deal conversation.

Which only proved how important it really was to her.

Her grip tightened on the notepad, white-knuckled, even. Chase's chest tightened at the pressure. He *needed* to like this design—because she needed him to. How would their truce work if they couldn't ever agree, or compromise, for that matter? He'd seen the crestfallen way she'd taken every one of his "not right, try again" comments.

But this was business. He couldn't pacify Stella at the risk of hurting her feelings. This was work—both of their reputations were stamped on this theater, and he was just getting started again in Bayou Bend. He needed a solid stand in the community.

But it was more than that—he knew Stella had what it took. All the years he knew her, her entire life was flashes of color. The gold of her hair. The pink of her smile. The blue of her eyes. Her very natural self resembled a living, breathing Photoshopped model with zero effort on her part.

But that light had dimmed since he'd moved to Houston. Her color had faded, her spark dulled. And it wasn't just because of the drab clothes she seemed to favor now, or the lack of makeup. No, this was from the inside out. Even her eyes weren't as striking as they were before. Something—someone?—had turned this rainbow of a woman into a gray cloud.

He recognized the color, because it was the exact shade he struggled to hide every day in the mirror.

"The Bayou, huh?" He'd wait until she offered the sketch. His instincts shouted for him not to reach for it. Maintain distance. Avoid eye contact. Slow and easy. Same instincts that applied to a snarling dog, or a frightened toddler.

The trouble with Stella was that you never knew which one you'd get. His interactions with her so far in the last week had been half terrified child, half rabid beast. She'd run the gamut from insecure, to paranoid, to defensive, to overly confident and insulted in a matter of minutes.

He missed the old Stella. The one who knew who she was, what she wanted, and how to get it, even if it was borderline too much. He'd much rather deal with saucy, mildly arrogant Stella than this shell of a woman he barely recognized. He missed her sass. And her—what was the word? An old classic movie word . . . *moxie*. That was it. Stella used to have moxie.

"Yeah, the Bayou inspired me. Think I'd just been inside too long." Her grip loosened slightly, the sketch pad sliding an inch lower in her hands. Letting down her guard?

He should probably keep her talking. "You still go to that same spot with the picnic tables?"

She hesitated, a wall shooting up around her tightening shoulders. "Sometimes."

Dang it. That was a miss. He probably should have thought about the fact that was the same spot they'd had more than one conversation together—alone, in private—while he was still dating Kat.

Ugh.

He shoved his hands in his pockets to avoid smacking himself in the face. Why had he stirred that up? Now he was being beat with memories:

Shooting paper straws at Stella that afternoon they met for coffee under the pretense of needing advice about Kat. *Whack.*

The night he ran into her at the movies, and stayed for two more flicks afterward because he couldn't bear to leave her side. *Whack.*

That time he and Stella sat on those very benches, shoulder to shoulder, denying the chemistry between them as they stared at the murky water and talked about the difficulties of life and the mysteries of God for hours. *Whack. Whack.*

"That carving is still there, by the way." She said it carefully, like an inspector stepping onto a bridge for the first time after its construction. Not sure of the steadiness, unwilling to fall, but even more afraid not to try.

Because someone had to try.

"The one where we used to guess the owners' initials?" He smiled at that memory, which dug in softly, not connecting nearly as hard as the solid thuds of the others. "D. M. and H. M."

The letters were carved into a tree inside a wobbly heart, which wouldn't have been all that noteworthy if it weren't for the crude sketch of an umbrella under the letters. He and Stella used to sit and guess who the couple could be, and what the umbrella meant. A couple stuck in the rain? A couple under a cover of love? Their guesses had been abstract and vague and they'd never figured it out, but he'd also never minded the mystery because it kept Stella there, by his side, laughing at his corny guesses and wrinkling her nose as she considered all the options.

Stella nodded her confirmation, almost shyly, and for a moment, he considered begging. Throwing away his pride, throwing away the professional truce between them, and clutching his hands in a plea to hear her story. What had rocked her world so completely and left her so . . . uncertain?

She'd always liked Disney movies. What was that one where the chick hurt her finger? Sleeping Beauty. That was it. Stella had turned into a lifeless version of herself, still beautiful, like the princess in the show as she'd lain motionless on a flower-strewn bed.

Or was that Snow White, after she ate the apple?

Either way, he'd been painted to be a villain by the Varland family, and maybe deep down they were right. He'd changed a lot since those naïve evenings in Stella's company.

But even in the movies, the villains always had their side of the story. She'd never really gotten his.

And he still didn't have all of hers.

"Stella . . ." His voice trailed off, and he shifted his weight, hating the guard that already slipped into her eyes the second he said her name. "Will you tell—"

"Here. See what you think." She surrendered the sketchbook, and he wondered briefly if it was because that's what she assumed he'd been about to ask—or because she considered it the lesser evil compared to opening up to him.

Fine. He'd get the design first.

And her story second. This wasn't over.

He ran his fingers lightly over the cover, intentionally, slowly, shooting up a prayer for the right words to speak in case he hated her entire design. *Again*. And had to ask her to redo it. *Again*.

He opened it to the first page. Which was blank.

Um. He raised his eyebrows at her. "Is this a joke?"

"What?" She craned her neck to see around the notepad, then snorted. "Sorry. Next page." She leaned away and stepped fully aside, as if giving him room to view her creation in private. Maybe she just didn't want to watch. If he was nervous, he could only imagine how she felt right now.

He turned the page.

And the design stole his breath.

His inner gasp must have been out loud, because she flinched like she'd been pricked. "Is it that bad?" Her tone held the word she didn't utter afterward. *Again?*

"No." He shook his head, wishing he could find the words to settle her unease but still rendered speechless at the beauty in his hands. She'd kept the gold theme, but replaced the silver with a shade of turquoise. A deep aqua that reminded him of Caribbean waters and Montana skies and her own eyes when she got angry.

She'd found her color.

"Is it worse than bad?"

"NO!" He shook his head harder, her frown only deepening in confusion as he struggled to speak. "It's . . . it's Stella."

He hadn't meant to say that, but the design was just so very *Stella*. The Stella he knew still existed, the one he'd been trying to dig out since he first laid eyes on her in the Cameo lobby with Bob. This was what he knew she'd been capable of.

All that expectation on his part, and she'd still managed to blow him away.

"It's me?" Her confusion lingered, but a wary hope lit her eyes, as if trying to decide if he was complimenting or teasing.

"It's beautiful." And so was she. He focused on the colored

sketch in his hands, not on the way her igniting spark of life turned his grip shaky. It was as if the real Stella was awakening from slumber, and watching the beauty of the process turned his knees weak. Like a sunset. He couldn't look directly at it without it burning his eyes, yet somehow, neither could he bear to look away and miss a moment of the miracle.

She came closer, an intrigued moth to a flame. *His* flame? Or just acceptance from someone in general?

He wasn't sure which scenario would be worse.

Her voice hitched higher. "You really think so?"

That was still the shell of Old Stella talking, the reform not having quite made it to her voice, though it had consumed her expression and body language by now. The confidence was returning, the sass, the moxie . . . taking over even as he watched. Her arms unfolded from across her body and her cheeks flushed pink. She stood on tiptoe, rocking up and down as she peered over his shoulder at the sketch.

"I know so." He cleared his throat, hating the emotion that deepened his voice to a rasp. His telltale giveaway only heightened her assurance.

Yet left him raw and vulnerable.

He handed her the sketch, as if he could pass the baton of emotion with it—and free himself of all that had shifted inside when he looked at that sketch book. "Well done."

He started to walk away, away from the sketch, away from Stella. He needed to get back to work. Needed to refocus, get his mind off the amazing creature half dancing beside him with joy, and get his crew together for an update.

Too bad the demo stage was over. He could stand to swing a

sledgehammer right now. Beat out some of these nails starting to pound into his heart.

He and Stella were done. A thing of the past. His relationship with Leah deserved to be honored—it was too soon for anything else, for anyone else. He wasn't ready.

Never mind that Stella wasn't just anyone. Their history ran deeper than his and Leah's, for that matter.

But no. He was back in Bayou Bend for a fresh start. Not a review of dusty old chapters better left unread. He walked faster.

"Wait."

He turned at her plea, slowly, the way a man might turn to view his own gallows. His heart stammered, and he raised his eyebrows in question, not trusting his voice to stay steady enough to speak.

She lifted her chin a little, eyes narrowing as she considered him. "Well done? That's it? No stipulations? No conditions? No 'well done, *but . . .*'?" A longing for an extra measure of assurance flickered in her eyes. She believed him, but needed just one more confirmation. And the stubbornness lingering in the aftermath proved how much she hated the fact that she needed it.

And like a man tightening his own noose, he gave it to her.

He glanced at the open sketch pad in her hands, then let his gaze travel pointedly to her face. "Beautiful. Just the way it is."

ceee

That hadn't gone as planned. Or, rather, as expected.

Stella stood at the bathroom sink in the ladies' room of the theater, staring at her reflection in the cracked glass and wondering what in the world Chase saw. Both in her design . . . and her image. She squinted at herself. No makeup. Navy T-shirt, slightly wrinkled from her dresser drawer. Jeans she used to save for her "fat days" that now sagged all the time. She'd lost weight after Dillon left, and never put it back on even after the initial shock and depression had faded, even though she'd stopped religiously carb-counting and actually enjoyed meals from time to time.

When she remembered to eat, anyway. Or stopped painting long enough to do so. Or bothered to cook for one instead of two.

He'd said it was beautiful. Her design . . . or her?

Both?

And why did the thought give her butterflies?

She pressed her hand against her stomach. The butterflies turned to gavels, thumping judgments in her stomach, sealing orders unspoken yet so very permanent. She and Chase were history. A moment of connection over her new design didn't change anything. It didn't change how he'd ultimately betrayed and hurt her sister. Didn't change how he'd pitted them against each other. Didn't change the fact that Chase had no idea she'd already been married and divorced and knew nothing about her current life.

Didn't change the fact that the door between them had been slammed shut and dead-bolted a long time ago.

She stared hard into her own eyes in the mirror, half wishing she could see what Chase had seen and half terrified to try. He'd inspired a flash of creativity, prodded her to do her best. That was all. A connection like that could easily be misunderstood as attraction.

No big deal. Right?

So why did he keep using the word beautiful?

And why did she see a ghost in the mirror? A faded, colorless image of who she once was, before Dillon stole the best parts.

Or had he? She still wasn't convinced the "best parts" had been all that great in the first place. She might have wowed the judges on a regular occasion during the pageants, but the judges saw the made up pieces of Stella Varland. The lipsticked, glossed up, highlighted, bronzed version of herself.

Dillon saw the real her, and had bailed.

That had to mean something.

What would Chase do if he knew she'd been divorced? Rejected? Dried up and cast aside like last month's prize-winning bouquet? She might have been a queen on the stage, but at home—in her marriage—she was nothing better than runner-up.

There was no "well done" for that. No prize for imploding before the five-year wedding anniversary. No award for becoming an ex-wife before she could become a mother.

She'd failed.

Her beauty had failed.

With a cry, she threw her notebook hard at the mirror. The corner cut into the already cracked glass, and a fragment clattered onto the dusty countertop. It bounced and slipped into the sink, but she grabbed it before it could make it down the drain. The pointy end pricked her finger, and she winced as she dropped the shard back on the counter. Great. Now she was bleeding, the mirror was even more destroyed than before she got there, and she'd pitched a fit like a toddler.

But Chase liked her design.

The fact that had blown her away and driven her to the privacy of the restroom in the first place. Now it returned to the forefront, perking her spirits.

Chase liked her design. She had a mission now, a purpose to accomplish for the Cameo, without having to fight Chase along the way. She could make some real headway now that the design had been approved. Brainstorm ideas for the bathrooms. Head to the fabric store for samples and measurements. Get to work on her computer programs.

Breathe life back into the Cameo.

It didn't matter that she didn't have a whole lot of breath to offer.

She had enough.

It would have to be enough.

She gave the cracked mirror one more glance. Her counselor used to assure her that her strength was still there, deep down, whether she felt it or not. She dug deep, searching.

Strength, she wasn't so sure about.

Determination? There was that, at least.

Hope?

Ha. That'd be more likely found in a funhouse mirror, as twisted and distorted as that notion remained.

She reached toward the mirror, her finger growing closer until it connected with its reflection, blending into one image. It was a mirror. Just a mirror. It didn't define her. Just a reflection—and an inaccurate one at that.

One day, she'd be strong enough not to look.

With a deep breath, she shoved her shoulders back, tucked her notepad under her arm, and, on second thought, dropped the mirror shard into the outer pocket of her purse.

Broken.

She could relate.

eight

Row after row of fabric bolts spread before Stella like a meadow of rainbows, each color-coordinated section blossoming wild-flowers of potential. It was a creative artist's dream. And it was hers for the plucking.

As long as she stayed within budget, of course.

"Oops." A bolt of gray wool slid off the end-cap display and landed on the floor with a thump.

And as long as her unlikely sidekick didn't trample the flowers before she could form her bouquet.

"How old are we?" Stella hissed as she side-stepped Chase and grabbed the bolt from the floor, avoiding the owner's sharp glare from across the room. This was Stella's favorite store, despite the hawk-like watching of management. They treated their stock as if it were fine China instead of material. Chase bumping into every-thing wasn't going to help her reputation there.

He was already making her nervous enough just tagging along. What if his acceptance of her final design attempt was just a fluke, and they continued to fight over every other decision for the Cameo? What if it was only downhill from here?

"Be nice. It was an accident," he whispered back, wrestling the fabric into place and shooting a sheepish grin to the black-clad woman behind the counter. She lifted her chin and sniffed.

"Wow," he snorted. "It's not a library." He didn't whisper that one quietly enough, and Stella elbowed him in the ribs, nearly knocking him back into the same display. "Hey, stop that."

"*You* stop that."

"And how old are we *now*?" Chase grinned. "What's next? I'm rubber and you're glue?"

Stella rolled her eyes. "You're impossible. Why are you even here, again?" She continued her way down the aisle toward the blue section, simultaneously enjoying and hating how easy it was to fall back into their old banter.

Yet somehow, the fact that they could pick right back up where they left off just seemed cruel. Not to mention confusing.

If her sister could see her now . . .

Stella stopped her train of thought as she halted in front of the rows of turquoise, aqua, and cerulean fabric. All of which perfectly complimented her design with the gold. Regardless of what Chase thought, regardless of the careful truce between them, regardless of her sister's opinions, she was here to buy fabric.

And somehow make the Cameo look classic and modern and brand new and vintage all at the same time.

Easy peasy.

"I already told you. I'm here to monitor any bright ideas you get about going back to black or red." Chase shuddered, the intentionally overdramatic shiver both annoying and funny.

"I'm not changing the design again." Her tone held equal parts warning and acceptance. They'd agreed on the design. That was it. "I promise I won't go back to my old ideas." She shot him a pointed look. "As long as you don't try to nitpick what you've already agreed to."

He held up both hands in surrender, the sudden motion nearly knocking over an end-cap display of bagged sequins. He caught one bag before it hit the ground. "Scout's honor."

He wasn't a Scout. That she knew of. Hardly reassuring.

Not that she could fully trust Chase's word anyway, Scout or not.

She smirked at the idea of him in that khaki uniform.

"What? You think that's funny? The idea of me keeping my word?" He was joking. Maybe. Mostly? His grin seemed hesitant. Unsure.

Well, join that club. She was already president.

She narrowed her eyes, wishing she could x-ray his thoughts and then decided, no, that would probably make things a lot more complicated. "Not funny. More like amusing."

Something flashed in his eyes so fast she wasn't entirely sure she'd seen it in the first place. "I hear ya."

"I was kidding." She reached to touch his arm, then stopped herself at the same time he stepped slightly away. Wow. "Chase. I was laughing at the idea of you in a Boy Scout uniform."

His features relaxed slightly. Had he really taken that much offense to the idea of her thinking his word wasn't reliable?

But *did* she believe his word to be reliable?

And did it even matter, either way?

"You're right. Beige is definitely not my color." He grinned, suddenly looking so much like the laid-back Chase she used to know that she briefly wondered if she'd made up the whole exchange. Chase, open and vulnerable? Never in a million years.

Even now, since he'd been back in Bayou Bend, he'd been on permanent warp speed. Racing ahead with his conversations with Bob and the plans for the Cameo. Racing ahead with her designs and the steps that were *her* job to take toward progress on the project. Even now, he was racing down the aisle ahead of her at full speed, leaving behind a faint hint of cologne that lingered over the bolts of blue and green fabric.

She struggled to keep up, torn between wanting to go back to the serious moment and dissect it and wanting to pretend it never happened. Regardless, she couldn't let him have the last word.

"You know what else isn't your color?"

He glanced back over his shoulder. "What's that?"

"Black and red."

He laughed. Out loud, long and loud. A sound she hadn't heard in years but never fully forgot. "Well played, Tiara."

Her heart stuttered at the old nickname. Their eyes met, and the panic registering in his gaze convinced her he hadn't meant to say it. Funny how one word could stir up a hundred memories, flickering through her heart like images in a flip book. One brief sketch after another, crudely drawn portraits of the past.

The past that he had divided into two periods of time.

When she and Kat were close.

And when she and Kat were distant.

She stiffened as the memories bristled, rubbing and scratching raw. She hated to hold grudges; they were so pointless. Hadn't her counselor harped on that enough in the aftermath of Dillon?

If she could learn to forgive her ex-husband for all he'd committed against her—though admittedly she used that term somewhat loosely—why was it so much harder to forgive Chase, a man she'd not even been fully committed to in the first place?

Maybe that was the problem. Her heart had never had a solid place to land with Chase. And now, it still floated around, a restless ghost with nowhere to haunt.

"Sorry. It . . . slipped out." He looked remorseful enough. But hadn't he *looked* remorseful when he'd broken Kat's heart?

Hadn't Dillon *looked* remorseful when he'd gotten caught with the truth?

Well, that might be a bad example.

She drew a deep breath, willing her pulse to slow to a normal rate. How had a shopping trip for fabric turned into a psychoanalysis of the past?

She was going to turn into a psycho herself if she didn't shut off this circular train of thought and get back to business.

This moment was in desperate need of lightening up. "Slipped, huh? Sort of like how you slipped when you knocked that fabric to the ground?"

He snorted, relief flooding his eyes. "Uh-huh. Keep it up, blondie. Keep it up."

Blondie. Still a nickname, but at least not one from Back Then. Progress. She'd take it.

And speaking of progress, they'd been on this row—and accidental topic—long enough. She rounded the corner to the next, still boasting multiple shades of turquoise and aqua and everywhere in between. The bolts seemed to beckon her forth, their spotless material intimidating and alluring all at once.

She trailed her fingers down the length of one, the silky fabric flawless under her hand but completely the wrong texture for the Cameo.

Hmmm. Maybe she could find those same colors in a tapestry . . . something thicker and heavier that would cover portions of the wall around the theater and by the stage. She glanced up and down the row of options. She'd have to try the back of the store for the wall hanging samples. But maybe she could use the lighter fabrics here, like the silk, as accents in the lobby.

Her mind raced with ideas. She could bunch it to form a bouquet. She'd seen that on Pinterest a few months ago. Or she could use some of the material in the restrooms, somehow, again with the bouquet, or as part of a collage wall mount. Or cut into strips and—

"You're not actually thinking of using that silk, are you?"

He had to be kidding. She risked a glance.

Yep. Kidding.

She ignored him.

But her traitorous eyes darted once again to his stubble-covered smirk, and her heart stammered a truth she couldn't keep denying.

She'd never been able to fully ignore Chase.

And in that regard, absolutely nothing had changed.

❦

He really shouldn't stand on ladders when he knew Stella would be around.

Chase wobbled and grabbed the top rung for balance as he tried not to watch Stella bustle into the lobby of the Cameo, toting several bags brimming with the material they'd bought a few days ago at the fabric store—the store he had almost gotten kicked out of. That owner hadn't warmed up to him after he knocked over that display, and then even less so after he kept talking too loud and making Stella laugh. Someone took her store a little too seriously.

Though maybe he had taken a bit of their conversation a little too seriously too. His running shoe still felt permanently wedged in his mouth. How could he have slipped that way with Stella, calling her Tiara, bringing up the past so flippantly? He was trying to keep all of that separate from the project at the Cameo, and yet here he was, waving old memories around like a red flag in front of a pacing bull. Would he ever stop asking for trouble?

Stella swept past him again, tossing her bags on the concession counter, and then began to pull out yards of blue.

Speaking of trouble, he really needed to get off this ladder.

He climbed down quickly. Meanwhile, Stella's presence in the Cameo hadn't gone unnoticed by his crew. Tim rushed to her side before Chase had even cleared the bottom rung. "Need some help, Ms. Varland?"

"No, but thank you." She smiled at him, all white teeth and shiny lips, and Chase briefly wondered if he should catch Tim or let the boy fall on his backside and get what he deserved for ogling.

Though he hadn't fully grasped that lesson for himself yet.

"Whatcha got there?" He joined Tim at Stella's side as she continued pulling fabric from the bags, ignoring the slight frown Tim sent him at being interrupted. He was doing this kid a favor. Equivalent to shooing away a fly about to get tangled in a web.

Not that Stella meant to be a spider. Not anymore, anyway, with this new demure thing she had going on.

Once upon a time, though—absolutely.

She folded up the now empty bags. "Just wanted to get a few more measurements, and hold everything up where it's going to be, so I can see if I still like it."

She'd better like it, after what they paid for all that fabric. There wouldn't be room in their tight budget from the city for her to start over. He shifted his weight. "Is there a chance you won't?"

She turned that smile on him, now, and he immediately berated himself for judging Tim's weakness. "There's always that chance. I'm an art—" She stopped, looked away, and smiled again, though it shone weaker this time. "I meant, I'm a designer. We have license to change our minds."

"Changing your mind isn't in the budget." Nor was there room in the budget for her to keep rendering him and his crew useless every time she stopped by the theater. Thankfully, the last few days, she'd been working from home on some computer program he'd never heard of, laying out her design in what she called layers, playing around with different visuals until she found a few that made her want to come pretend in person.

Designers. He'd never understand them.

Never understand Stella, for that matter.

"Relax, Moneybags. I'm not going to hurt your budget. If anything, I'm going to save you money."

Stella Varland? Save money? That'd be a sight to see. If her closet was anything like the way he remembered—brimming with sequined shoes and poufy dresses and about a hundred button-down shirts to "protect her pageant hair"—she could sell the entire contents and feed everyone in Bayou Bend prime rib for a month.

He'd only seen that closet once. That day he stopped by because he couldn't find Kat, and she wasn't answering her phone. Stella had opened the door and invited him in to wait. He shouldn't have, but at the time, Stella's spun web was too much for that fly to resist.

Not that she knew it. He'd never accuse her of being alluring on purpose, not like that, anyway. She knew she was beautiful, sure. And she used it to her advantage, but never to hurt someone.

Never to hurt Kat.

No, he'd done that all by himself.

He'd gone inside to wait for Kat, texted her again, and the next thing he knew, he'd put his phone down and forgotten to check it for the next two hours as he laughed at Stella's runway stories, joked with her about world peace, and gotten a rare glimpse into her heart. She'd shared how she worried over still not knowing what she would actually do with her life one day, shared how she still struggled with comparing herself to other contestants. Shared how insecurity could wedge deep like an injury, how there were flaws hidden in places the spotlight could never touch.

He had even opened up about his own concerns with his family, his future, his path in life. His own insecurities and doubts—the ones that still lingered today, if he allowed himself the chance to stop long enough to recognize it. Doubts that he had what it took to succeed. That he could make a life worth living one day, that he was capable, that he could ever commit to one career and make a difference to someone, somewhere.

When the conversation had gotten too heavy, she'd shown him her collection of pageant ribbons, pointed out the layer of glitter on the floor of her closet that was pointless to vacuum up, and wrapped him in a pink boa until the ridiculous feathers made him sneeze and he forgot how unsettled he'd been just hours before.

He and Stella had connected in a way that couldn't be reversed.

Thirteen missed calls from Kat later, he'd finally driven to Kat's town house as they'd originally planned. Sick to his stomach. Unsure what was happening in his heart, unable to get Stella's smile out of his head.

And scared to death.

"Here, Boss." Lyle interrupted his stroll down memory lane by setting a half-full industrial trash bag at Chase's feet. "This is the last of the trash we found off the side of the stage."

Chase stepped back to get the bottom of the bag off the toe of his boot. Slivers of wood poked through the sides, while the entire top was dusted with sawdust shavings. "Anything good in there?" He peered through the opening at the top, unwilling to dig through it without his work gloves.

"Yeah, anything good in there?"

Chase jumped at the sudden echo over his shoulder. An older woman he'd seen once at the theater before squinted over his arm into the depths of the bag, as if she had absolutely nothing better to do than evaluate garbage.

"Dixie!" Stella shook her head, with surprise or frustration, Chase couldn't be sure. "What are you doing here?"

"One man's trash just might be my treasure." She waggled her eyebrows, nudging Chase out of the way. He gladly stepped aside, rubbing his ribs. Who was this lady, anyway?

"Or . . ." Her voice trailed off dramatically as she held up one finger. "One man's treasure might turn out to be what he thought was trash."

Cryptic gypsy. A shiver skated down Chase's back. Was this woman crazy?

He smelled cinnamon.

Stella grinned, but he could tell she didn't fully get the woman's comment, either. Lyle backed away, hands up, as if surrendering the entire lot of the trash and the woman—who now, at second glance, might be homeless. That would explain why she hung out randomly at the Cameo and was interested in the theater's refuse.

But how did Stella know her?

The newspaper article, with the headline regarding the fire at the shelter, popped into his mind's eye. So that was how.

Lyle pulled an empty twenty-ounce soda bottle from his back pocket and spit into it, then called over his shoulder as he turned away. "Tim, come on, boy. You can use the sledgehammer."

Tim grudgingly shoved away from the concession counter. "Fine. I'm coming." He followed after Lyle, hands in his pockets, turning back twice to look over his shoulder.

Tim might want to stay and see what happened next, but Chase sort of wished he could disappear too. He hadn't figured this out yet. And after Stella's jokes about the Cameo being haunted . . .

He shivered again. Just bad timing. That was all.

Though was there ever really a *good* time to be renovating an old theater and have a crazy old lady appear out of nowhere to dig through the garbage?

"You gone through here yet?" Dixie directed the question at Stella as she pawed through the top of the bag, seemingly unconcerned about the sharp fragments piled within. "Find what you're looking for?"

"What do you mean?" Stella frowned, her gaze catching Chase's before she shrugged and shot a cautious smile back at Dixie.

"You've been searching. I've seen you. Seen you searching." Dixie kept digging methodically through the bag.

Chase couldn't look away from Stella's expression, a mixture of wonder and confusion all topped with a heavy layer of denial. She forced a laugh, her eyes darting between him and Dixie and the bag. "Dixie. I don't know—"

"Here," the woman interrupted by holding out a curved fragment of something that looked like it might have once been a stage prop. Three inches of metal with shiny rhinestones glued all over it. A quarter of the rhinestones were missing, leaving behind smudges of white glue.

Stella hesitantly took the piece. Dixie continued rummaging, then as quickly as she'd started, stood up straight, tipped an imaginary hat at Chase, and left the lobby, disappearing into the sunshine.

Then she popped her head back in and pointed at Stella. "You need an umbrella."

They both peered out the windows. Into the fully lit day, void of rain clouds.

No matter. Dixie was gone.

Chase watched the doors swing shut behind her. "So, yeah. That was creepy."

Stella was quick to defend. Too quick. "Hey, be nice. Dixie isn't creepy."

"How do you even know her?"

"She frequents the homeless shelter where I volunteer." The words rattled off Stella's lips. "Or she did, anyway, before I shut it down." She narrowed her eyes. "Don't even start with me on the newspaper headline."

"Wouldn't have dared." Chase waited a beat. "Is it going to reopen soon?"

"I think so. Kat was just telling me about a fund-raiser they're going to do there to raise money to expand." Stella picked up a pile of fabric and began folding it into a manageable size. She shot him a sidelong glance. "She's the one I volunteer with."

"You volunteer with your sister." He hated how his insides still cringed at Kat's name. Hated even more how Stella's lips straightened into a line and her entire body tensed.

Hated not knowing exactly what she was thinking. About the past. About his choices.

About him.

"Dixie thought you needed that." He pointed to the rhinestone stick on the counter. "Why?"

"Why does Dixie do any of the things she does?" Stella shrugged, and her motions at folding grew jerkier with every word. "No one knows."

"It wasn't creepy?" It *was* creepy. He just wanted Stella to admit it. And if she couldn't, then he wanted to know why she was so bent on defending the woman—the woman who gave her advice and rhinestone-covered trash.

She stopped folding and glared. "Dixie is unique."

"Not creepy."

"Right."

Wrong. But okay. He held out his hands for the fabric. "Want me to help you carry some of that into the theater?"

She folded the last bunch and began stacking the piles on top of each other. "I owe Dixie a lot."

He slowly lowered his hands. Right . . .

"I single-handedly put the woman's entire living space out of commission for over a week. And she was a big help to me after my—" Stella stopped short, stacking and restacking the fabric piles like a woman on a mission

"After what?" He wanted to know. Why he wanted to know so badly, he couldn't say, didn't want to evaluate the what-if behind it. Just wanted to know. He leaned forward, as if he could tangibly pull it out of her. "What happened?"

She met his gaze for a long moment, then looked quickly away, back at the material before her. She released a small sigh. "I just don't mind if she wants to come up here sometimes, okay? Because right now she doesn't have many other places to go. And she's not like the rest of the group down there. She's . . ."

"Unique?"

Stella nodded. "Exactly."

"And creepy." He couldn't resist. It was too easy. And Stella needed to smile more. He grinned.

She glared.

"I was kidding."

"Whatever." She shoved a pile of fabric into his hands, but he saw the corners of her mouth turning up slightly before she hid the smile behind her hair. "Follow me."

And he did.

He always had.

nine

Stella used to equate beauty with attention. She never felt lovelier than when she was onstage at a pageant, in a shimmering gown, hair cascading down her back in perfect ringlets, teeth shiny with Vaseline for a balanced, tireless smile. She could perform her "pageant walk"—the practiced strut and half turn, hip slightly cocked, feet angled, weight thrust backward—not only in high heels, but in her sleep. She had dreamed of it, many times. Dreamed of the next win, the next bouquet, the next ribbon.

Terrified to dream about what came after the last one.

Off stage, what was she? *Who* was she?

Then Dillon had come along and she had been rescued from having to answer. She could be beautiful for him instead of the judges. Could prove herself as a wife instead of as a contestant.

She'd never imagined marriage would be the one competition she'd never win.

Stella shifted through the shoe box of broken pieces she'd collected from the Cameo, some even from the area near the dumpster behind the building, and blew out a sharp breath of frustration. She rocked back on the stool and squinted at the tiny workbench in her apartment, hoping for a vision to appear. This project—dare she even call it that? A project required a plan, and she didn't have the least idea where this was going. It just wasn't coming together. Not in her mind, and definitely not on her worktable.

She picked up a few of the small pieces and let them slip through her fingers back into the box. She used to dream of art. Secretly, privately. Not even Dillon knew that part of her soul. The siren song that called to her to create beauty rather than simply to be beautiful. So much work and effort and practice went into those nights onstage, and when it was over, she just wanted the freedom to wear jeans and a sweatshirt and a ponytail—without being judged. Everyone expected perfection of her—most of all, herself.

But what would it be like to create beauty instead? A beauty no one could alter. To create something that wouldn't age or wrinkle or sag or become average.

Something timeless. Forever beautiful.

Forever worthy.

That project was definitely not in this shoe box. She shoved the box away from her but couldn't bear to throw the pieces away. They were fragments of the Cameo, and something within her heart connected to those slices of rejection, those broken bits no one else deemed usable.

She'd toss it eventually. For now, the pieces deserved at least the hope of a future.

Even if she wasn't qualified to give them one.

A knock sounded on her studio door, loud and confident. Not her mom's knock. And definitely not Kat's trademark tap. She shoved the lid on the shoe box of pieces, shut the door to her art nook, and peered through the peephole.

Chase.

With bags of fast food.

Which reminded her—she hadn't eaten. She'd come straight from the Cameo earlier that day, after having spent hours hanging fabric samples, hating her choices and doubting her entire career path, and then finally loving the design again. Come home to this failed artistic attempt with the boxed fragments.

Now it was almost eight o'clock. What was Chase up to?

And why did the thought of him at her door not send her into a frenzy, as it had a few weeks ago?

That might be more terrifying than his sudden reappearance in her life—the fact that he could be a comfortable thought in the middle of it.

She yanked open the door.

"I come in peace." He held out the bags like an offering. "And I come with French fries."

A few short years ago, she wouldn't have even allowed the greasy side dish into her apartment—or the French fries, for that matter. She snorted at her own joke.

How times change.

"Come on in. I'll grab the ketchup." She shut the door behind Chase as he began spreading their food on the coffee table.

"What's with the random burgers?" She raised her voice to be heard from the kitchen, her heart pounding an unsteady rhythm in her chest. Okay, so maybe there was still a little bit of frenzy . . . as long as he didn't see her art room, she could handle this. Burgers. Small talk. Then leaving.

Why was he here?

"I felt bad about what I said." Wrappers rustled from the living room. "About Dixie."

Ah. He never could leave things unsettled. If he thought there was any hint of conflict lingering . . .

"About her being creepy, you mean?" Stella rejoined him in the living room, tapped the ketchup bottle against her palm to shake the good stuff to the bottom, and offered the bottle to Chase first.

He squeezed a few dollops onto a napkin and slid it to her across the coffee table before serving himself. "It offended you. So for that, I'm sorry."

Wow. Chase Taylor, apologizing. The man *had* grown up— and for once, that fact wasn't indicated just by the muscles under his tee. No, it was showing in the manner in which he made sure her food was fixed up and accessible before starting on his own. Was showing in the way he carried himself, a little wearier around the edges than she remembered, but confident. Strong.

She settled on the couch beside him, a full cushion away, pulling the coffee table up to meet their legs. On second thought, maybe he was too strong. Maybe he had his own mask, his own secrets.

She was sure of it, actually. He'd been through something too.

What if *he* was divorced?

The thought made her choke on a fry.

"Is it that shocking? Me apologizing?" Chase swabbed a fry through a pile of ketchup and shook his head at her in exaggerated pity.

She covered her mouth and coughed harder, laughing now behind it. But the initial thought lingered, wouldn't quite dissipate.

"No, sorry. I just . . . choked." On a question she could never ask. But was dying to know the answer to. Why did it even matter? She wouldn't judge him for the same label she tried to hide herself.

It just . . . mattered. Somehow.

She wanted to know.

Wanted to know Chase again.

She stuffed another handful of fries in her mouth. Too bad she couldn't choke off the thoughts in her mind.

He put down his cheeseburger and leaned toward her. "So, you forgive me?"

Such a serious question for such a minor offense. "Of course. It's not a thing." Wasn't, really. She had been bothered by it a little for Dixie's sake, even though she knew at first impression—or sometimes, even second, third, and fourth impression—how Dixie came across. What had bothered her more than the comment was the judgmental attitude behind it. This was her town and her people—*he* had left. He had forfeited the right to tease and criticize and judge Bayou Bend.

But there was zero to be gained in pointing that out. She'd agreed to a truce, so she'd pick her battles.

For now.

"So how did you know I hadn't eaten yet?" Stella took a bite of her burger, wiping her mouth with a napkin and mentally blocking the calorie count prancing through her head. She didn't give much merit to the parade anymore, but it didn't stop the numbers from parading all the same.

"I just assumed. Remembered how busy you were at the Cameo, and you never did turn off of productive-mode very quickly." He shrugged, looking almost . . . shy. Sheepish?

No way. Chase? She fought the urge to rub her eyes to clear her vision. The man didn't have a shy bone in his body. This was the man who hit on her while dating her sister.

But it hadn't really gone down like that, despite Kat's version of the story.

He kept talking. "I figured you came home and started cleaning." He looked around and then shot her a teasing grin. "Clearly that wasn't the case, so you must have been working on the design for the theater again."

She snorted. Her house wasn't that messy. Just . . . cluttered, especially after her haphazard flight from her art room. She darted a glance at the shut door and drew a steadying breath. Her secret was safe. There was no way Chase could stumble into there.

She really needed to find a deadbolt for that thing.

Chase focused back on his fries then, his voice higher and a little too nonchalant. "Just assumed it'd be a safe bet to bring you a burger. You used to always be doing something to make you forget to eat."

So, he had put a good deal of thought into what she might be doing—and pretty much nailed it on the head. The idea spread warmth through her stomach, the type of warmth she hadn't felt in years. Maybe since her honeymoon days of being married. When was the last time a man—a real, flesh-and-blood man—had put that much consideration into her well-being? For no gain of his own?

Scratch that—had it *ever* happened?

Reality sucker punched her, jabbing away the short-lived warmth and comfort. An anchor dragged at her gut, pulling her emotions down into an endless pit. Dillon always had his own agenda. So did the dozens of men before Dillon. Always wanting a piece of her, wanting to break off a portion for themselves, rather than protect her or make sure she was taken care of.

Tears sprang, unbidden, from a well deep within and rarely accessed. She blinked them away before Chase could notice. She was done falling apart. Had already wasted way too many tears on Dillon.

And Chase, for that matter.

No more. She finished the last bite of her burger and began quickly gathering up her trash, wishing he'd never come. Wishing he'd stay forever.

Wishing he'd just leave. Like everyone else always eventually did. Just. Go.

"What happened?" Chase frowned at her, but she ignored him, kept wadding together her paper wrappers and shoving them into the discarded bags, refusing to cry. She was fine. Everything was fine.

"Stella." His hand covered hers, warm, traces of salt still on his fingers from the French fries. She jerked away as if she'd been burned. But she *had* been burned. By Dillon. By Chase. By the lineup of men before them.

Unbidden, the memories flooded through her. She let out her breath, but couldn't draw another one. She began to shake. The room dipped. She closed her eyes. Opened them again. It was hot in here.

"What did I say?" He reached for her hand again but didn't force it, allowing her to step back. Which she did. He stood up, facing her across the coffee table as her fists clenched at her sides and her breathing came in short gasps she couldn't control.

No. *Oh no.* Not another anxiety attack. Always at the worst times . . . was there ever a good time?

She struggled to inhale. She was fine. *Fine.* Her counselor and her doctor told her the attacks would pass with time, that she was healthy. There was no reason for these to continue. It was just stress, the sensation of being overwhelmed.

Yet somehow, knowing she was fine didn't quite push back the darkness.

She faltered, then strengthened. She could not—would not—faint in front of Chase Taylor twice.

Determined to beat it, to fight, she tried to breathe, but the apartment was shrinking by the minute. Like Alice in Wonderland standing before the tiny door, she was too big. Nothing fit. Nothing made sense.

Chase Taylor was in her apartment.

Black crowded her vision and she opened her eyes wider, forcing back the darkness. She tried to pray, but it stuck in her throat. Stuck in her thoughts.

"Stella? Are you okay?" Chase was in front of her then, swaying. No, she was swaying. She reached toward him to steady the room, still pressing in tight. But the electricity shooting up her fingers at the contact with his shoulder let loose a fresh burst of adrenaline.

Everything burst with light.

And then went dark.

❧

Either Stella had some sort of blood sugar issue, or his way with women was getting worse by the minute.

At least this time, he caught her.

Chase laid Stella's limp form on the couch. She moaned, and he relaxed slightly. She didn't seem quite as out of it as she'd been that day on the Cameo stage. He adjusted the couch pillow under her head and watched her take several deep breaths and stir. What was he supposed to do? Calling 911 seemed extreme, especially since she hadn't hit her head. Maybe a cold washcloth?

He looked around for the bathroom and headed for the shut door near the curtained off area he assumed contained Stella's bed. He eased it open, reaching for what he figured would be a light switch, expecting to see a sink and a toilet.

Natural light shone through a window, illuminating an easel with a half-finished painting. He blinked. Not a bathroom. A watercolor? A beautiful blue sky . . . hidden behind an angry red X. He frowned. Why had someone ruined the work?

And yet the one on the wall . . . a woman, dancing. It was stunning.

He turned a slow half circle, taking in the rest of the tiny, packed room. To the left of the half-finished canvas sat a low workbench, holding a shoebox full of broken pieces of random objects. He gingerly reached into the box, rustling the contents. They were from the Cameo.

This was Stella's room.

Stella was an artist.

A *talented* artist.

"Chase?"

He spun at the sound of her voice, which sounded sleepy and disoriented, and hurried to the doorway so she could see him and ease her confusion. "I'm right here. Are you okay?"

She sat up on the couch, her hair mussed, and squinted at him like he was an illusion. "What are you doing? Were you . . . why is the door . . ." The blood rushed from her face, leaving her even paler than before. "Did you go—" She jumped to her feet and wobbled slightly.

"Stella, you fainted. Don't move too quickly." He took three long strides in her direction, ready to catch her again if she was still weak.

But the firm set of her jaw was all strength. "Get out."

He stopped short of touching her, hands hovering. "What's wrong?"

"Get. Out. Now." She pointed to the door, her entire arm shaking, betraying the steel in her eyes. What had happened? Was he not supposed to have gone in that room?

He backed away, giving her space even though he just wanted to pull her into a hug. Find out if his hugs still helped at all like they used to. "I was trying to find a washcloth for your head. You fainted."

She pushed toward him, the anger sparking in her eyes propelling him backward. "A washcloth? The bathroom and kitchen are both over there." She pointed in the opposite direction from her art room. Her secret art room, apparently, if he was reading the situation correctly.

Their truce was rapidly slipping through his fingers. Maybe she was just afraid of his criticism again. He knew it had affected her when he hadn't approved her first designs for the Cameo. Maybe she just feared his rejection again.

Maybe he could fix this.

"It was an honest mistake." His back was against the front door now. He held up both hands in surrender, attempting to talk her off the ledge "Stella. Listen to me. You're good. Really good." So good, it was pure relief. Relief that the Stella he knew still resided somewhere in there. The colorful, flashy Stella he missed so much.

Cheeks flushed red, she reached around him and grabbed the doorknob, knocking into his side as he stumbled out of the way. "I *said* get out."

Apparently compliments weren't going to work. He obediently stepped onto the porch, but leaned forward and braced both arms against the door frame, preventing her from shutting the door in his face. "This isn't like you, Stella."

"Don't even pretend to know a thing about who I am now." Her voice shuddered with intensity. "Don't you dare."

"I'm sorry I went in the wrong room." More than sorry. He should have just wet a paper towel in the kitchen and been done with it. Who knew stumbling into the wrong room could cause all this? Whatever *this* was. "I'm really sorry."

"It doesn't matter." She started to shut the door.

He blocked it with his foot, frustrated. Confused. Hating that he had ruined something he'd just started putting back together, however fragile it'd been. "What, it's some unpardonable sin? That's not fair." Not that much was these days, but this . . . he couldn't lose this. They'd had a truce. They were going to be friends again, redeem the past.

No more regrets. He couldn't have any more regrets.

And this was rapidly careening in a direction he couldn't control.

"You don't understand!" Her resolve was slipping now, cracks evident in her voice. Were those tears?

He'd made her cry.

Again.

He was really good at making girls cry. "Make me understand."

She shook her head, crossed her arms over her chest. Hid. Hid within herself. He hated when she did that. It was almost as bad as her pageant smile. He lowered his voice, tried again. "What are you so afraid of?"

She uncrossed her arms, and his hopes lifted. Putting down her defenses? Tearing down the wall she'd started building before his eyes?

She put both hands on the door and pushed. "The truth."

He stepped back just in time.

And the lock clicked into place.

ten

Stella had a dream once. One of those nightmares that lingered long after you woke up, that stayed on the fringes of your subconscious for weeks or even months.

In the dream, she'd been onstage competing in a pageant, and her bathing suit had been too big. It'd been a one-piece, red polka-dotted suit, and it kept slipping as she made her way down the catwalk. Every time she grabbed the straps to hold it up, the material slid through her grasp like oil and disintegrated until, by the time she'd reached the end of the stage, she'd been completely naked.

She remembered that bad dream vividly, even years later. The memory of it burned, that awful feeling of exposure. Helplessness.

But this was worse.

This was a reality she couldn't wake up from. Chase had found her secret.

She couldn't hide anymore.

"What is with you today?" Kat transferred a tray of cupcakes from the oven at Sweetie Pies and then bumped the door shut with her elbow.

Hot air from the oven billowed through the small industrial kitchen. "What do you mean?" But Stella knew exactly what her sister meant. If she looked even half as betrayed as she felt, then she could only imagine Kat's level of concern. Yet she couldn't explain herself without admitting Chase had been in her apartment, which would bring up all kinds of questions from Kat that she really didn't want to answer.

And she also couldn't explain without revealing her own secret to Kat.

It was lose-lose.

Kat deposited the hot trays on the countertop and waved her oven mitt in the air. "You're moping. Even more than usual. And why aren't you at the Cameo this afternoon working?"

Because she couldn't face Chase after she'd kicked him out of her apartment.

Stella rubbed her hands over her face. The smooth complexion under her fingers still caught her off guard sometimes. She never used to be able to touch her face without coming away with layers of foundation and powder caking her fingers.

Good thing she'd made that change, because with all the stress of the past year, she'd end up with finger tracks down her cheeks daily.

"I'm going over there later. To discuss the stage." She didn't have a choice. They wanted her opinion on what color stain to use after they finished sanding it. Would Chase play it off and be professional, or would he pull her aside and insist they hash out what had happened last night?

For that matter, she still didn't know for sure what had happened. She'd fainted. Another anxiety attack when her thoughts got the best of her, apparently. Then she'd come to and found Chase standing in her private sanctuary. Where she sweated and prayed and placed the only remaining untouched piece of herself on tentative, private display.

And now her last secret place had been revealed.

Kat took out the next tray from the oven. "The shelter reopened, by the way. I wasn't sure if you'd heard."

Thank goodness. There would probably never be a day that whole situation didn't rub against her nerves in some form. She'd never fully live it down.

Hazards of a small town.

Hazards of an easily pricked conscience.

"It wasn't your fault, Stella."

Stella squinted. Pursed her lips. "No, I'm pretty sure it was."

Silence tucked itself around the kitchen. And then Kat snorted. "Okay, maybe it was. But you've been through so much. Everyone does stupid things when they're hurting."

"Sure they do. They impulse-buy musical instruments they'll never play and go on rebound dates with the biker down the street. They don't typically ignite and flood out homeless shelters."

Kat coughed back her laugh but Stella heard it anyway. "Seriously, it's going to be fine. They've got the fund-raiser planned out now. It's in a few weeks. Remind me and I'll text you the exact date and time."

"Okay. I'll help." It was the least she could do.

"Have you thought about what you'll donate?"

She had some ideas, but nothing that was worth enough. "Still debating. I'll need to go through my closet again." The image of her wedding rings still danced in her mind, but she didn't know if she could go through with that. It wasn't like she'd wear them again—if anything, they'd burn a hole through her finger if she tried. And she didn't have a child to pass them on to.

Still. It was a decision to make.

"So how are things going with Chase at work?" Kat slid the next tray of batter-filled liners into the oven and shut the door. "And I want a real answer. None of that fake mess."

"What fake mess?" Stella straightened her spine, feigning offense.

It didn't work.

"Don't even pretend to be offended. You know you can slap on that pageant smile and give all the big-white-teeth right answers you want all day long, but I want the truth." Kat tossed the oven mitt on top of the counter and grinned. "And I can say that right now because I'm pregnant and you can't get mad at me."

Oh, she could. But she wouldn't. Because her sister was right. She'd perfected the crowd-scene expression and tone and could slip back into the practice faster and more automatically than she liked. Old habits died hard.

Some of them, anyway. Others labored for breath and refused to die at all.

"The truth is . . . it's rough." Stella let out a long sigh. Should she tell Kat the whole truth, or just the highlights?

And what were the highlights, anyway? That Chase's ridiculous truce was a farce? That too much water had flooded that particular bridge to ever have a chance at staying dry?

That she still had feelings for Chase?

No. She grabbed a cupcake from the counter and pulled off a hunk from the top, shoving the almost-too-warm bread into her mouth, sans icing.

"That bad, huh?" Kat tilted her head, studying her in that way only a sister could.

Stella looked away, terrified the truth would start radiating out of her bare pores. "It's confusing." Which might be the understatement of the decade.

Kat narrowed her eyes knowingly. "You can't trust him."

"Are you asking me or telling me?"

"Telling. You can't." Kat shrugged, turning to peek through the oven window at the baking cupcakes. "Just know that up front and get through the project, and then you'll be done. After the Cameo is renovated, you won't have any reason to have to talk to him again."

The thought tightened something in Stella's stomach she hadn't realized was loose. She tore off another bite of cupcake, the sudden urge to defend Chase welling up from somewhere deep within.

But not to Kat.

Not ever to Kat.

And where did that urge to defend even come from? He'd betrayed her. Invaded her space and her heart.

But he hadn't known. He'd been looking for a bathroom. To *help* her, because she was unconscious, for crying out loud. *Again.*

Could she really stay mad over that kind of an accident?

She bit her lower lip. "It'll be fine. Just . . . it's been complicated, because of—well, everything." Stella wondered how it was possible to keep saying so many words without actually saying anything at all. And wondered further if Kat noticed. She needed to redirect, quick, before Kat picked up the scent. "On a funny note, I think the cleanup guy on the crew, Tim, has a crush on me."

Kat nodded. "He does."

Huh? "How do you know? You haven't even met him." Stella frowned.

Kat rolled her eyes and blew a wisp of hair out of her face. "Is he eighteen or older?"

"Yes."

"Is he a male?"

"Yes."

"Then he has a crush on you, Stella."

"Whatever." Those days were long over.

And if they weren't, they sure as heck needed to be.

She changed the subject again. "At least Chase and I finally agreed on a color scheme for the theater."

"That's good news." Kat turned away and began plucking the cooled cupcakes from the tin on the countertop and setting them on wire racks. "See, you can work together and be professional. That's a good exercise, really, for any time you have to deal with difficult people in your career." Her voice grew tighter. "And it's great you finally agreed on the design, because you can't let people like Chase run you over."

Was it just her, or was Kat tossing those cupcakes a little harder than usual onto the racks?

She continued. "Like I said before, just be careful. If you know up front you can't trust him—"

Yep. Her sister was definitely throwing cupcakes.

"Then it won't matter how he acts or what he does because

you're already prepared for the worst. For the inevitable, really. So you can just do your job then and not worry about anything personal." Kat finished her tirade and faced Stella, pointing the oven mitt at her. "Don't worry about anything personal."

Not a suggestion. A command.

Stella bristled at the order, then reminded herself that her sister was hormonal, and they were discussing her ex-boyfriend. And not just any ex, but *the* ex that very nearly devastated Kat's heart. Lucas was part of God's plan for Kat, and she knew her sister would have gladly gone through the same heartache again to land where she'd landed now in her marriage and family. But exes were still a tricky subject—even for the relationships that ended well.

Kat and Chase had not ended well.

And her sister was always going to hold that tiny spark of blame over Stella's head.

Talk about preparing for the inevitable. "Nothing personal." She was simply restating. Not agreeing. Right?

So complicated. She let out a low sigh, finished the cupcake she'd systematically started mutilating earlier, and dropped the liner in the trash. "I've got to get to work." She pushed out of the kitchen before she could say things she shouldn't say. Because saying anything in defense of Chase would only fuel the embers that still glowed.

And she really didn't need to be setting any more fires.

"Want to take some cupcakes to the crew?" The old Kat was back now, the normal one, the one who didn't rage with hormones and conjure jealous green eyes over the distant past.

Stella smiled. She loved her sister. Wanted to smack her, but loved her. "No thanks, sis. You know the saying about the way to a man's heart being through his stomach. And, well . . ." She purposefully let her voice trail off.

Kat raised one eyebrow, waiting, a warning gathering on her face like a storm cloud.

"I'd hate to give Tim the wrong idea." Stella winked before disappearing into the front of the store, Kat's laughter ringing loud.

Good. Maybe she'd stay oblivious to the obvious a little bit longer. The inevitable.

If only Stella could do the same.

❧

He figured he'd regret letting Memphis use the sander, but a boy had to learn how to use power tools eventually, right? He winced as the machine ground against the stage floor, and leaned down to adjust his oldest nephew's grip. "Like this, dude." Thankfully he'd had enough sense to give eight-year-old Aaron sandpaper strips, and a back corner of the stage where he couldn't do any damage.

"Sorry." Memphis frowned, concentrating, as he resanded the same portion he'd gone over twice already. Talk about being afraid to step out of the box and give it a real go. The boy was beyond hesitant with new things. Might be why he'd been benched all season in football.

It was something to work on. There was no time for second guessing or doubting—in school, in sports, in work . . . in relationships. Chase had learned that particular notion through and through, and if he had anything to offer his nephews after his hiatus from their life, it would be that singular important lesson.

Time mattered.

Speaking of time . . . he glanced at his watch. Jimmy had brought the boys by earlier to check on the renovation progress and bring him and the crew coffee—a nice gesture, very unexpected for his brother.

Then the truth had become clear less than three sips into his coffee when Jimmy admitted he needed to run an errand, and could do it faster without the kids. So now the foreman and contractor for the Cameo was officially a hired babysitter—paid for in coffee and arm wrestling contests.

He had let Aaron win.

"Is that better?" Memphis called over the construction noise as he looked up, his need for affirmation and perfection practically glowing in his eyes. Chase recognized himself in the boy.

Life had taken care of that neediness. Not a lot of compliments to be found when you had to start over at almost thirty, nothing to show for your time except a trail of broken hearts and the fragments of your own still trying to remember how to beat.

And no time for perfection when there was so much to do, to achieve, to accomplish while he had the opportunity. If you hustled fast enough, nothing much could catch up. Memories. Pain. Failure. Regrets. They were all left in the dust, where they belonged.

Except that lately, certain pieces of that dust pile had been reforming itself into bones.

He nodded at Memphis. "Much better." Somewhat better, anyway. But at least now his nephew saw that trying counted. A lesson Chase wished he had realized sooner in life.

And speaking of teaching lessons . . .

"But you've got to speed it up if you want to finish what you're doing." Starting a project well was important, but completing it was crucial. He gestured to the expanse of stage still needing to be sanded. "You have to finish what you start."

"Even if you don't know what you're doing?" Memphis frowned up at him, his trendy-long hair falling into his eyes. He shook it back and waited for an answer.

"Well, yeah, dude. If you can't deliver a promise on time, it's as bad as breaking the promise in the first place." Or worse. If his word was all a man had . . .

The conversation with Stella in the fabric store jumped to the forefront of his mind, and he winced.

You think that's funny—the idea of me keeping my word?

Not funny. More like amusing.

Like a sucker punch to the stomach. Not funny at all.

And she definitely hadn't been laughing last night when he'd stumbled upon her art room. He still had no idea why she'd flipped out on him, shoving him out of her apartment while crying. No idea why it'd been such an unpardonable sin.

No idea why she fainted two-thirds of the time she was caught in his presence.

Memphis persisted, oblivious to the battle raging in Chase's head. "But this is just a floor, Uncle Chase. It's not a promise."

"Well, yes and no." Chase squatted down beside his nephew, turned off the electric sander so they could hear each other. "I told the city I'd get this project done in a certain amount of time. So that's like a promise. Any time you give your word it should be your guarantee as a man."

A throat cleared softly from stage right, and Chase looked up at Stella in the wings, her giant purse pulled around in front of her body but doing little to shield her beautiful, lithe frame, clad today in washed-out jeans and a black tank top.

Last night's debacle rose to the surface, and he stood up quickly. "Hi." That was smooth. He tried again, motioning at Memphis. "This is my nephew, Memphis. He's been helping me sand."

Memphis stood, held out his hand, and shook Stella's firmly, all charm and manners. His grandma would have been ecstatic. "Nice to meet you, ma'am."

"Likewise." She grinned, shyly, and met Chase's eyes before flitting her glance away. "Do you have the stains for me to choose from?"

Business. Right. He wished he could bring up last night but knew he couldn't in front of Memphis. Probably shouldn't, even if he could. The in-your-face, tell-it-like-it-is Stella still seemed pretty dormant 99 percent of the time, but he knew better than to taunt a volcano.

"Aaron's guarding them pretty well over here." He introduced Stella to his youngest nephew, who offered her an arm wrestle.

Stella grinned and politely asked for a rain check.

Aaron shrugged and went back to rubbing his sandpaper strips on the stage.

Chase pointed to the stain samples he'd displayed on a large sheet of poster board. "These were the best options in the hardware store. They had others, but these are the most commonly used, according to the owner." He shrugged. "I've never renovated a theater stage, so I can't vouch for the validity of that, but he seemed to know what he was saying."

Stella ignored his rambling, knelt down next to the board, and pulled some of the gold and turquoise fabric from that giant purse of hers. She carefully held the pieces up next to the different options. "Too red."

She dismissed the first, which he'd secretly preferred until she'd said that, and he realized the stark truth in it. "Too yellow."

They finally agreed on the fourth option, a deep, rich brown that made Stella's eyes light up when she held the turquoise next to it.

Chase couldn't help but smile. Too bad they couldn't find the exact shade of her eyes for the fabric samples. Talk about a design hit if he'd ever seen one.

He jerked back from that train of thought. Stella was beautiful, no doubt about it. But dwelling on that had only gotten him in trouble in the past, and from the way she'd been trying to hide her beauty lately, it appeared she felt the same.

He wanted that story. Wanted to sand down the past and remove the blemishes and the scars and have a clean slate to work with, like the stage beneath their feet. Wanted them to have a foundation again . . . To build what? A relationship?

Impossible.

A friendship?

Maybe.

But they'd tried a truce before, and that had lasted about forty-five seconds before proving difficult. Should he bring it up? Would Stella even try again?

He should probably figure out first why it mattered so much to him that she did.

But if he discovered the real answer to that, he'd likely never ask.

"Daddy's back!" Aaron shot up between them so fast, Chase reeled backward. Stella grabbed his arm to balance him, probably on instinct and unplanned, judging from the way she dropped it. Aaron and Memphis jumped off the stage and rushed up the main aisle to Jimmy, who waved and hollered his thanks.

Chase saluted him with a nod. "Anytime, bro."

"Anytime? What about tomorrow at four?" His brother winked. "Kidding. Holler if you need more coffee." They paraded up the aisle toward the theater doors, and Jimmy called out over his shoulder. "It's looking great, by the way."

It wasn't. Not yet. Still looked like a giant mess, but Jimmy had always been able to envision the final outcome of things before Chase could.

Was that why he'd warned Chase about Leah the one time they'd met?

She's not the one, dude. He'd said it so casually, the equivalent of picking out a suit or a fantasy football roster. He couldn't explain why. Just seemed so sure.

But Chase didn't operate by instincts like the rest of his family. He needed facts. Evidence. When he chose to have faith, he had it in spades. He had faith in God. And had faith that his relationship with Leah would be just fine.

Death had other plans.

"Well, I guess I'll head home too." Stella gathered the fabric samples she'd used and deposited them carefully back into her purse. "I've got a few more things to plug into my design program and figure out for the restrooms." She hesitated, her blue eyes seeking his with questions beyond interior design. "I guess I'll run the final plans for that by you in the next few days."

"I can't imagine having a conflicting opinion about a bathroom." He grinned, attempting to take the edge off, but it fell flat.

"I can." She smiled back, but it faded faster than he'd have preferred.

"Stella, I—"

"Chase, about—"

There they went again. He held up both hands. "I'd say ladies first, but I need to apologize. I still don't really know what happened last night but apparently I offended you and I'm sorry. Whatever I did by going in that art room was an accident, Stella. Totally unintentional."

"I know." Stella rubbed her hands over her face, leaving temporary pink marks on her cheekbones. "You had no idea, and I overreacted. It's just . . . that's—"

"That's your space."

"Yes." Relief flooded her eyes, and he wished he actually understood as much as he apparently gave the impression that he did. "No one knows about that room, Chase. Not my mom. Not even Kat."

She didn't flinch this time at the mention of her sister. Progress. Maybe they were ready for this truce after all. A real one.

But looking into her hopeful eyes, he knew it couldn't be a mere truce. It'd have to be a full-on friendship, or nothing at all. A truce in itself wasn't nearly enough. It'd be a tease.

He wanted Stella back in his life.

As a friend, of course. Anything more than that was asking for regrets.

And he was done with those.

"Your secret is safe." He took a chance—a big one—and reached for her hand. "What I was telling my nephew about a man's word . . . I believe that."

Something uncertain flickered in her eyes, and he wished she'd say it. But he knew better than to push. "I hope you believe me."

She hesitated, then nodded. She didn't pull her hand away. More progress. "I do."

Huge progress. He released her hand, reluctantly. Contact was dangerous, the current between them still strong. He shoved his hands in his pockets instead. "Since I already know about the room, I'd really like to hear why it's a secret."

She opened her mouth, then shut it. Opened it again.

"I meant it when I told you that you were good, Stella. Your art . . ."

She held up one hand, her expression gentle, but firm. "Later."

Yes, ma'am. He nodded, accepting her terms. "Whenever you're ready."

She inhaled an unsteady breath, nodded back, and offered a half smile, tucking the strap of her purse higher on her shoulder. "*Ready* is debatable. But one day." Her smile wobbled. "This time I promise."

She made her way offstage before he could comment. Probably for the best.

And probably for the best she didn't turn and notice how he watched her the entire time she walked out of the theater.

eleven

Claire Varland was the epitome of southern charm and hospitality. Full of honey-coated, coaxing words that brought to mind images of sweet tea and homemade pie and all things charming west of the Mississippi.

Until crossed. Then she could intimidate the green off a grass blade.

"I can't believe that man has been in Bayou Bend for weeks and you didn't even tell me."

From her vantage point on the couch, Stella watched her mom pace the width of her apartment, which didn't take a lot of steps, and alternate wringing her hands with glaring. Sometimes accomplishing both at once. "You're the one who got me the job at the Cameo, remember?"

"I didn't know Chase Taylor was the contractor, or I'd have never arranged that with Bob!" Those perfectly manicured hands flung high in the air so fast they caught the long chain of pearls around her neck and tossed them in her face. Stella bit back a snort.

155

Dealing with Chase had grown more complicated than she'd have preferred, but watching her oh-so-proper mother freak out almost made it worth it.

Almost.

The reminder that this job was paying for her apartment so she didn't have to live with said mother definitely made it worth it.

Stella gave up and headed for her closet. She'd promised Kat tonight she would start finding things to donate to the shelter's fund-raiser sale, but her mom's impromptu visit after she'd heard about Chase through the grapevine had thrown her off schedule. Stella had been waiting for her mother to finish venting, but at this rate, she better get started. Didn't look like Mom was going to run out of steam anytime soon.

"What did you tell your sister?"

Stella opened her closet door and began rifling through the contents. "That I'm working with Chase?" It came out as a question, even though it was fact. But why had she even asked in the first place? She bent down and began opening shoe boxes. Ah. That's where her photo album had gone.

"So?" The pacing had stopped, judging by the lack of noise and lack of shadow passing in front of her living room lamp, but now the foot tapping had begun. *Tap tap.* "How'd she take it?" *Tap.*

"Better than you."

The tapping stopped. "Stella Michelle Varland."

"Weeelll. She did." She hated the high pitched tone her mother always brought out in her. But constant defense did that to a voice.

"I find that hard to believe."

Of course. Unless something was *her* idea, that was always the case.

Stella sighed. "Mom. Listen. It is what it is. Chase and I are working together just fine. There's no need to gather the posse and run him out of town."

The tapping began again. "Who said anything about that?"

"You didn't have to. I know you were already scrolling through your mental list of contacts to find someone who could get him to move back to Texas."

The tapping stopped. "Maybe."

"Don't deny it. You were." Stella turned to face her mother, who now stood silently, rubbing her arms with both hands. "Kat is fine. I'm fine. It's ancient history. So let's just drop it, okay?"

Her mother opened her mouth, and Stella beat her to it, pushing the issue. "*Okay?*" She could threaten to call Dad, but they both knew it would be a useless bluff. He might wear the pants in the family, but he also knew good and well who washed, dried, and ironed them.

"I just don't want any more drama from that man."

Stella bit back a sigh as she squatted down in front of more boxes on her closet floor. "None of us do, Mom. Trust me." There had already been more than enough since Chase's return to Bayou Bend. But some things her mother was better off not knowing.

Stella got back to work. "If you want to stay, you can help me find some things to donate to the shelter's fund-raiser. But I'm not going to talk about Chase anymore."

"All right. I understand." Her mom joined her at the closet, then shot her a sidelong glance. "So, is the job going well? Just in general?"

Sincere concern and interest radiated from her mom's eyes for one of the first times in . . . well, a very long time. Maybe the first time since Stella had quit entering pageants. The warmth of the acceptance spread through her chest. She nodded slowly. "It is. Was a little rough at first, but I'm finding my way." She hesitated. "I'm really glad you helped me get the position." Ironically enough, she meant it.

Her mom made eye contact, then nodded briskly. "You're welcome."

They filtered through the closet in silence for a moment, the shock of the connection nearly knocking Stella off balance. She opened the lid on another box, staring blankly at the contents as her mind raced. She and her mom, bonding? Not arguing? That was rare. They used to be close, back when Stella had big hair and did everything she was told to do with a shiny white smile onstage for hundreds of people.

But since her divorce, she felt as if her mom looked right at her but just didn't *see* her anymore.

Which was probably fair enough, considering Stella didn't really see herself, either.

Maybe things could change between them after all. The relationship between Kat and their mom had improved radically after Kat and Lucas got married and Kat learned to stand up for herself. Maybe Stella and her mom could find that same common ground of mutual respect.

Maybe then she'd finally stop being thought of as the baby who needed taking care of.

For that to happen, of course, she'd actually have to stop needing to be taken care of.

The prick of tears came, as it always did when she thought about her divorce and all the consequences afterward. She blinked rapidly. No. She wasn't sad about Dillon. Not tonight. It'd just been a long week, and with Chase and work . . . just emotionally overwhelmed, was all.

She pushed the emotion back and replaced the lid on the shoe box she'd just opened. "Any luck?"

"I'm not sure. What kind of things do you want to get rid of? Old clothes?" Her mom slid hanger after hanger across the rack over her head. "All of this looks old, Stella. When was the last time you went shopping?"

Stella tilted her head. She honestly couldn't remember. "Um, last spring?"

"That's not possible, dear. None of this was in stores this spring." The hangers screeched across the iron bar.

"I meant *last* year. Like, a year ago spring."

"Oh, dear heavens." Her mother let out an exasperated sigh. "If you needed money that badly, Stella, you could have asked."

It had nothing to do with money. She didn't want to be seen anymore, so why spend money on new things that would just draw attention? Put her back in the spotlight?

Bad things happened in the spotlight. Dangerous things. Things like men thinking they were in love. Thinking she could be worth something beneath the glitter and the tiaras.

Tiara. Chase's nickname rubbed a raw spot on her heart, and she cleared her throat in an effort to rid him from her thoughts. "I'm good, Mom. Don't worry."

"Well, I do worry, dear. It's a mother's job."

"I thought preachers' wives were supposed to pray instead of worry." She stood up beside her mom and started shoving hangers from the opposite direction, working to meet her in the middle.

"We do that too."

She abandoned the middle ground and traded it instead for the far end of her closet, where she'd stuffed all her pageant dresses. A rogue thought began to form. "There. This. It's perfect."

"What's perfect?" Her mom craned her neck to see in the shadowed corner of the deep closet.

"My pageant dresses. I can sell those at the fund-raiser." She began pulling them off the bar, eight in all. No, probably ten. They wouldn't bring in a ton of money, but it would definitely be a real contribution. Some high school girls could probably use a discounted dress for Homecoming or Prom. Save their parents the trouble of going to a high-end store.

Besides, there was no reason to preserve the dead in her closet.

"Are you crazy?" Her mom grabbed for the teal one on top of the stack in Stella's arms, sending a smattering of sequins to the carpeted floor.

Stella widened her eyes. "Um, no, but you might be." What had gotten into her mom? They were just dresses. Old dresses that wouldn't even fit her anymore, most likely. Not that she had anywhere to wear them, even if they did.

"These aren't fund-raiser type dresses, Stella." Mom took the heap of material from her. "These are memories. These are mementos of an . . . an *era*."

"I'm glad you're not being melodramatic." Stella rolled her eyes and exaggerated a swipe of her forehead. "Because *whew*. That would be really unfortunate."

"I'm serious." Her mother's southern accent grew stronger when she was on a mission, and right now, it was thick enough to wade across. "You can't sell these."

"Mom. You have to let go." Stella tugged at the dresses her mom clenched with both arms. "And I mean that literally and figuratively."

"Maybe you were too quick to let go. Did you ever think of that?" Her mother finally released the material and watched as Stella moved the dresses to the couch, spreading them out one by one. She followed her, running her fingers across the taffeta and silk and beaded designs. "Don't you miss it, at all?"

No. Yes. Sort of. Maybe some parts. But the aftereffects—the misplaced identity, the overconfidence, the sass—they'd only brought heartache. It'd hooked Dillon.

She just hadn't realized she'd been fishing catch and release.

She straightened the skirt of her favorite dress, a deep pink that had complimented her skin tone so perfectly back in those days. All of these dresses held memories. Some good. A lot of bad. "Some eras need to end, Mom."

Her mother crossed her arms, sinking onto the couch in defeat. "Maybe. But maybe you need to realize not all of your past is terrible."

"I don't think that." But she did, didn't she? She continued smoothing the fabric, avoiding her mother's gaze. She'd connected all the yarn of her past into a big, tangled ball until now, it was so knotted she just wanted to ditch the entire thing. She might have had a misplaced identity when she was caught up in the world of pageants, but today she didn't have one at all.

She wasn't sure which was worse.

"That one was your favorite, wasn't it?" Her mother pointed to the pink dress.

Stella nodded.

"This was mine." Mom touched the shoulder strap of a royal blue gown that had done amazing things to Stella's eyes. "You were always so stunning."

Were. Yeah, that stung, a bit. But not as much as she used to fear it would. That part of her had died. That desperate need for attention, for compliments, for security in her appearance . . . gone. Buried.

But nothing had been born in its place.

Her gaze darted to the closed door of her art nook. Well, maybe something. Nothing worth anything to anyone else, though.

But at least she was hidden. No more lights. No more pressure. No more perfection. She could eat what she wanted, wear what she wanted. Actually feel her face instead of layers of makeup. She'd traded her high heels for flip-flops, and she was *safe.* Tucked away.

Invisible.

So why the constant ache, if she'd achieved what she wanted?

"Maybe we're both right." Mom stood up, moving in front of the dresses and picking up the hangers one by one. "Maybe it is time to let go." She draped the heap of dresses off to one side of the couch, then pulled the royal blue and the deep pink gowns off the top of the stack and laid them in a separate pile. "And maybe it's time to realize not *all* of the past is bad." She shot Stella a pointed look.

Stella studied the two piles, the one containing everything she had to give away, and the one containing her and her mom's favorite gowns. Preferred memories of an era long gone. Pieces of the past.

She nodded slowly. This wasn't just about the dresses. This was about her and Mom. This was a truce, a compromise on her mother's part, an offer of acceptance that went far beyond mere fabric and beads.

"What do you think?" Her mother was wringing her hands again, which meant she was worrying. And probably praying, too, by the furrowed line between her perfectly plucked brows.

And in that moment, she wasn't intimidating at all. She was a mom—her mom—who probably had been affected by the last few years of Stella's life a lot more than Stella could ever realize.

They all needed to be cut a break.

And she'd start here.

Stella gave her a soft smile in return. "I think you've got a deal, Mom." Maybe this compromise would hold her mom for a while, last her until she got a new bee in her proverbial bonnet.

"So you'll try the dress on for me? Just for old time's sake?"

Nope. Never enough. Stella fought back a groan. But the hope in her mother's gaze made her wonder if maybe it'd be worth being seen again, just for a moment.

A very brief moment.

"Fine. Why not?" She took the blue dress and tried not to be hurt by the beaming expression on her mother's face. It still mattered too much to her. But they'd reached a new line in the sand, and it seemed like a good one so far. What was one more dress in the grand scheme of things?

She disappeared inside the bathroom, pulled the dress up over her now-slimmer hips, and twisted around for the side zipper. She latched the hook at the top of the seam and adjusted the spaghetti straps.

Then she faced the mirror.

And saw a ghost.

A wan gray ghost swimming in an ocean of blue that once hugged her curves perfectly, but now hung loose on her thinner frame. Her face looked hollow and gaunt, her eyes pale and stark against a cream background of surprise.

Despite the royal blue gown, a colorless existence stared back at her.

Where had she gone?

Her mom knocked on the door and Stella jumped, clutching the loose top half of the dress against her chest, heart pounding. "You okay in there?"

No. She shook her head, then realized her mom couldn't possibly see her.

"Do you need help with the zipper?"

She shook her head again. And then she remembered.

This was the dress she'd worn the first time Dillon had seen her.

With a strangled cry, she dropped the dress into a heap on the floor, puddled blue on the tile. Voices echoed. The judges' comments that night, Dillon's approval afterward. The victorious announcement of her win ringing over the loudspeakers. *And first place goes to Stella Varland!*

The winner's tiara being set carefully on her head.

Isn't she a vision, folks?

Dillon's eyes lighting up.

You're beautiful.

Constant applause.

Want to grab some coffee?

The scratch of thorns against her bare arms as she accepted the paper-wrapped roses.

It wouldn't stop. They wouldn't stop. The voices wouldn't stop.

She shoved back the shower curtain and crawled into the bathtub, still in her underwear and cami, and huddled in the corner, arms wrapped around her drawn knees. Her hands shook, and she squeezed them into fists. The room dipped and darkened, and she shook her head, eyes focused, concentrating on her breathing.

Her mom kept knocking. "Stella? Stella, let me see."

No. No one could see her. No one ever had.

"It doesn't fit, Mom." Understatement. Or maybe, *she* just didn't fit anymore. "Sorry."

About so many things. So very many things.

"Stella? Are you sure?" Her mom's voice pressed close to the door.

She reached over and turned on the water, raising her voice above the flow and struggling to keep it even, hide her meltdown. "I'm just going to take a shower." Weak excuse. She tried again. "I got a lot of dust on me from the closet."

"I can wait."

"No, you go on, Mom. I'll call you later." Go. Now. Please, just go.

"All right, then." A reluctant acquiescence, followed by fading footsteps and the shutting of the door.

Then, wet, alone, and invisible, Stella buried her face in her knees and cried.

☙❧

Chase knocked on Stella's apartment door, then again, louder. He'd been outside on the street when he saw her mother leave. She had even turned and called something back into the apartment before she'd left, so Stella had to be inside. He had wisely waited in the car until Claire Varland drove away.

He wasn't scared of the woman, exactly. Just figured there was no reason to deliberately throw himself before a firing squad.

He knocked again, his stomach roiling with nerves. He'd had an idea earlier at work, one that wouldn't go away, and when Stella hadn't answered her phone a while ago, he'd decided to pop by and ask her about his idea in person.

She'd be less likely to say no to his face.

He waited, one shoe scraping the concrete outside her door in an anxious rhythm. Nervous to talk to her? Maybe. He really wanted her to say yes to his idea—not only would it help the Cameo, but it would help her. Well, them.

Okay, maybe *him*. It was probably two parts selfish, really. He just wanted to see her. But if they were going to be friends, they needed to spend some time together away from the construction, and it made sense to go live out his plan tomorrow while the plumber was finishing up the restrooms. He needed this truce of theirs to be real.

He knocked again, hating the anxiety in his gut, hating that it mattered so much that she say yes.

Hating that she wasn't answering the door.

Was she avoiding him? They'd made up at the theater yesterday—he hadn't even had time to tick her off or offend her again. Unless she and her mom had argued, and then, well. He'd probably hide out too. Claire Varland could do that to a person. But hiding wasn't healthy, and it wasn't like Stella.

And if they had fought, she probably needed a hug.

That was the reason he told himself why he kept knocking, anyway. "Stella?" He yelled louder, knocked harder. "Stella!"

No answer. But what was that sound inside the apartment? He pressed his ear against the door but couldn't identify the noise. A vacuum cleaner? Maybe she just couldn't hear him.

But his instincts told him otherwise. Something was wrong. The way Claire had stomped to her car, the way Stella refused to answer the door . . .

Even when she'd been upset with him that first day, she'd answered.

Slammed the door shut in his face afterward, but she'd answered.

What if she'd passed out again . . . and she was in there, alone? What if she'd hit her head this time?

She could be hurt. He couldn't leave. Not without knowing. He looked under the welcome mat for a key but found only piled up red dirt and a crunchy leaf. There was no other decorative rock or figurine nearby. He stepped back, studying the door, then felt up and around the top of the frame. Ah, there. Cold metal met his eager fingers. He made a mental note to remind her to quit hiding her keys in such obvious spaces.

He inserted the key in the lock, twisted, and turned. The door released and he eased it partway open. "Stella?" He knocked again, called louder. Opened it halfway.

Then the constant rush of noise registered. Running water. Was she in the shower?

He suddenly felt foolish. He'd all but broken into her apartment, and she was simply getting ready for bed.

He started to ease back out the door, then stopped. The water had been running the entire time he'd been outside knocking. And there was no breaking up of the rushing sound, the way water beat an interrupted, sporadic pattern when a person typically moved about in a shower.

Something was wrong.

He rushed to the bathroom door, knocked hard, called out, and then knocked again. If he went in and she was in the shower . . . he couldn't even fathom that level of embarrassment for both of them.

But the water wasn't changing, and there was no other noise inside. No humming. No splashing. No clank of shampoo bottles or snaps of soap container lids.

He covered his eyes with one hand and opened the door. A rush of steam billowed out. "Stella?"

Silence. Just the constant rush of running water.

He risked a glance between his fingers.

And saw her crumpled form on the floor of the tub.

Unmoving.

Adrenaline shot a headache straight into his temples, and he sucked in a hard breath. He quickly shut off the water. It had grown lukewarm, almost cold. She wasn't moving, though her position was more sitting and slumped than sprawled. It didn't look like she had fallen.

Still.

Towel. She needed a towel. He flung open the nearest cabinet door and grabbed the first one he saw. Why had she taken a shower in her underwear? He was grateful for the detail, for both of their sakes, but why?

Something was definitely wrong.

He leaned over the tub and draped the towel over her still

form. "Stella?" He patted her cheek, moved her dripping hair off her forehead. She stirred, and the knot in his heart loosened. *Please, God.* He quickly checked her temples, felt the crown of her head for knots. Nothing. No bruises or lumps forming. She didn't seem to have hit her head.

He shook her arm, gently, then squeezed her hand.

She squeezed back, stirring again, until her head lifted slowly and she squinted at him. "Chase."

Her weak, weary voice sparked a flame inside him that made him want to climb a mountain. Fight a war. Wrestle a bear. She didn't even sound surprised to see him.

That fact almost scared him more than finding her passed out in the bathtub.

He adjusted the towel to cover her wet form more fully, then stepped back, close enough to help if needed but far enough away to give her some privacy. "I'm here."

She still looked out of it, not fully comprehending where she was or why he was here. "Do you see me?" She squinted again, blinking hard, and his heart tripped and stumbled.

"I see you, Tiara. I see you."

He always had.

twelve

Fifteen hours ago, Stella had been having a panic attack in her bathtub. Now, somehow, she was buckled into the front seat of Chase's truck and heading west.

To an art museum, of all places.

She had argued at first—a lot.

We have work to do at the Cameo, Chase.

Aren't you worried about Tim working unsupervised?

I'm behind on the bathroom design.

No excuse had been good enough. He'd been adamant.

Get in the truck, Stella. I'm taking you to see some art. You need to get inspired again.

Hours earlier he had rescued her from an anxiety attack, not to mention potential drowning and hypothermia, so she'd quit arguing. She was tired of debates. Fights. Conflicts.

Sometimes it was just easier to get in the truck.

She shot Chase a sidelong glance, noting the way the muscles bunched in his forearm as he gripped the steering wheel with one hand, the way he twisted and cracked tension out of his neck, nervously fiddled with the dials on the radio.

He was worried about her.

She was sort of worried about herself.

He wanted to call 911 last night. Take her to the ER. See a doctor.

But she was already seeing a doctor. The panic attacks were getting fewer and farther between—not that she could have told it lately. Counseling was helping. The flashbacks to Dillon's betrayal were lessening, the fear was subsiding. Gradually, gradually.

She didn't tell Chase any of this, of course. Not about the unfaithfulness, the divorce, the therapy. Not about throwing herself into art, even amid the abject terror of failure. Not about any of it.

All she had said was, "Trust me. I'll be all right."

And he hadn't asked another question. Not a single one. Not about why she'd been unconscious in her underwear in the bathtub. Not about why she kept fainting on him. He had simply saved her, covered her. Waited outside while she'd changed into dry clothes and then sat on the couch with her while she towel dried her hair, never saying another word.

He'd only asked one thing of her—that he could pick her up the next morning for a field trip. It was work-related, he said, and she'd agreed, partly to get him out of the apartment before he caved and started asking real questions, and partly because if he didn't leave soon, she'd collapse into his arms and never let go.

Now she adjusted her seatbelt, crossed her arms over her chest, and turned to watch the white stripes on the road zip past.

Here they were. Driving. Not asking questions.

Which just made her want to answer them all the more.

If she had any answers to give, that is.

He hadn't said more than two words the entire drive out of the city limits. Bayou Bend wasn't a big enough town to have a real art museum, so they were going to the larger city of Hollis.

At last he turned into a parking lot, mostly empty, and cut the engine. Looked at her. "Ready?"

Not even a little. "Yes."

The lies were starting to feel familiar on her tongue at this point. But were they lies, if they were what she hoped to be? She wanted to be brave. Be adventurous again. Be *ready*.

But the largest part of her still felt like hiding in the bathtub.

Inside, the rush of air conditioning offered a welcome respite from the midmorning sun already heating up. Chase pulled a credit card from his wallet for their admission, and Stella tried to remind herself this was business. This was inspiration for the Cameo, nothing more. Not a date.

Definitely not a date.

They received their museum maps, nodded at the brief instructions from the door attendant about not touching any of the exhibits, and then set off. Chase to the left. Stella to the right.

"Hey, wait. This way." She motioned him toward her just as he said and did the exact same thing.

They laughed, the ice not exactly breaking between them but cracking, at least. Stella held up her map, unable to hide her smile at his mock exasperation, and pointed to the creased paper. "Watercolor art is this way."

He nodded. "And western sculptures are this way."

She really wished she could arch one eyebrow like her sister did. "How are statues of horses and boots going to inspire me for the Cameo?"

"They won't. They're just cool." Chase grinned, dimples flashing, and Stella rolled her eyes. "We can get the useless stuff out of the way first."

His words rang deep. Maybe they could.

Maybe that's what this whole trip was about.

She followed, one step behind, into the Old West exhibit. The bronze and metal figurines, some inches tall, some as large as four and a half feet, shone under the carefully placed spotlights. She paused in front of a cowboy on a horse, the stallion's front legs pawing the air as the rider held on with one hand, the other swinging a wire rope high above his head. "Looks dangerous."

"Looks amazing. What an adrenaline rush." Chase started to touch the statue, then must have remembered the attendant's warning because he quickly withdrew his hand. "I'd do that in a heartbeat."

"Ride a bucking bronco?" Crazy. Absolutely crazy.

Chase shrugged. "Yeah. But that horse is rearing, not bucking."

"Same difference."

"Actually, no. Rearing is when a horse rises up on his back legs; bucking is when he puts his weight on the front and kicks his back legs up."

Stella settled for raising both eyebrows. "I had no idea you were such a cowboy." She edged closer and nudged him with her elbow. "Should I call Bob? See if he needs to borrow any spurs?"

"Very funny." He nudged her back. "I'm not a cowboy. But I like . . . that."

"What? Near-death experiences?" She snorted.

"No." He quieted then, something flickering across his gaze she couldn't place. "Living on purpose. Living out loud."

She watched him, the way his eyes darted over the statue, as if he was memorizing it. Memorizing the feeling. Living vicariously. And she grew convinced. He really would ride that horse, right here, right now, if it came to life and gave him the chance.

When had Chase become such a daredevil? He'd never been like that while he was dating Kat.

Or her.

She tugged him away from the statue, uneasy over his fascination and equally uneasy over how simple it was getting to read him. "Come on. There's a bronze sombrero over here that looks fascinating."

They wandered through the remainder of the exhibit, but the restlessness never left Chase's eyes. He finally led the way out of the room and toward the watercolor exhibit. "Your turn."

She followed, not as eager as before, a little afraid of the transformation between them. The closeness that suddenly seemed to reveal how far apart they still were.

She gazed at the portraits on the walls, the still lifes, the landscapes, and felt empty. Hazy, foggy flowers painted on hillsides, smeared bowls offering muted bananas and shadowed grapes.

This didn't speak to her. It wasn't alive. It wasn't vibrant.

It wasn't who she used to be.

Wasn't who she feared to be again.

And then it hit her. She loved art because it could be everything she wasn't, with no fear. No expectation. No threat.

It could just be beautiful.

She pressed her fingers against her forehead, closing her eyes and breathing in the revelation. No wonder.

"This is depressing." Chase's hushed voice in the stillness jerked her out of her reverie. "Do you like any of these?"

Stella opened her eyes, turned a slow circle, and took in the room. She didn't like a single piece in the space.

She shook her head, unable and unwilling to voice her thoughts. "Let's try the next room." The description on the map was vague, but it should be some sort of eclectic mix of art. Statues, sketches, clay. Surely she'd appreciate *something* in there. She hated for Chase to spend his money on her—on them—and it be a total waste of inspiration and time.

Unless that single revelation was the reason she had come . . .

She led the way, already exhausted, Chase's steps shuffling a few feet behind. The next room was cooler, so she unwrapped the thin hoodie she'd tied around her waist and slipped her arms through the sleeves. She looked to the left, to the right, noting the clay formations, the abstract art on the walls, and then froze. A giant framed piece took up a huge portion of the wall in front of her, lit by a single canned light above.

She moved toward it, eyes soaking in the details. Mosaic tiles. Broken pieces of stained glass, carefully pieced and coordinated into a profile portrait of a beautiful woman. Long flowing hair, the color of daffodils. Electric blue eyes. An off-the-shoulder white toga draped over her form. Her face was raised slightly. Toward heaven? Her expression peaceful. Serene.

The background behind the woman was a deep, rich red, almost burgundy, setting off the yellow and blue and white from the rest of the portrait like a beacon.

She couldn't look away.

"Come on." Chase nudged her, apparently oblivious to her fascination.

She held up one hand in a plea to wait.

"What? The girl?" Chase stood by her side, glancing at the portrait, then back at Stella. "I don't get it."

"Don't you see it?" She kept her voice to a whisper, feeling as if a normal tone of voice would be completely irreverent. She couldn't get past the woman's expression, made up entirely of little fragments. Completely broken—and completely at peace.

"See what?"

He was right; he didn't get it. She didn't blame him. But he wasn't really trying.

And she had to know something.

"You said you saw me." She felt his gaze burning into her, but she refused to turn her face. Refused to look away from the peace that woman in the portrait held. Despite her brokenness. Despite being rendered into shards. "Last night. You said you saw me."

Chase looked back and forth from the picture to Stella, as if trying in vain to connect what she was saying with the portrait before them. "You're right. I did say that."

"Did you mean it?" She held the woman in the frame's gaze, fearing what would happen if she looked into Chase's eyes while he answered. Fearing a positive answer. Fearing a negative one.

She was tired of being afraid.

With a shaky breath, she tore her gaze from the art and met Chase's head-on. He blinked, took a step backward. Then regained the ground between them, reaching for her hand and squeezing it briefly before letting go. "Absolutely."

The contact burned her hand like a brand. But she couldn't focus on that right now. Not yet.

This was more important.

"But you don't see her?" She pointed to the glass portrait, Chase's head swiveling to follow her movement. "How is that possible?"

"What do you mean, how is that possible?"

She swallowed hard, reaching toward the portrait despite the rules. Her fingers brushed against the display, feather light. "We're the same."

ഇള

How do you eat an elephant?

One bite at a time . . .

Chase knew the expression. But the idea of ever being able to consume the one that always lingered in the room between him and Stella overwhelmed him to the point of near depression.

There weren't enough forks in the world.

He shoved his basket of fries across the table toward her. She plucked one and dragged it through a pile of ketchup, thanking him with a tired smile. They'd toured the majority of the museum already, and her growling stomach had convinced them both to stop by the snack bar for a junk-food lunch before heading back to Bayou Bend.

At this point, he needed the break. The relief. The opportunity to drown his confusion in nachos and make small talk about the weather and the progress of the Cameo.

The last half hour of their museum tour had been so heavy, he felt more exhausted than if he'd sanded the entire stage at the

Cameo by himself. Or reroofed the entire theater, for that matter. Something had happened to Stella back there at that mosaic tile portrait, something he couldn't quite grasp and something she couldn't quite explain, despite trying.

They weren't connecting over it.

And it bothered him more than he wanted to admit.

Stella ate quietly. Now and then she brushed her hair back, her deep blue eyes even more prominent against her beautiful bare face. The more he was around this new version of Stella, the prettier he thought she looked. Though pretty wasn't near enough of a word. More like beautiful. Gorgeous. Stunning.

Able to rip his heart out with one glance.

The girl couldn't help it.

God knew she was trying. But for the life of him, he couldn't figure out why. And he wished Stella—or God, for that matter—would tell him. He'd been praying for her. For them both, every night when he lay sleepless on the uncomfortable bed in his cousin's guest room, staring at the popcorn ceiling and wondering how it was Stella had found her way back to his nighttime thoughts instead of Leah.

Was he a horrible person?

He missed the woman he saw every day more than he missed his late fiancée.

So yes. Yes he was.

He shoved a fry in his mouth. They needed salt. Or maybe he just needed to get this bad taste out of his mouth. There was so much he wanted to say to Stella. Ask her. Tell her.

But the elephant just wouldn't shrink.

And maybe it shouldn't.

"Why do you go so fast?"

He looked up from the fries. "Go so fast where?" He didn't remember speeding on their drive to the museum.

She gestured with her fry around them. "Here. Everywhere. You rushed past all the art. So much so that you lost me twice."

It was true, he had. He had thought she was right behind him, but she had still been back in the exhibit room, gazing at the artwork as if she were listening to what it was saying. And maybe it did speak to her. Especially, that one—that woman in the mosaic tiles.

In fact, he was sure of it. So sure, he didn't even fear his next question. "What did she say?"

Stella knew exactly what he meant. "That it won't hurt forever."

"What won't?"

"Being broken."

He nodded slowly, wishing he had a translator, wishing the dang portrait would say something to him to help him understand. He wanted to get it, so badly. Wanted to get Stella.

It mattered more than anything lately. More than his job. More than the Cameo.

What had broken her?

Had *he*?

That was so long ago . . . surely not. No, Stella had a secret, something else in her life that had robbed her of her life and color.

She took a sip from her soda, shaking the cup to rattle the ice inside. "Why do you rush, Chase?"

It was a fair enough question. He ran his finger around the rim of the paper basket between them, glancing up as a mother and son walked past their table to order. The boy's navy backpack bumped his arm, and he smiled, remembering childhood days when his own mom would accompany him on a school field trip or randomly check him and Jimmy out of school for the day for an adventure.

"I've always been sort of go-go-go." The words slipped out easier than he thought they would. "Trying to keep up with my brother. Keep up at school. But after . . ." His throat closed, and he swallowed, unsure how much to reveal and unsure how much Stella really wanted to know. "Something happened in Texas. I realized I didn't want to live in slow motion. Regrets are, well . . . my biggest fear." He shook his head. "I don't want to waste any time. Or miss anything."

Stella nodded, and he wondered if she really got it.

"That's why I'm back. In Bayou Bend." He picked up another fry but didn't eat it. "I missed so much time already with my family, my nephews. I'm not going to waste anything else."

"That makes sense." Then her eyes narrowed at him thoughtfully. "But isn't rushing only robbing you of the moment?"

Yep. She got it.

"You didn't see half of the art here because you were so determined to get through each exhibit. You never lingered and just . . . looked."

The disappointment in her eyes ran a lot deeper than her point merited.

And then *he* got it.

She was afraid he wouldn't see her.

"I'm not into art as much as you are, Stella. I don't see it the way you do." He reached across for her hand, brushing his thumb across her knuckles before he could change his mind. "When I walked into this museum, though, I noticed a bunch of things you probably never even thought of."

"What do you mean?" She looked at their joined hands, her expression a blank canvas. He wished he could choose what to paint on it.

"The ceiling joists. The wiring of the lights above each framed piece of art. The pattern in the tile floor." He grinned. "I was here about twenty minutes before I noticed three things I'd have done differently if I'd built this place, and two things that could have saved them money."

She shook her head, rolled her eyes, grinned.

"I can't help it. I do that to every building I walk inside. And you probably redecorate every lobby and doctor's office you go into."

She nodded slowly.

"So yeah, sometimes I rush and I don't see things the way you do . . . but that doesn't mean that I don't *see*." He held her gaze until he was sure she caught his double meaning.

"I gotcha." A slow rush of red crawled up her neck, and he didn't let go of her hand until she tugged gently away and reached for her drink. "Just . . . be careful not to rush too fast." Her piercing eyes landed on his.

And her double meaning didn't go unnoticed, either.

༄

The truck ride back felt a hundred miles longer than it had on the way there. Maybe because she was tired. Maybe because of all the walking they'd done and the junk food they'd consumed after.

Or maybe because of the random longing in her stomach to slide across the bench seat and buckle in next to Chase. Prop her feet on the dash and turn the last half hour of drive time into the lyrics of a country song.

Their conversations, so heavy, didn't weigh on her as she'd expected. In fact, she felt lighter, having shared even a portion of her hurt with Chase. It'd been in abstract form, no details, but he'd seemed to get it. Get her. And it made her brave.

Courageous enough to tell him the next piece.

"I'm not whole."

She didn't mean to blurt it out quite like that, but the sun dappling warm pockets of gold on the legs of her jeans and flickering through the passing tree limbs coaxed her out of her hiding place.

To Chase's credit, he didn't even flinch. Just changed hands on the steering wheel and cast her a sincere look. An interested look. He wanted to know what she had to say. "You mean, you're broken. Like the mosaic tile portrait."

Stella nodded, fingers clasped around the strap of her seatbelt, her fingers zipping back and forth over the slightly frayed edge. The material scratching into her flesh gave her comfort, kept her grounded. Gave her something to hold on to.

Because she was about to leap into midair.

"I'm divorced, Chase."

The truck veered slightly to the left, but he recovered quickly. Shook his head fast. "What?"

"I know. I never thought that'd be the case either, trust me."

"You were . . . married?"

He was definitely slower to catch on here. Unless he was truly just *that* shocked. She nodded. "For a few years."

"A few years?" His voice rose an octave, and he gripped the wheel with both hands. "What—what happened?"

She didn't know what he meant. What happened, as in, after he moved and she clearly met someone else? Or what happened as in why the divorce came about?

She didn't have solid answers for either scenario, really.

"A lot." She inhaled and exhaled deeply, watching the dimple in his cheek twitch. He was holding back. Way back. But holding back what? Sympathy? Anger? Judgment?

She suddenly didn't feel nearly as brave.

"It didn't work out." This conversation wasn't going the way she'd hoped. She was making it sound so flippant, so distant, so vague. Like it hadn't literally ruined her life and scraped her soul raw and left her bleeding to die.

"I'm sorry to hear that." His voice, now strained, pitched as if he wanted to say more. Or maybe as if he wished he'd heard less.

Stella gripped the seatbelt tighter. "It happens." No, it didn't. Or shouldn't, anyway. Why wasn't this conversation flowing the way she'd imagined?

Without another word, Chase pulled the truck to the side of the road, flipped on the hazard lights, and twisted in the seat to face her. "Stella. What *happened*?"

And the whole story erupted. Dillon. Meeting her at a pageant one night. Their first date. His fast proposal. Their whirlwind marriage. The other women. The pressure. The expectations. The betrayal.

He'd left. *Cheated* and left, which was a double whammy. She'd been willing to try, to keep her side of the vows regardless— but apparently she wasn't even worth winning second place.

Marriage was supposed to be a lifetime.

They'd made it less than two years.

By the time the story was out, she was tearstained, unbuckled, and sitting in the middle bench seat neat to Chase, his arm around her as he rubbed a comforting pattern with his thumb on her shoulder.

"Can I kill him?"

His first response, through all of that, and it was a death threat. She snorted back a strangled laugh. "There's a waiting line for that, I think. My dad's at the front. I think Lucas is a close second."

"Nah." Chase shook his head. "Your dad is a man of the cloth. And Lucas . . . he might have the brother-in-law protective streak, but I can handle this better." His grip around her arm tightened. "I can definitely handle this."

His desire to defend her, to avenge her, warmed a part of her heart long frozen. She reached up to his hand on her shoulder and squeezed. "I'm not mad anymore. It's been official for a year, and the resentment and bitterness are gone." She wrinkled her nose. "Mostly." She hesitated. "Now, it's just this lingering sensation that things aren't as they should be. Or what they seem."

"Unfamiliar. Unknown." Chase nodded.

"Exactly. It's . . . *Alice in Wonderland.* I fell down this rabbit hole, and now nothing quite makes sense. It's all upside down and too small and too big, all at once." She swallowed. "I'm not me."

"Exactly." He cleared his throat. "'*You were much more muchier. You've lost your muchness.*'"

Now she'd heard everything—Chase Taylor, quoting *Alice in Wonderland.* "You've seen that movie?" She reeled back in surprise, twisting her neck to meet his gaze. Then wished she hadn't. The proximity of his face, his dimple, his stubble, was too much. Too familiar.

Too wonderful.

"My nephew Aaron loves that movie, because of Tweedledee and Tweedledum. I've watched it twice with him just since I've moved back." Chase shrugged, his hand once again rubbing comfort into her shoulder.

Muchier. Yes, that was it. She'd lost her muchness. She closed her eyes, reveling in the light touch on her arm, in Chase's nearness, in the fact that a man was sitting with her, enjoying her, listening to her—*seeing* her.

And she was safe.

"It's why I get anxiety attacks." She let the admission slip from her lips. It was embarrassing, but the desire to let Chase know the truth—to know *her*—pushed her forward.

"That's understandable. You've seen a doctor about them?"

"Yeah. It's just stress. When something happens to throw me off balance, the memories recur, and even though I know better in my head, my body reacts as if it's happening all over again. I let my mind get overwhelmed and it takes me away." She drew a deep breath. "They're actually getting better, believe it or not. Used to be more frequent. "

"I've never been divorced." Chase spoke slowly, as if he was choosing his words carefully. "I don't know that kind of pain. But I do know pain." His voice cracked. "I know what it's like to have all your dreams and plans shattered at your feet."

She twisted again to face him, his arm sliding halfway down her back as she turned. Her heart thudded. How had Chase been hurt? No wonder he understood how she felt so well. Deep spoke to deep.

And some wounds could only be identified by someone bearing a similar scar.

"What happened?"

"I was engaged." He started to say more, then paused, tucking a strand of her hair behind her ear. The contact of his palm against her face made her forget the question hanging between them, and on instinct, she closed her eyes.

It only took a moment. His lips were just the way she'd remembered, but so much more. The last time she'd kissed Chase Taylor, he'd been a guy with an agenda, just like the others. Respectful and appropriate enough, but subconsciously intentional toward a goal.

This Chase had no agenda, no intention of taking. His lips moved over hers in a gift, generous. Offering. Giving.

She reached up as his kiss deepened, and her fingers found the hair at the back of his neck. Her other hand gripped the front of his shirt as ancient history and the present collided into a single moment.

Chase's phone rang from the dashboard, and they jumped apart, Stella's breath releasing in a quick gasp.

What. Had. Just. Happened.

She started to slide away, but Chase caught her arm, eyes imploring her to stay as he grabbed his phone. "Hello?"

Engaged. He'd been saying he'd been engaged.

Surely he wasn't still. She shook her head. No, that was crazy. She pressed a hand against her racing heart, trying to look casual as she watched Chase from the corner of her eye.

He listened, the male voice on the other end of the call garbled and distant. He pushed his free hands against his ear, frowning as he concentrated. "Tim? Slow down. What about Jack?" He listened again, then his eyes widened. "The hospital?"

Stella reached up and touched her fingers against her lips, unsure if the kiss had jump–started her heart or if the source of her adrenaline was the emergency that was apparently happening right now.

Chase jabbed off his hazards and turned on his blinker as he checked his side mirror. "All right. If you're sure he's okay." He shot Stella a glance, then checked his mirror again before pulling out onto the main road. "I'll be there in an hour, max. Call me if anything changes."

Stella buckled her seatbelt as Chase merged onto the highway. Something was changing, all right.

It already had.

thirteen

So much for not rushing too fast.

He'd just pushed the speed limit by about fifteen miles per hour. Jack had fallen off a ladder at the Cameo and was at the ER with a broken ankle.

He had kissed Stella.

That was probably pushing the limit by fifty.

Chase pulled into a parking spot near the emergency room and cut the engine. He'd filled Stella in on the way there. Tim swore Jack was fine and would be going home soon, but he wanted to see for himself and make sure Jack had been taken care of. Make sure Jack wasn't going to sue. Make sure no one was responsible for the injury and it was a true accident.

Sort of like that kiss. Pure accident.

One he'd gladly repeat.

No. Had to stop that train of thought. Jack came first.

But Stella . . . divorced . . .

The conversation of the past hour wouldn't filter through his mind. It clogged up his brain and consumed him as he opened Stella's door and led the way to the sliding double doors of the hospital. Who would be so stupid as to divorce Stella?

Then again, who would be so stupid as to kiss the woman he'd come back to Bayou Bend to avoid?

He rushed up to the front desk, his mind still racing a mile a minute with concern for Jack and the unfinished business between him and Stella, and suddenly realized he couldn't remember Jack's last name.

"Old guy?" He gestured with his hands, like that might help the confused, scrub-clad nurse behind the counter. "Um. He has a beard." He gestured again at his chin.

Stella neatly elbowed him aside. "Hi. We're looking for a man named Jack. He was admitted about an hour and a half ago for a broken ankle." She pointed at Chase. "Despite the fact that he sounds like a five-year-old playing charades right now, this is his boss."

For someone who panicked regularly, Stella sure remained calm in an emergency. Chase smiled sheepishly at the nurse, who raised two perfectly arched brows in obvious doubt. "She's right. Sorry. We were out of town, and one of my employees called to tell me there was an accident. But I didn't get all the details—"

"Mr. Taylor! Over here!" Tim's voice rang through the crowded waiting room. He stood from a seat under a TV in the back corner, and waved with both arms, as if he was flagging down a friend at a football game.

Not that Chase had been a whole lot more professional. Relief flooded through him. Finally, someone who could tell him the truth.

Someone who could distract him from the whirlwind of the last two hours.

He put one hand on Stella's back to guide her through the crowded lobby toward Tim, narrowly avoiding a teenager on crutches. "Tim, is he okay? What happened?"

Tim shoved his hair back with his hand, then replaced his ball cap and shrugged. "I don't know, Boss. He was on the ladder, then all of a sudden he wasn't."

Chase had been in construction long enough to know that might just be the whole story after all.

"Where is he?" Chase looked away, but the curtained off areas of the emergency room were all tightly drawn. "And where's Lyle?"

"Lyle was with the plumber when it happened, so he asked me to drive Jack to the hospital." Tim's shoulders squared by an inch, his chest raising with pride. "We got here quick. I even ran two red lights."

"Why didn't you just call an ambulance?"

Stella's innocent question threw Tim off guard, and he looked at her fully for the first time in all the excitement. His composure flustered considerably. He glanced back and forth between Stella and Chase, unsure. "Jack said not to. He didn't want to pay for it."

Chase shook his head. Sounded like the old man.

"I'm fine. The lot of you worrying about me is going to make me crazier than this blasted ankle." Jack's gruff voice echoed behind them, and they all turned at the same time. Jack sat in a wheelchair, one foot propped up and surrounded by a white cast. He held crutches length-wise across his lap. "They won't even let me walk out of here on crutches."

"Hospital policy, sir." The straight-faced nurse behind the

chair said it as if she repeated the same sentiment a thousand times a day to grouchy patients. She probably did.

"So you're fine."

"Fine as I can be. Won't be doing much work at the Cameo for a while." Jack shifted in his chair. "Just a few fractures, but they won't let me put weight on it for six weeks."

"At least six weeks," the nurse corrected.

Jack crossed his arms and grunted, the crutches slipping halfway off his lap.

"It's no problem, man, don't worry about us." Chase took the crutches for him as they began a processional toward the automatic front doors. "Tim said you fell off a ladder?"

"Didn't fall. Just stepped off."

"And that broke your ankle? What'd you land on, a spike?" Tim asked, incredulous.

Jack glared as the nurse snorted. They wheeled outside into the late afternoon sunshine. "I stepped on the ground as I intended." He paused. "Just didn't realize I had an extra rung beneath me. Ankle rolled."

Ouch. Chase winced. "Let me drive you home, at least." He was glad Jack was okay, but they'd have to hire someone to replace him on the crew or their production schedule would get thrown way off.

"No, you've got company already." Jack gestured at Stella, who looked away and pretended not to hear.

"You know Stella is our designer for the Cameo," Chase corrected him, hoping to put Stella at ease. Though his own heart pounded a rhythm far from easy. "Tim can drive Stella home."

"Yeah!" The boy lit up so bright he shone like a Christmas tree, and Chase immediately regretted his words. Especially at the way Stella's head snapped back around to give him a pointed stare.

"No need to mix it up. Tim can take me."

Tim deflated as the hope of being alone with Stella was rudely snatched away.

"He drove just fine over here," Jack continued, and the compliment puffed Tim back up a little. But behind Tim's back, Jack made the universal signal for crazy, whirling a finger by his head and then pretending to clutch a steering wheel. Stella snorted and Chase bit back a laugh as he handed the crutches off to Tim.

"Good luck." Chase lifted a hand in a wave as the nurse wheeled him to the passenger side of Tim's truck. "Let us know if you need anything."

"I'll be fine." Jack made a face as he managed to get his crutches under his arms. "If you have a sit-down job at the Cameo, holler at me."

They both knew that wouldn't happen. But it made them both feel better to say it. A man needed to work, and Jack was facing six weeks of staring at a television. While Chase faced the challenge of hiring someone who knew construction and could start, like, the very next morning. On second thought, today hadn't been the best day to take off work after all.

But as he and Stella climbed back into his truck—in unison, as if they did it all the time—he second-guessed his second thought.

Maybe things happened for a reason after all.

It didn't hit him until he pulled up to Stella's apartment fifteen minutes later that he hadn't had a single flashback while at the hospital. Not one single memory of Leah's accident or the aftermath thereof.

Not sure what that meant, but he'd take it.

He breathed a prayer of relief and gratitude, trying not to feel guilty, then hopped out to open Stella's door. "Well, today turned out a little more exciting than I intended."

She slid out of the cab and faced him with a tired smile. "I'll say."

And then he wasn't sure if she meant the hospital trip or the kiss. Or both.

Which did he mean?

Both.

He shut the door behind her, bracing one hip against the bumper of the truck, wishing he could kiss her again. "I'm glad Jack is going to be okay. That could have been a lot worse."

"No kidding." Stella shaded her eyes from the sun as she looked up at him. "Are you going to have to replace him at the Cameo?"

"Definitely." Chase hesitated as he briefly ran through potential options in his mind. He didn't love any of them. "I guess my best bet is to check with Lyle and see if he knows anyone."

"There's someone at the homeless shelter who could use a job . . ." Stella's voice trailed off and she twisted her lips to the side, eyes widening in silent question.

Homeless shelter. Dixie. Surely not her, specifically, but someone like her? Did he have the patience to deal with someone like that at work all day? More importantly, did they have the skills needed to do the job well and not get hurt? Accidents happened to the best of crewmen, as evidenced by Jack today—but when you weren't familiar with the tools involved, they happened a lot more frequently, and usually more severely. "I don't know, Stella. Is he certified?"

"No, but he's an amazing builder. He's handcrafted all kinds of things he's brought up to the shelter before, things he sells on the side sometimes or trades for food. Rocking chairs, rocking horses. Stuff like that."

"Just because he can build a chair doesn't mean he can build a theater."

Stella held up both hands. "I know that, obviously. I'm just saying you need someone to work as soon as possible, and he needs a job as soon as possible." She shrugged. "Could be an answered prayer for you both."

She could be on to something. And unless Lyle had a recommendation, Chase didn't have any solid leads at the moment anyway. And they really couldn't waste any time. "What's his name?"

"Howard. He's friends with Dixie."

He knew it. Chase paused, wondering how to proceed without offending Stella. "Is he . . ."

"No. He's not like her. Not like that."

At least she wasn't offended this time. "If he's interested, tell him to come by the theater tomorrow, and I'll see what he can do. I'll pay him for a day's work, and if he proves himself, he can keep the rest of the job."

"Sounds fair." The smile that lit up Stella's face made the entire risk worth it. She reached out and touched his arm, eyes shining. "Thank you. For giving him a chance. I really doubt you'll be disappointed."

No matter. If she kept smiling like that, he wouldn't have a care in the world. Chase touched her hand, then realized he couldn't quite let go. "You're very welcome." They held hands for a moment longer than necessary.

No disappointments here. Not a single one.

·ee·

Four days later, Stella breezed into the Cameo, arms full of bags containing everything she needed to decorate the theater's restroom. She deposited the bags in the ladies' room, grateful the plumber had been able to make his original deadline, and then headed back into the lobby, looking for Chase. Since that evening he dropped her off at home after the hospital trip, they had barely spoken except for two nights ago, when he called her to tell her that Howard had been doing a great job so far, contributing above and beyond what he'd expected.

The compliment warmed her as directly as if she'd done the work herself. It was good news for Howard, of course. But beyond that, she had been able to give Chase advice—and have him heed it and appreciate it. It was affirming, being part of a team, bouncing ideas off someone who truly cared.

Not that she was sure, in hindsight, that Dillon had ever *truly* cared, but regardless, she'd still gotten used to a default, a habit, a pattern of behavior that she now missed. Being able to assist Chase in even small details at the Cameo and strengthen not only his reputation but the project itself felt . . . good. Foreign and familiar all at once.

She wanted more.

Just a little more.

Chase met her inside the lobby before she could barrel through the theater doors, sweat staining the front of his T-shirt, his hair mussed and covered in what looked like sawdust.

And it still didn't deter her from wanting a hug.

"Hey, you're here!" He looked happy to see her.

Really happy, for that matter.

Relief and apprehension mingled in a single tidal wave. She drew a deep breath, calming her nerves. Relief that he was glad to see her, because she'd been a little curious why they hadn't run into each other over the last few days, or why he hadn't sought her out after that kiss in the truck. She knew he'd been busy, especially in Jack's absence, but still . . .

And apprehension, because, well . . . he was happy to see her.

Exciting. Scary.

Complicated.

Then reality tapped her on the shoulder. Even though they'd talked about their recent pasts and were getting along well on the theater progress, she was still a Varland and he was still very much Chase Taylor.

If her mom freaked out because they were simply working together . . . well, that kiss would slap the Baptist right out of her.

Best to forget it.

If only she could. Her stomach dipped. "Chase, we should probably—"

"I have a surprise for you." His eyes danced with a secret.

That alone was a surprise. Stella raised her eyebrows. "Okay?"

"But you have to go home first."

She frowned. "Okay . . ."

He laughed. "It's a good thing, I promise. Or if you need to work in the women's restroom, that's fine. You just can't come in the theater until tonight."

"What time?" Meeting Chase, alone, in the theater, after hours? The thought made her want to throw up and turn a cartwheel, all at once.

He checked his watch, also covered in flakes of construction dust, as he began easing backward toward the theater doors. "Seven o'clock. Maybe seven fifteen."

"I'll be here." And she would be a nervous wreck until then. They still had yet to discuss that impromptu kiss in his truck. Was that part of his plan for that evening? Or was it just something to do with the theater progress? She'd have to wait to find out.

Why did it seem like she was always waiting on men?

Chase lifted one hand in a quick wave and disappeared back inside the theater, taking care to make sure the door didn't open too far and allow her to see in as he slipped through. She shook her head. If patience was a virtue, she was no saint. Looked like she'd be killing some time decorating the women's bathroom.

At least if she opted for throwing up instead of cartwheels, she'd be in the right spot.

❦

The summer rain shower came hard and fast, taking Bayou Bend by surprise. The streets couldn't keep up, and the gutters flooded within minutes.

Good thing she wasn't worried about her hairdo. Stella squeezed out the excess water from the damp strands that hung over the hood of her teal sweatshirt. She had finished up the restrooms a lot faster than anticipated, then gone home. Better to pace her own apartment than the bathroom of a theater.

The door swung shut behind her, and she shivered against the frigid air conditioning. The temperature had hit ninety-two degrees earlier in the day, but the rain dipped the temps, and her wet hair did little to convince her it was still summer outside. She shivered.

"I was worried about you driving in all that." Chase's voice echoed through the dimly lit lobby before he appeared. He grinned, approaching her slowly, giving her stomach way too much time to react.

She played it off as a joke, as if the chemistry between them couldn't possibly start a forest fire, and held out both arms, revealing hoodie sleeves splotchy with rain. "I'm here. With bells on, as you can see."

"If I had known we'd get a monsoon, I'd have waited until tomorrow." He hesitated as he began leading the way toward the theater. "I just really wanted you to see it without the crew around."

Why? She wanted to ask, bad, but instead she bit her lip and followed him. She waited once inside the dark room, but he didn't turn on the theater lights. "Chase?"

"I'm right here." His voice near her ear brought more sparks of danger than reassurance.

She shivered again, this time not from the cold. What was wrong with her? She was suddenly reacting to his proximity like a high school girl with a crush on the school jock. This was Chase. Chase, who had dated her sister first. Chase, who was the archenemy of her entire family. Chase, who left her for Texas and for some mysterious life she didn't understand.

She shoved her hands into her hoodie pockets, struggling to breathe in the dark space. Was it the lure of the forbidden driving her hormones this way? If so, she had to stop it immediately. She was done with the proverbial Bad Boy.

Especially the ones who hid that particular label under an entirely different wardrobe.

"This way." Chase's hand found hers in the darkness, tugged her forward down the main aisle.

She hesitated, knowing in the darkness there were stairs coming.

He prodded her forward. "You're safe. Just a few more steps."

Safe? Hardly.

From falling down the stairs, yes. From falling for him? Not even.

She swallowed.

"Okay, ready?"

No.

"Surprise." The lights flipped on simultaneously with his voice, and she blinked at the sudden brightness. She glanced around the empty theater, then realized why such pride echoed in his voice.

The stage.

Newly sanded and polished, gleaming with fresh stain, the deep brown of the wood looked like liquid bronze flowing across the boards.

Stella caught her breath, covered her mouth with her hands. "It's stunning." More than beauty, though, it radiated *potential*. She could envision the plays that would take place on that stage now, the talent that would grace its floors, the laughter and tears it would coax from its audience. The stage would be the foundation of it all, the stoic witness to hundreds of memories yet to be formed.

Chase beamed almost as brightly as the stage. "I knew you'd be happy with it. I knew it."

He sounded almost relieved, as if maybe he hadn't been sure. And the sudden switch in who valued whose opinion most made her grin. Then sober.

Maybe she wasn't the only one afraid of falling.

"Come see it up close." He began the trek down the main aisle steps, and she followed at a slower pace, taking in the sight of the completed stage from each level. Flawless. Truly flawless.

They reached the front and she looked up from the ground level, reached out to gingerly touch the edge. Smooth as silk. "I'm surprised it's dry."

"It's fast-drying stain, but yeah. That was part of why I had to keep you out of here this morning. Was still sticky."

"It looks amazing. You did a great job."

"You picked a great color." He smiled, his hand almost brushing hers as he, too, touched the stage floor. "We're a good team."

Teamwork. Her earlier thoughts flooded with the present, and she winced. Why did this have to be so complicated all of a sudden? Chase returning to Bayou Bend should have been nothing more than a fact.

Now it was a truth that consumed most of her daily thoughts. When had that switch happened?

If she was truly honest, it'd happened the moment they'd stood toe-to-toe on that very stage mere weeks ago, her first day on the job, and shouted at each other like old times.

The theater knew—drama sold. Drama seeped through trap-doors and velvet curtains and stage wings and consumed everything in its path. Her drama with Chase hadn't ever ended—it'd just taken an intermission.

And Act Two was in full swing.

fourteen

They sat on the edge of the completed stage, feet dangling. Laughing. Talking. Just like they used to. Just like that one time Chase had accidentally ended up visiting with Stella for hours instead of hanging out with Kat as promised. Easy conversation, no pressure, no expectation.

As if they had become best friends from that first conversation they shared.

And tonight, nothing had changed in the least.

Chase watched as Stella reclined back on her elbows, blonde hair spilling onto the dark wood, peering up at the stage lights above their heads and studying the layout of the grid. "It looks so complex."

"Nah." He lay back in the same way, the hard wood of the stage digging into his elbows. "It's pretty simple, considering. Not everything that looks complicated has to be that way."

She glanced at him then, and he heard himself, what he'd just said, and wondered briefly if he should apologize or just own it.

Because it was true, wasn't it? Not everything had to be so difficult just because it was expected to be that way. Managing the stage lights was a learned skill.

Navigating a friendship—or even beyond—again with Stella would be the same way. Something to learn, to discover, to work on.

Not easy. But not impossible.

So why the doubt in her eyes?

More importantly, why the overconfidence in his own thoughts? Was it simply this new urge to take life head-on, full-force, no regrets, prompting him back toward the woman he'd left all those years before? Or was it something more than that?

Maybe it wouldn't be that easy. Maybe they did have too many skeletons between the two of them to empty that particular closet. She still didn't know about Leah. And while he knew about her divorce, he didn't know her life these last two years. Or why she hid her art. Or how her relationship with her family would ever mesh into a relationship with him.

He was pairing up two pieces that might or might not fit. Despite his instincts, he needed to backpedal, quick.

But for the life of him, he couldn't even find the brakes, much less reverse.

"Thanks for showing me like this. You know, privately." Stella laid fully on her back, continuing to stare up at the lights. "It's hard to give the stage its proper due and respect with guys like Tim and Lyle lurking around."

Chase snorted, lying back to mirror her position. "It deserves better attention than that." So did Stella. But she seemed content out of the spotlight, despite the one positioned directly above her on the grid. He wanted to know for sure. "Do you hide because of your divorce?"

He loved that they could still ask each other random, direct questions, with no hint of pretense or games, and not freak each other out. Like his questions from the other day at the museum, Stella took this one in stride as well. "I wouldn't call it hiding."

"I would." Chase rolled over on his side to face her, propping his head up with one hand. "Most women tend to hide behind makeup and fashion. But somehow, you hide behind your bare skin."

She turned her head and looked at him then, eyes even bluer than usual with surprise and indignation. He almost regretted his words. Almost.

"Don't pretend to know me, Chase Taylor." Her voice held a teasing tone, but it also contained a solid warning. "You might know a secret or two of mine, but I'm not as easy to figure out as you might think."

"Oh, trust me. There's nothing easy about it." He refused to let her go back into hiding again. He'd rather her be honest and real and mad than stow away. "But I do think I have it somewhat pegged." He took the slightly arrogant route on purpose, determined to get her to open up a little. He wanted to know the rest of her story.

"Is that so?" She laughed, short and hard. "Do tell."

"Your heart got broken." He said it calmly, simply. "And you didn't see it coming." He could relate all too well to that notion. He'd tell her that next.

She stared straight up at the lights, her jaw tight, not acknowledging with her expression if he'd hit the jackpot or not.

"You probably think your fast relationship with your ex means he was only into you for the superficial reasons." He watched, waited—yep, there it was. A tremor in her chin. He kept going, not to hurt her, but to free her. "So now, you hide. No more girlie clothes, no more makeup, no more complicated hairstyles. You traded your nail polish and high heels for security and safety."

A tear slipped from the corner of her eye and rolled down her cheek.

"You exchanged all your colors for neutrals."

She closed her eyes, both of them now streaming.

"Stella." He hated to make her cry, but she had to get these lies out and sometimes the only way to purge the false was with infusions of truth. "Look at me."

She shook her head.

"Please?"

Slowly, painfully, she turned and met his gaze. He rolled an inch closer to her, cupped her face in his hands. Still propped on his elbow, he looked down into her eyes, those same eyes he could never quite get out of his daydreams or his nightmares, for that matter, and whispered the truest thing she needed to know. "Your beauty has nothing to do with your appearance."

She closed her eyes again, swallowed, a tear dripping from her chin onto the shoulder of her hoodie.

He waited, praying, hoping the words would sink in deep. Had they made an impact at all? Had he helped heal even a portion of her pain? He knew that was a job bigger and deeper than any mere man could take on, but if he could even put a single dent in that armor, he wanted to.

Needed to.

She opened her eyes then, but instead of the expected glimmer of relief or gratitude in those baby blues of hers, he saw anger.

Unmatched, unfiltered, unprecedented anger.

She sat up so fast she almost caught him in the chin. "How dare you."

He scrambled to sit up, too, rubbing his elbow now indented from the hard wood of the stage. Scrambled to keep up. "What are you talking about? How dare I what?"

"How dare you any of it!" Stella stood, then, glaring down at him, arms stiff at her sides. "How dare you do this to me and my sister? Tease us. Love us. Leave us." Her voice cracked. "I had no idea why you left, Chase Taylor, except for the fact that you left *me*. You destroyed my relationship with my sister and then vanished before I could even begin to pick up the pieces." Her voice shuddered with unshed sobs. "You have no idea what you did."

He froze, paralyzed, unable to move or even comprehend the depth of pain radiating out of the woman he'd never been able to forget.

"Now you're back, and you're sweet, and you're . . . you're saying all the right things. You're romantic and kind and yet—you're doing it again! Rescuing me. Teasing me. Lov—" She stopped short then, cut herself off. "Just stop it. Stop it!"

He slowly rose to his knees, then his feet, hands held out carefully as if he could somehow stop the nonsense flowing from her mouth. "Is that how you see it?"

"I'm seeing it for exactly what it is."

He shook his head. "False."

"True!" She shouted then, her voice bouncing off the stage wings.

He tried to keep his composure, but he just wanted to shake her, shake the facts into her. She wasn't always right. Usually, maybe, but not this time. Not about this. "You have no idea why I left. Or what happened since I left, for that matter."

"Well I know you didn't waste much time. You said you were engaged."

"Are you kidding me? You were married!" He didn't mean to shout back, but the hypocrisy of it all pushed him over the edge. She was treading on ice now, and had no idea the temperature of the water below that razor-thin surface.

She glared, unable to counter his truth, and he lowered his voice, trying to pull them away from the cracks. "Stella. We both were a lot younger then. We've had different lives since then. Why does that have to change anything that's happening right now?"

"Your whole *live for the moment* mantra isn't always convenient, Chase." She poked her finger at his chest. "Because the past and the present are tied together. Irrevocably."

"Maybe. But one doesn't have to dictate the other."

"Of course it does. You left. You made a mess and you left me to clean it up, and it took years to even begin to get close." Fresh tears slipped over her flushed cheeks, eyes so vivid against the teal of her sweatshirt he thought he might never be able to look away from them. "I lost my boyfriend and my sister in the same moment."

"You didn't lose me, Stella." He reached for her, needed to hug her as badly as she needed to be hugged, but she shoved him away.

"You. Left."

Yes. He had. A decision that haunted him for years, a regret he would never overcome. "I know. But I'm here now."

She didn't have to say a word—the look on her face screamed that wasn't good enough. And he didn't blame her. "Everything that happened with me and you and your sister . . . it was bad timing, I'll admit. But I never meant to hurt her. Or you."

The fight returned to her eyes, the rigidness to her posture as she crossed her arms. "But you did. You hurt us both."

"I was scared!" His voice shattered the stillness of the theater. He yelled again, just for the release of it. "I was terrified, okay? I had made a promise to your sister and thought I was happy with her, and then there you were. You, in all your beautiful mess. You, with your flouncy dresses and shiny crowns, the exact opposite of anything I ever thought I'd like."

Love, his heart corrected. But he wouldn't say that word right now, not now.

Maybe not ever.

She rolled in her lips and pressed tight until they whitened, then motioned for him to continue.

But he was afraid he'd already said too much.

"I didn't expect you."

That got to her, by the way she quickly looked away. He wished he could touch her again, wipe away the tears hovering on her cheeks.

He needed her to understand. To forgive. Needed it more than he wanted to admit. "Look, I made a mistake, yes. I handled it all wrong. But it wasn't a mistake to tell your sister the truth, Stella. She deserved to know." Now, looking back as a man at a situation he'd handled more as a child, he'd probably change the wording he'd chosen. "I've grown up since then, realized how I could have done it differently. Done it better."

He ran his hands over his head, wishing he could shove away his frustration as easily as he could shove aside his hair. "I panicked, okay? Your sister was great. But you were . . . you were . . ."

"What?" She met his gaze for the first time in several minutes, seeking confirmation and affirmation and a dozen other things he couldn't even begin to identify.

He simply didn't have the words to explain the feeling that had taken over his heart that first afternoon they talked for hours. Or the day they sat on the benches at the bayou and speculated about the carving in the tree. Or the time he'd caught her doodling designs for her dream house on a sketch pad.

There were just no words.

"You were . . . Stella."

She sighed with exasperation. "That's vague and convenient."

That did it. "Quit hiding from compliments if you're going to beg for them."

"Ouch." She flinched, literally backed up a step, closer to the edge of the stage than he preferred. He reached for her, but she dodged him. At least she eased away from the edge. "I can take care of myself."

"That's evident, seeing how you've fainted three times now in front of me." She wasn't going to play fair, and he was tired of being the only grown-up in the room.

"You can't save me." She shook her head, arms pinned tight across her stomach. "No one can."

"Then why are you waiting for someone to try?" He lost it now, frustrated with the one-eighty in the conversation. Frustrated at himself for somehow screwing it up *again*. Frustrated with Stella for believing so many lies. "I understand heartache, Stella. Trust me."

"How is that even possible? You're always the one doing the hurting."

"Not always."

"What do you mean?" Her eyes sparked a challenge, "Did your fiancée leave you? Hit on your brother?"

That hurt. He looked down. Then away. Then at her gaze, shooting out confidence that she'd won. "Actually, she died."

All traces of victory fled Stella's eyes. "Chase." She covered her mouth with both hands, then reached toward him, then covered her face again. "Chase, I'm so sorry."

So was he. Sorry for starting any of this. For thinking he and Stella could ever go back into the past and create a positive future. For thinking he was capable of ever making a big decision that didn't lead to a huge regret.

He hopped off the edge of the stage, landed on his feet, and strode up the main aisle toward the doors. The Cameo might not be done yet.

But they were done here.

❦

Her stupid car wouldn't start.

Stella turned the key again and again and listened as her car attempted to crank and failed. Rain beat incessantly against the roof and windshield, and she pounded the steering wheel with her fist.

Pain shot through her wrist, and she stifled a cry. She'd cried enough that evening, enough to compete with the rain soaking her car and drenching everything else that was unfortunate enough to be outside in Bayou Bend tonight.

How could she be so foolish? The words she'd thrown so flippantly at Chase seemed to grow teeth in midair, biting them both before landing. She'd been so harsh.

His fiancée had died. *Died.*

And she'd denied his pain. Denied his ability to understand brokenness. Defended her hurt above his own.

No wonder he'd left the theater so fast. She didn't really want to be around herself, either.

She grabbed the steering wheel in both hands and leaned forward, resting her forehead against the edge. It was just that he'd been so—so right. He'd figured her out exactly, to a T. And on top of that, he wasn't intimidated by her. Wasn't put off by her broken pieces.

It scared her to death.

She closed her eyes, pressing her head against the smooth wheel, wishing she could just float away in the rain. She didn't want to call her dad to come bail her out. Would she *ever* stop needing her parents to rescue her? Didn't want to deal with her mom, who would ask about her puffy eyes and quiz her mercilessly.

Stella really didn't want to give her the opportunity. Not right now, not while she was like this. All vulnerable and exposed and raw and open. Bleeding, again. Over Dillon. Over Chase. Over an entire future full of what-if's.

Would she ever stop breaking?

Slowly, reluctantly, she reached for her cell phone. Dialed her parents' number. And then stopped as headlights cut through the rain and parked directly in front of her. She disconnected the call before it went through just as Chase's number lit up her screen.

Her stomach knotted. "Hello?"

"Why haven't you left?" His question, rough around the edges, held a measure of concern she couldn't deny.

"Car won't start." If she'd had any pride left to swallow, it would have gotten stuck in her throat for sure. But she didn't. She felt numb. Indifferent. Too hurt to allow any of the broken shards a place to cut.

"I've got jumpers."

"Isn't that dangerous in the rain?" She didn't know a lot about jumper cables, but she knew electricity and water wasn't the best combination.

"I'll be careful." He hung up before she could think of anything else to say, before she could protest that no, she deserved to be left in the rain to freeze all night. That she wasn't worth risking electric shock for.

She'd shocked them both enough for the night.

A few moments later, a shadowed figure cut in front of the headlights, carrying long cables. She had presence of mind enough to pop the hood, and he lifted the lid, holding an umbrella over the top as he connected the jumper cables. He went back and started his car, then jogged around to her passenger side.

She unlocked the door and he slid in, shaking water off his hair as he slammed the door against the rain. "We'll give it just a minute to charge. Then you should be good to go."

But she wasn't. She didn't deserve this. Didn't deserve a knight after she'd practically stabbed him with his own sword.

"You should have left me here." She didn't mean to say it out loud, entirely, but now that it had happened, she didn't regret it. Chase shot her a level stare as he folded up his umbrella and dropped it on the floorboard. "Stella."

"I mean it. I was awful, and you came back." Her voice trembled, and she willed a strength into her tone that she didn't fully possess. "You should have left me."

Should have left last time, too, if she wanted to be honest. That's what men did. They left her.

And the only common denominator she could see was the tear-stained face in her rearview mirror.

"Stella." Chase leaned his head against the back of the seat and let out a long sigh. Rain drizzled down the side of his temple, catching in the dark end-of-day stubble lining his jaw. "Don't be ridiculous. I'm not going to leave you in the rain."

She couldn't stop staring at him, couldn't stop feeling as if every fractured shard of her heart was being broken again.

He rolled his head to the side to meet her gaze. "In the snow, maybe." A tiny grin lifted the corner of his mouth. "Or a sandstorm."

She couldn't help but smile back despite the ache consuming her insides. "But not rain?"

"Never rain." Chase reached for the hand that rested on the gearshift, and squeezed it tight. He held it like a brother or a friend would, palm to palm, not threading his fingers through hers like a lover. "Don't be afraid of the rain, Stella."

"Are you going to quote me something about dancing in it, instead?" She tried to smile again, but failed miserably.

"I'm more for stomping in the puddles than dancing in 'em."

She raised her eyebrows. "I don't get it."

"Think about it. What did you do as a kid, when it rained and you wanted to play outside?"

She squinted, then nodded as it sank in. "Put on my rain boots and stomped in the puddles."

"Heard it taught in church one time that God tells us to come to Him with faith like a child. I figure that means with our storms too." Chase traced his thumb over her knuckles.

"So instead of hiding under umbrellas, we . . . stomp in the puddles?"

"More fun that way, don't you think?" He cupped her hand between both of his, sending a rush of warmth up her entire arm. "I mean, if it's going to rain anyway . . . might as well make something out of it."

She watched the water drip down the windshield. Bead and bunch and collect in the grooves of the windows and the lip on the raised hood. "Every storm runs out of rain, right?"

"Eventually." Chase released her hand, reached up and pushed her hair back from her face. "But that can't be the point, can it?"

No. It couldn't.

"Your battery should be ready to go now. If you need someone to jump your car in the morning before you can get to a mechanic, let me know. I can swing by." Chase put one hand on the door as if he were about to open it.

"Wait." She reached for his hand this time, caught it and held it tight. "I'm sorry."

His gaze lingered on hers. Dropped to her lips. Her stomach quivered. She wanted him to kiss her, wanted him to so badly. More than she had in the truck the other day. More than she had earlier tonight before their fight. This time, she was sure the kiss could heal something. Put a few of her fragments back together.

Even temporary glue would be better than none at all.

He watched her eyes, almost as if he could read the storm

brewing inside her, and leaned closer. She closed her eyes, held her breath, waiting, longing, desperate to be made whole.

His breath neared her face, and her heart thudded in expectation. Hope. Eagerness.

He planted a kiss on her forehead and opened the door. "Drive safe."

And then he was gone. Into the rain. Face uplifted.

No umbrella.

fifteen

The bathrooms were finally done at the Cameo.

Stella stood back from the row of photos she'd pinned to a clothesline in her living room to survey her handiwork. She always liked to view pictures of the spaces she'd decorated, as she would in a magazine, rather than only view the room itself as a whole in person. She noticed quirks and minute irritations a lot more clearly that way.

But this time, so far, there weren't any.

The turquoise and gold accents popped against the white tile. The tiny stage lights above the mirror lit up the room and gave it an elegance that hinted at sophistication far outreaching Bayou Bend. Vintage art decorated the wall space near the counters, above the hand dryers. A gold and glass beaded soap dispenser waited beside each sink.

Stella's favorite piece, a framed collage of leftover fabric pieces, hung by the giant gold-plated oval mirror to the left of the bathroom door.

She backed up another step, tilting her head to view the final photos. Yes. A woman could easily touch up her lipstick in that mirror and like what she saw. Feel appreciated and valued and yes, even glamorous. Be given the spunk and sass to own her reflection, to go back to her date or friends or family with confidence.

It was asking a lot of a bathroom.

But Stella felt satisfied with the final result—more so than with the final result of the other night's fiasco in the rain. She hadn't talked to Chase since he disappeared into the storm.

Unwilling to bother him again the next morning, she'd called her dad and had him jump her car and meet her at the mechanic. He had insisted on negotiating with the guy, and since very few folks liked telling local preachers no, she'd come away with a bill a lot cheaper than expected.

Still. She hated having to be rescued. Even when she and Dillon were married, she leaned too much on her parents. Dillon could never be counted on to take care of business, whether from lack of know-how or lack of effort, she still wasn't sure. But if there was a car repair, she'd had to go to her dad. If there was an issue in the house with wiring or plumbing, she called her dad for advice. A monster bug to kill? Dad.

She'd tried to go to Dillon first. Tried to trust her husband first.

Turned out she couldn't trust him at all.

She pictured Chase in the scenario of a busted pipe or a leaky faucet or a flat tire, and almost laughed. There wouldn't be a single task in any house that he wouldn't be able to repair himself—or, at the least, know exactly who to call to help him out. And probably learn something new in the process.

Chase. She groaned as she began carefully taking down the strung photos. Why couldn't he have been a hero when she'd really needed him to be? When her family was falling apart and she was seemingly all to blame? He hadn't been there to back her up, to explain, to convince Kat it wasn't Stella's fault he'd broken up with her.

No amount of heroism today could make up for those years of being estranged from her sister.

Because even if she and Chase could figure this out and get on the same page, Kat was still a factor. A very intimidating, very pregnant factor. She couldn't lose her sister again. Not for Chase. Not for anyone.

Especially not for someone who hadn't chosen her first, but rather, had bailed when it got complicated.

That made two men now on that list.

She wandered back into her art room and laid the photos in the basket near her canvas. She'd look at them again in a day or two, with fresh eyes, to make sure she hadn't overlooked anything. But she was very satisfied with the completed bathroom.

Her mosaic tile project, on the other hand . . . she pulled the box of pieces out once again and settled onto the stool at her workbench. She'd laid a few pieces on a blank canvas flat on the bench, but wasn't convinced they were in the right place. In fact, she was sure they weren't.

She rearranged a few pieces, but the picture didn't resemble anything at all. Just a mess of broken shards.

There was nothing beautiful here.

With a frustrated sigh, she dropped the pieces back into the box. She'd never figure out how the artist who created the mosaic tile woman at the museum had done it. How did one envision such beauty from a mess of brokenness?

She couldn't even see it—much less create it.

She plucked a new shard from the box to try again, a piece of metal she'd found at the Cameo and thought interesting. Then she laid another piece next to it, filling in the spaces with random fragments like a collage.

Nope. Not working. It still just looked like a canvas full of lost causes.

She put the pieces back into the box, replaced the lid, and shoved the box away.

Maybe not everything broken was meant to be beautiful.

ↄℓℓↄ

He had wanted to kiss her. But every instinct in his heart had shouted no, every conviction of the Lord had called to wait. To honor. To respect.

Chase jabbed the punching bag at the fire station and dodged it as it bounced back in his face. He couldn't fill Stella's empty places. And in that moment in her car, in the pouring rain, that look in her eyes—that was exactly what she needed him to do. Fill her.

He refused to contribute to her brokenness. Only God could heal her. Only God could fill the empty places.

He just wished God would give him a chance to help.

He pounded the mini-bag again, and for a minute thought he should have brought gloves. But then again, any cracks or fissures in his knuckles would only serve as a much-needed reminder that Stella wasn't his to fix.

He punched again.

"Pretty poor form, cousin." Ethan joined him in the truck bay, still in his fire department uniform, and grinned, stealing a jab at the bag as Chase paused to wipe the sweat from his brow.

"Very funny."

Another uniformed man with Ethan, a taller African American man, chuckled and flashed Chase a row of even white teeth. "Sometimes release is more important. Isn't that right?"

"Whatever! What's this guy got to be stressed about?" Ethan jabbed playfully at Chase's ribs. "He's living all but free at my place and eating all my groceries."

"Oh so that hundred dollar bill I left you for food the other day was just Monopoly money, huh?" Chase tucked in and dodged Ethan's attempts at connection, then neatly popped him on the shoulder. "Next time I'll just leave a ten, then."

"Hitting him where it hurts." The other man laughed. "Chase, I already like you. I'm Darren. But everyone around here calls me Chap."

"Ah, the coffee-killer." Now he remembered; Ethan had mentioned Chap that first day in his apartment, when he'd brewed coffee thick enough to cut with a steak knife. "I've heard about you."

"My reputation precedes me." Darren steadied the bag for Chase and held it. "Front center."

Chase obeyed, his shoes squeaking against the concrete floor.

"Left jab."

He connected solidly.

"Right upper cut."

The bag let out a satisfying thud.

Darren eased away from the bag. "Release is important. But so is knowing how to properly channel it."

"That's why I'm here." Instead of tearing down all the hard work he'd put into the Cameo and blowing his fist through fresh Sheetrock. They were starting to paint today, and he needed to get back up there. But Stella had taken over his thoughts to the point where if he didn't let off some steam soon, he'd end up putting them both exactly where they didn't need to be.

Together.

"Must be a woman." Darren looked at Ethan, who shrugged.

"Don't look at me, Chap. He just lives with me and eats my food." He nudged Chase playfully to show he was kidding.

Chase shook him off.

Ethan started to smirk. "Hey, now. *Is* it a woman?"

He didn't answer, just connected soundly with the bag again.

"That's a yes. I speak kickboxing." Darren slapped Ethan on the shoulder. "Go hook a man of the cloth up with some coffee. How about it?"

"You could have just said you wanted to talk to Chase alone." Ethan headed toward the bay doors, then pointed back at Chase. "I'll water it down for you so you can handle it."

Chase shook his head. He loved his cousin, even if joining the fire department had boosted his ego a notch or so too high.

"He means well. Just doesn't get it yet—hasn't ever loved and lost." Darren held the bag again as Chase continued his workout. "He'll figure it out soon enough, and then be glad he hung this bag."

Exactly. Chase whaled on it again, then stopped to catch his breath. "So, have you?"

"Loved and lost?" Darren waited for Chase's confirmation then nodded. "A few times."

"Death?"

"Death. Failed engagements. I've seen my share."

"But you're married now."

He wiggled his ring finger. "Yes sir."

"How'd you get past the failed engagement?"

"The Lord. His Word. Church." Darren spread his hands wide. "Those are the easy answers, though they're true enough. Also friends and family. Realizing I wasn't alone, didn't have to carry the pain alone."

He'd done all of that while healing from Leah.

So why the guilt now of even thinking about pushing ahead with Stella? The condemnation that lingered in the wake of their one kiss. And even in the almost-kiss from the other night in the rain.

He started pounding again. "But you obviously moved on. Married someone else?"

Darren nodded, the bag slipping from his grip. He readjusted his stance. "Took time."

"How much time?"

He grinned, steadied the bag. "There's no formula, man. My time line isn't going to be yours."

True enough.

"I'll tell you what I told my good friend Lucas, though. Don't stir up or awaken love until it pleases."

He nodded. He'd heard that verse before. Song of Solomon, maybe? He punched again. How did one know when it did please, though? How did anyone ever determine the when of it all without sinning in the process?

Wait. Lucas?

Kat's Lucas?

He stopped midpunch.

Darren continued, oblivious to the bomb he'd just dropped. "I don't know your story, man, but I'll listen if you ever want to tell it. That's why I'm on staff here at the department. To listen. To help. Pray, if you want."

Maybe. Chap was a stranger. It felt awkward, but on the other hand, an unbiased opinion might just be what he needed.

But this was Lucas's friend? Would he piece any of it together, tell too much to Lucas or Kat too soon? It seemed risky.

He swallowed the urge to spill his guts, confess it all. "Prayer would be good. For wisdom, and timing. It's hard to let go of the past, you know?"

"Oh, I know. Trust me. And I'll pray for you." Darren came from around the back of the bag and clapped his hand on Chase's shoulder. "Just remember one thing for me."

"What's that?" He'd never felt so comfortable with a stranger before. Something about the chaplain just spoke peace and certainty. The man was good at his job, and Chase wasn't even a fireman. So good, he almost reconsidered his decision not to tell his story.

But at the price of Kat finding out too soon . . . he couldn't do it. He couldn't dredge all that back up, even if she was happily married now. It didn't seem fair. Not really fair to Stella, either.

But then again, not much of how he'd treated either sister had ever been fair.

Darren squeezed his shoulder tighter, as if trying to drill his words directly into Chase. "Whatever is holding you back . . . make sure it's of the Lord."

"How do you do that? How do you know for sure?"

"What's the root of it, man? Fear? Guilt? Discouragement?"

Chase looked down at his hands, rubbed his fingers over his cracked knuckles. Yeah. Basically all of the above. Fear of failing himself, his family. Fear of failing Leah and her memory.

Guilt over not mourning just a little longer the woman he'd promised to love forever.

Discouragement that he'd ever be able to run fast enough to catch up to the life he'd intended to have—the life that was stolen from him. Or to outrun the memories that snapped at his heels.

Darren let go of his arm after another hearty tap. "God doesn't roll that way, dude. Fear, guilt, discouragement? That's from the other side of the camp."

Chase agreed, in theory. On paper. But his heart and his thoughts remained more jumbled than that. Not so clear-cut. So what was Darren saying—that this was the right time to stir up the old embers of love for Stella? To move forward, to awaken what was put to sleep years ago?

He looked up, halfway willing to get more specific and actually grab some answers, but at that moment, Ethan burst back into the bay, coffee mugs in hand. "Don't worry, cousin. I made yours weak."

He winked and Darren laughed as Ethan handed Chase his cup. He looked at the dark brown liquid and decided he valued his life too much to even taste it.

"And here's yours, Chap. Just the way you like it—unable to be poured."

"Perfect." Darren blew on the top of it and took a sip, then raised his mug in a toast to Chase. "I've taught him well."

Maybe so.

And maybe Darren still had more he could teach Chase too.

Chase took a sip and grimaced. Not as bad as the coffee at the apartment that night with Ethan, but pretty close to it. "How long did you brew this stuff again?"

Ethan shrugged, taking a long sip of his own coffee. "I don't know. How long was I gone?"

Well, that explained it.

"It's all about timing, brother." Darren met Chase's gaze over Ethan's head and raised his eyebrows pointedly. "All about knowing how long to wait."

He didn't know if it was a revelation from the Lord, the coffee sludge in his cup, or Darren's advice—maybe all of it sinking together. But Chase looked at his mug, then back at Darren, and nodded.

He had his answer.

Now he'd see if Stella had hers.

❧

The grave site was exactly the way she'd left it a few weeks ago.

Stella crouched beside her great-aunt Maggie's tombstone, pulling the dried purple flowers from the dusty holder and gently wedging the new bouquet of daisies inside.

"Miss you, Aunt Maggie." She wasn't entirely sure if the woman could hear her from heaven, or how all of that worked, but regardless, it felt comforting to come and talk to God, next to the memory of one of the wisest women she knew.

She missed Aunt Mag's advice.

Stella sank into a sitting position in the short grass by the headstone and crossed her legs, the dirt warm beneath her jeans.

"Hope you're letting her do some baking up there, Lord." She plucked a grass blade from the earth and began to shred it into tiny pieces with her fingernail. "She makes a mean cupcake."

Not as good as Kat's gourmet creations, of course, but Aunt Maggie's cupcakes had always been tried and true classics. Even after she was diagnosed with cancer, she kept baking as long as she could stand up in the warm kitchen. Then Kat had taken a break from her thriving business long enough to make her aunt's favorite strawberry, vanilla, and chocolate cakes for her upon every request.

Stella tore the grass into another strip. Aunt Mags would know what to tell her about Chase being back in town. She closed her eyes, wishing she could still hear the woman's voice, but the more time that had passed since the funeral, the more it faded.

Stella wrestled another piece of grass from the dirt. "Aunt Maggie knew the whole story, God. About what happened with him and Kat. And between me and Kat after that." She shuddered, not missing those days for anything. She and Kat had never been close, and one day not too long ago Kat had finally admitted that she had felt invisible in Stella's beauty queen shadow.

How little she realized that Stella longed to live up to the potential, maturity, and drive that her older sister always had in spades. Kat never had to prove herself as wise or even just prove herself as an adult. She was never coddled and overly taken care of. She relied on Lucas for a lot of things, but after entering *Cupcake Combat*, her sister developed a backbone Stella knew had been there all along. It just needed strengthening.

Funny how that worked out.

A summer breeze lifted the hair from the back of Stella's neck and breathed relief across her flushed face. Maybe this situation with Chase would work itself out too. Maybe she was overthinking, overreacting. She just couldn't stand the thought of things going back to the way they were with Kat those years ago. She was about to become an aunt, for crying out loud. Hardly the time to distance herself from her only sister.

But maybe she was assuming the worst. She did that a lot after her divorce—expected the negative before it could catch her off guard. Maybe Kat wouldn't be opposed to Stella pursuing something with Chase after all.

She should probably just talk to Kat.

In fact, if she tried, she could almost make out Aunt Maggie's voice right now, exasperated. "Talk to your sister, girl. Y'all are both grown-ups." Then she'd probably throw in a wink and add, "And if conversation doesn't work, a good ol' fashioned food fight usually does."

Wouldn't that be something? She pictured Kat covered in raspberry lemonade torte icing and smirked. "Good one, Aunt Mags."

Then again, there might not be anything to pursue with Chase. She couldn't figure him out. First the kiss in his truck. Then the kiss she'd offered that he'd rejected in her car, replacing it with a friendly peck on the forehead instead. What did it all mean?

She waited a moment, listening with God in the silence. If she would just stop and do this kind of listening more often, she'd be a lot less stressed. A lot less passive aggressive. And a lot less insecure.

But would she be made whole?

She pulled a new blade of grass from the dirt and opened her palm, letting the wind catch the blade and whisk it away. "What do you think, Aunt Mags?" She waited a beat, wishing she could pull an answer from her memory files of her great-aunt's wisdom, much of which was shared at her hospice bedside while the cancer raged.

A lump knotted in her throat, and she forced her whispered words past it. "Do you think anyone is ever too broken to be healed?"

"Of course not."

At the sudden voice behind her, Stella sprang to her feet so fast that she stumbled and fell right back down to the grass. Landed on her own foot. She winced, twisting her ankle free from underneath her. "Dixie?"

The older lady stepped from the shade of a nearby oak tree and walked toward her. She sat down next to Stella in the dirt. "Did you find the gold?"

"The gold?" Stella's mind raced. "At the Cameo?"

"Right. The Cameo. The gold."

She remembered then, Dixie's help with her design that had led to the final product, and nodded with a laugh. "Oh, yes. That. Yes, the gold looks great. You'll have to come see it when it's done."

"I've seen it."

Stella frowned in confusion. "Then why did you ask—"

"Did He answer the question?"

"What question? Who?" Somehow, when in Dixie's presence, all Stella seemed to have were questions.

"God. That's who you asked, right?"

Stella twisted to look back at the tree where the homeless woman had stood. How had Dixie possibly heard her whisper from that far away?

At this point, she was done even trying to figure it out. Just let

Dixie be. There was no harm in it. Stella relaxed her tense shoulders and turned her face up to the sun. "Not yet." A bird chirped from a tree branch overheard, and she found a measure of the peace she'd been starting to seek before Dixie arrived.

The woman stretched out her legs, one of her knees popping. She didn't seem to notice. "I did. I answered."

She had, hadn't she? What had she said before she scared Stella half to death? Her exact question had been, *Do you think anyone is ever too broken to be healed?*

A chill skated down the length of her spine, despite the sun heating her bare arms and cheeks as Dixie's answer sprang to mind. *Of course not.*

Dixie tugged the edge of that same old blazer around her middle. "Brokenness is a method."

"For what?"

"God has methods." She looked Stella straight in the eye, and she seemed almost 100 percent normal. Like talking to one's grandma over coffee.

Like talking to Aunt Mags over a bowl of cake batter.

"He's in the method business, child." Dixie pointed to the headstone. "That dash right there? That's all that matters."

"The in-between." The life lived between the numbers. Aunt Mags's life had been one of impact in her family, her church, her community.

Dixie nodded. "Broken is just a method. A means."

"A means to what?" For a moment Stella forgot she was talking to a potentially crazy woman, and just simply craved wisdom and an answer to her question as strongly as if she were talking to a renowned teacher or speaker.

Maybe she was.

"A means to what matters."

Stella's heart raced. *No.* Dixie was getting vague again, slipping off into that distance. She desperately wanted the woman to stay close. Stay sane. Just for another minute.

"Don't be afraid of the broken."

Stella nodded. Their coherent moments were slipping through her fingers like sand. "Okay. What else?" There was more. There had to be more. *Please, God, let there be more.*

Dixie squinted at the headstone, then up at the sky, as if listening for a voice only she could hear. She grinned wide. "Don't be afraid of the healing."

Don't be afraid of the healing? Now *that* was crazy talk. Healing was all Stella wanted, all she had ever wanted since first learning of Dillon's infidelity. No way would she be afraid of it. "What else, Dixie?"

But the woman stood and brushed at the baggy old dress pants with a hole in the knee. Stella determined to buy her a new pair, just as soon as she got paid from the Cameo.

Maybe two pairs. No one deserved to walk around in holes.

"What else what?" Dixie's voice hardened a little, took on that snappy edge she got whenever she was getting low on sugar. "You better get back to work, girl. That theater won't open itself."

True.

Stella stood as well. She smiled at Aunt Maggie's tombstone and wondered if God let her aunt overhear even a portion of that odd conversation. Aunt Mags would have loved Dixie. Maybe that's why Stella kept feeling drawn to her. She knew her aunt would have seen past the façade and the shell, too, and would have drawn out the wisdom that lurked beneath the surface. Aunt Mags was good at that—revealing what hardly anyone else saw. Seeing the best in people. Coaxing them to be more than they believed they could be.

Sometimes it just took being pushed a little to realize you were actually being drawn.

Dixie headed back toward her tree, and Stella headed the opposite direction to her car. She turned as Dixie hollered against the wind.

"Told you you needed an umbrella."

sixteen

She almost didn't want to go inside the homeless shelter for fear there would still be dripping water somewhere.

But, as usual, her fears were unfounded.

Stella followed her sister inside, lugging another giant box of dishes Kat was donating to the fund-raiser sale. The director of the shelter, Nancy Martin, broke from the crowd gathered to help, and pointed to the far corner of the living area, where boxes were already stacked into several neat piles. "Thanks! Find the pile marked kitchenware."

She dumped the box in the appropriate stack, then took the next box from Kat. At least that one was full of clothes and not too heavy. "You're too pregnant to be lifting anything."

"I'm tired of being helpless." Kat looked down and rubbed her protruding belly. "But I know. I need to slow down. I had some contractions yesterday."

"What?" Stella reached out to touch her sister's stomach, as if doing so could convince the baby to stay put. "Don't say that."

"They were minor ones in my back." Kat shrugged it off. "Doctor said it was just from being on my feet so much. I was told to take it easy."

Figures. "And yet, you're here helping coordinate and organize a fund-raiser."

"I'll sit down and help. I promise." Kat held up one hand as if swearing an oath.

"Here, then, take this." Nancy shoved a label maker into Kat's hand. "You can sit and make price tags."

"Perfect." Stella tugged her sister over to the frayed loveseat in the corner of the room by the dusty fireplace, smiling at one of the older residents who sat half-dozing in the recliner nearby, a folded magazine in his lap. "I'll unbox and bring you the stuff to price."

"How do I know what to label everything?" Kat called toward Nancy as she brushed past with another box.

Nancy paused and juggled the box in her hand long enough to point to a stack of papers on the coffee table in front of Kat. "I printed price estimates earlier today. You can follow along as a guide and if anything isn't listed, just make it up. They're only for suggestions, anyway." She continued her mission toward the shelter's kitchen. "I think people are just going to end up making offers, for the most part."

"That's easy enough." Kat settled in the chair, label maker at the ready. "Let's do it."

Stella opened the nearest box and handed Kat a striped throw pillow that had seen better days, but wasn't nearly as ratty as the shelter's furniture.

Kat ran her finger down the printed list of furnishings. "Two dollars." Then she carefully typed in and printed a label, smoothing it onto the front corner of the pillow.

This was going to be a long night.

But as long as they had time on their hands . . .

Stella handed Kat another pillow. "I've been meaning to talk to you about something." She wiped her palms on her jeans before digging another pillow from the box. Ever since leaving Aunt Maggie's grave site the day before, she knew she couldn't postpone having The Conversation with her sister.

And now Chase had left her a voicemail about an hour before, asking if they could talk at some point before work in the morning. He asked her to call him tonight when she was done volunteering, or come over. But he insisted it was important, that it couldn't wait longer than that.

Not knowing was making her slightly crazy, almost crazy enough to cancel the fund-raiser prep and go talk to him first. Was it work related—or about them? Maybe he'd been asking himself the same questions since they last saw each other, as she'd been.

Or maybe he just wanted to talk about the Cameo.

Either way, one thing was certain. Whether Chase was interested in her or not, she had to know what was going on in her sister's head about the whole situation. Because if Kat shut her down, then it wouldn't matter what Chase did or said or wanted later tonight. She'd already have her answer.

And then maybe she could spare them both some extra heartache.

"Why is everyone donating pillows?" Kat frowned as she slapped another two-dollar label on the fringed fabric in her lap. "Anyway. Sorry. Rhetorical question. What'cha got?"

Stella moved to the box marked kitchenware and handed Kat a used but quality blender. "It's about Chase."

Kat kept her eyes on her label. "Is he being a jerk again?"

"No." Hardly. In fact, he'd been quite the hero lately, which was half the problem. Assuming attraction to Chase was a problem.

Yeah. It was.

She swallowed hard, trying to force a casualness she didn't feel. "Actually, he's been really helpful."

Kat looked up, her expression wary. "How so?"

"Just, you know. Working. At the Cameo." No, oh no. This wasn't going as planned. "And beyond."

What? How had that even slipped out of her mouth?

"What kind of beyond?" Kat narrowed her eyes, the blender forgotten as she stared at Stella.

Her stomach did a double flip. Why did she even try anymore? She was bombing every serious conversation she tried to have lately. "I mean, he jumped my car the other day when the battery died."

"I thought Dad helped you get to the mechanic." Kat still hadn't finished her label.

"He did, the next day. Chase helped make sure I got home in the rainstorm."

"How noble."

Stella pointed to the blender and Kat reluctantly slapped a label on it and handed it back. "It was. We had been fighting over something stupid, and yet he still—"

"Fighting?" Kat snorted. "Now *that* sounds more like Chase. What trouble did he start this time?"

Trouble? Oh, there'd been Trouble. With a Capital T.

"Ladies! Working hard, or hardly working?" Howard grinned

as he wandered up to them, fingers hooked through the straps of his overalls. He stopped beside Stella and took in the scene before him. "One more than the other, maybe?" He nodded at Kat's stomach.

Only Howard could get away with such a comment. She'd seen her sister erupt over much less.

Kat smiled and shook back her hair, batting her eyes with intentional overdramatics. "Howard, if you're going to flirt, you should really check with my husband first."

He let out a hearty laugh. "I'll do that, ma'am. I'll do that. I know my place, though." He elbowed Stella in the ribs. "First in line for her cupcakes."

Stella elbowed him back. "You're a smart man, Howard." She wanted to ask him about Dixie, but wasn't sure what to say. She'd had enough relational awkwardness to last her a lifetime the past few weeks. Besides, how did two homeless people date? Where did they go? They were just friends who probably cheered each other up, helped provide for the other. All of the homeless community stuck together, as evidenced by the turnout for the monthly meals and even the fund-raiser preparation.

"What did you make for the big sale?" She knew Howard would contribute something, even if it was an animal he whittled out of a spare hunk of wood he'd discovered in the forest off the interstate.

"Rocking horse." He pointed behind him to the area designated for toys. "Someone donated the wood for me, and I took care of the rest around my schedule at the Cameo."

Stella craned her head to see. The piece was somehow basic and crude, not stained or polished, but it looked as if it'd been sanded smooth. It was a sweet contribution, one that showed Howard's skill, but further proved how frustrating it must be to have the talent to succeed but not the means to do it with. She made a mental note to ask Chase if she could give Howard the leftover stain from the stage. It'd look beautiful on the horse.

"You did a great job, Howard."

"What'd you make, little missy?"

Stella pointed to the pile of dresses peeking from a garment bag that was draped over the back of the couch. It'd taken them two trips to get everything in from Kat's car, and those were the first things she'd dumped.

Including the royal blue gown.

Mom would have to deal. There was no coming back from that memory.

"I'm donating an era." Apparently.

Howard nodded as if he understood. "I see. Well, you ladies get back to work." He winked at Kat. "Or hardly working, anyway."

"You're giving away all those dresses? How did I not see those earlier?" Kat looked back and forth from the garment bag to Stella in surprise.

"You were busy with all your kitchenware and baby-toting." Stella brushed it off, not wanting to make those dresses any more of a big deal than they'd already been. She'd already decided to wait and not sell her wedding rings. Not yet. She didn't feel near the panic over letting them go as she had before, but still the timing wasn't quite right.

Baby steps.

"What did Mom say?"

Stella set the blender down at the product table before digging through the box for another item in need of a label. "She helped me clean out my closet."

"But what did she *say*?"

Darn her sister's intuition. "She's supportive."

"Uh-huh."

"Now, anyway. It took a minute, but she's cool." Well, a minute was an understatement, and cool was probably one too. But at least it was done.

"Whatever. I'd grill you on that, but I'd rather get back to what you were saying about Chase." Kat pointed as if she could pull up the interrupted conversation on an iPad screen. "You were saying he started some kind of trouble. Picked a fight with you."

Stella pulled out a toaster for Kat. "Actually, I was the one who started the fight—"

"Stella! You've got to be kidding me. He's gotten in your head, hasn't he?" Kat leaned forward, ignoring the toaster Stella extended toward her. The older man in the recliner nearby stirred from his doze and stared at them both.

Kat lowered her voice, but not enough. "I told you to be careful."

"I was. He hasn't done anything."

"Do you hear yourself?" Kat hissed, loud enough to be heard in the outside back ally. "He's manipulating you. Just like he always did to me."

Indignation flared. "That's not true."

"How do you know?"

"Because, it's different. He's different now." She came and sat on the arm of the loveseat, close enough to force Kat to use her real inside voice. "We've had a lot of talks while working together. He's been through a lot in the last few years."

More than she felt comfortable sharing. It didn't seem fair

somehow to publicize Chase's secrets to her sister—his ex. Even if it would help Stella's case for him.

"I'm sure he has. But so have you—which makes you a little vulnerable to being manipulated." Kat yanked the toaster from her sister's hand and put the label she'd finally printed on the front. "Especially by someone who is as good at it as he is."

This was getting ridiculous. Why was Kat so convinced Chase was a monster? "I'm not totally blind to things, Kat. Dillon taught me a lot about trust, you can be sure of that."

"I'm not saying you're an idiot, Stella. I'm saying Chase is a mastermind. And out of your league when it comes to mind games."

Now she was forgetting to whisper. "That was ages ago. Why are you so sure he hasn't changed?"

"Why are you so sure he has?"

They stared at each other, eyebrows raised, the toaster ignored between them.

Stella finally broke the stalemate and carried the toaster to the table. Then she turned and put her hands on her hips, trying to keep her voice level. The ladies working across the room in the kitchen area and folding towels on the buffet counter didn't need to know their dirty laundry. "Kat, you have Lucas."

"I know that." Kat patted her stomach. "Daily reminder here."

"Then why are you still jealous?"

Kat went so still, Stella almost snapped her fingers in front of her face to see if she was awake. "I'm not jealous." The words came out low, monotone, almost robotic. When Kat was that level and even, it meant the calm before the storm.

She'd awakened the hormonal giant.

"Well, if you're not, you sure are acting jealous. Why are you so against the idea of Chase and me?" She was panicking now, desperate to get her sister to see her side. And that desperation nearly did her in. What had changed? Fifteen minutes ago, she was willing to have a brief conversation and then tell Chase whatever she needed to tell him later that night. If it even came up. Casual. Easy. Nothing life changing.

Now, somehow, if Kat didn't give her blessing, her world was over.

Stella took a deep breath to calm her nerves, willing her heart to settle in her chest before her panic reached a point of no return. She grabbed another throw pillow waiting to be labeled and squeezed it against her chest.

"I don't like what Chase represents." Kat's voice, still calm and even, stilled even further as she placed her hands protectively over her belly, almost as if attempting to cover the baby's ears. "I don't like the way he treated either of us."

"I agree. But why can't he have another chance?"

"Do you not remember, Stella?" Kat's voice turned less offended and more imploring. "Just stop for a minute. Remember. Remember all of it. The lies, the betrayal. He was a wedge between us for years. *Years*, Stella."

Yes, he was. But part of that had been a lot of miscommunication and a lot of fault on Kat's part. It was Kat's grudge, not Stella's. Why did she have to pay for it now? She hadn't done anything wrong, hadn't intended to steal her sister's boyfriend.

That wasn't the way it went down.

But Kat had told her side of the story so often by now, Stella wasn't sure if she even accurately remembered the full truth.

"You deserve better than that." Kat held out her hands for the pillow, and Stella reluctantly released it to her. "After all you've been through with Dillon . . ." Her voice trailed off.

"Don't bring him into this. It's different." She yanked the pillow back, tossed it on the end table. Handed her another one.

"It's not different, Stella. It's all part of the same wound. You deserve a man you can trust explicitly. With your whole heart."

True. She did deserve that. Could she trust Chase that way?

Would she ever be capable of trusting *any* man that way?

Kat leaned back in the chair, pressing her hands behind her waist and arching her back. "There's another one."

She was stressing her sister into labor. "Sorry. I didn't mean to start an argument."

"It's not an argument. " Kat took one of the newly labeled pillows and shoved it behind her lower back. "I'm just trying to protect you."

Once again, the baby of the family. Needy. Dependent. Unable to take care of herself. The barbs, unintentional as they might be, sank in deep.

"Promise me you won't date him?"

That wasn't fair. How could she make such a demand? But the pleading in her sister's eyes ran deeper than the barbs had penetrated. "I don't know."

"Stella. I'm trying to help you." She leaned forward in the chair and held out her pinky as they used to do when they were kids, back in the days when their biggest fight revolved around who ate the last Little Debbie snack and whose turn it was to set the table. "Promise me."

Stella hesitantly reached out her hand, and latched her pinky around her sister's. "I promise." She tried to tell herself the tightening feeling in her chest was just indigestion.

Certainly not yet another piece of her heart snapping off from the rest.

✑✑✑

Thank goodness, Ethan was working tonight. Chase really didn't want to have this conversation with an audience, especially not someone in his family. They'd have to cross the family bridge at some point, but for now, he just wanted to talk to Stella. Tell her the revelation he had at the fire station the other night with Darren.

Just wanted to sit with her on Ethan's back patio swing and watch the stars and tell her that he had begun to feel a little closer to God than he'd had in a while. As if maybe something in his life was lining up, for the first time in a long time.

Her timid knock on the front door rang through his heart like a gunshot. He flung open the door a little harder than he intended.

"Hey, there." She looked beautiful as always, though a little tired, weary around the edges. "How did tonight go?" She'd been at the shelter for the fund-raiser, and if it hadn't been for her volunteering that night with Kat, he'd have gone too. But there was no need to push Kat's acceptance of them before he even had a chance to tell Stella what was on his heart.

The other stuff could wait.

"It was okay." Her tone said a lot more than her words, and he gestured for her to follow him through the kitchen and out the back door. "We got a lot of stuff labeled for the sale." She stepped outside onto the patio and settled onto the swing.

"That's good." He turned on the patio light and joined her, pushing them off gently with his feet. "Was Howard there?"

She smiled now, a real smile, one that threatened the stars above their heads. "Yeah, he was. He built a rocking horse for his donation. I was going to ask you if he could use the leftover stain from the Cameo stage to paint it. It needs a little finishing touch."

"Sure. I'll send it with him tomorrow." He rocked them again. "That's pretty cool that the residents of the shelter are helping too."

"I know what you mean. I don't think anyone would judge them for just stepping back this time and letting others who can give more easily contribute." Stella tilted her head back to look up at the night sky, and he averted his eyes to keep them from tracing the long length of her neck. "They're good people."

"Even if they are creepy?"

She shoved him, then, so hard and unexpected, he almost fell off the swing. "Sorry! Sorry. I couldn't resist."

She was laughing now, almost as hard as he was.

"You got me. I deserved that." He settled back into the swing beside her, this time draping his arm around her shoulders.

She hesitated for a minute, then slowly relaxed against his side. "I think maybe you were right about Dixie. She is creepy in a way, but not in a bad way. More like in a hears-from-God kind of way."

He nodded, pushing them higher in the swing with his foot. He could see that—especially after his conversation with Darren the other day. God spoke to people through people, and He definitely chose to use Chap.

243

Just ironic that He also chose to use Chap to speak to Kat's husband.

"I've had some interesting conversations about God myself lately." He let out a slow breath, unsure how to dive in, unsure exactly how much to say. He knew the timing was right—just didn't know how to express that sentiment in the right way.

"Dixie showed up in the graveyard the other day."

That was unexpected.

Stella kept gazing at the sky, adjusting her head slightly on his shoulder. "I was taking flowers to my aunt's grave, and she was just there, out of nowhere, by a tree. We talked for a while."

"What did she say?"

She hesitated. Maybe, she, too, was wondering how much to reveal? The thought gave him hope, and he tightened his grip slightly around her shoulders. "She said several things, but the most noteworthy was for me not to be afraid of being broken."

"That's wise."

"And then she said for me to also not be afraid of healing."

"That's creepy."

She half sat up and nudged him in the ribs. Hard. He grinned. "What did you say to that?"

"Not a lot." She shrugged, settling back against his side and getting comfortable again. Her shoulder was digging into his rib cage, but he wasn't going to move for the life of him. Not with her tucked so safely under his arm. "What *can* you say to that?"

True. Not much.

"Do you think you're afraid of healing?"

"No." She said it too quickly, though, and he filed that fact away for future thought. He didn't want to start another argument tonight—and if you disagreed with Stella Varland, you were going to get at least a temporary argument. "Who would be afraid of healing?"

Stella, he thought. But he wasn't going to say it without a solid example to back himself up. And right now, he didn't have one.

"Anyway. You didn't ask me over to talk about Dixie." She twisted her neck and wrinkled her nose up at him. "I'm assuming?"

She was adorable, and had no idea. Not anymore. He tapped her nose. "Nope. You guessed right, Tiara."

Her eyes flickered with emotion, and she twisted back to face the night. "So what's up?"

Her. Them. *Us.* He wanted to say it, but knew he couldn't be too abrupt or she'd take off running. Literally and figuratively.

Then again, she'd been the one attempting their last kiss. So maybe she wasn't as much of a flight risk as he thought. "I had a thought the other day. One that won't go away."

She stilled, listening, so quietly he could feel her heart beating through the contact of his arm wrapped around her.

"I thought about the past. And about all we've been through. Divorce, engagement, death of loved ones . . ." His voice trailed off, and he half wished she'd look at him and half wished he could just talk to the top of her head all night. Safer that way. "I'm tired of living with regrets, and Stella, you've been one of my biggest ones."

She turned to look at him then, her eyes searching his for . . . sincerity? Confirmation? She pulled in her lip and studied him, so intently he felt almost as if he were taking a quiz.

And had no idea of the correct answer.

"I don't want you to be a regret anymore, and well—if I don't tell you how I still feel about you, then I'm going to regret it forever." He reached up and smoothed the worry crinkle between her eyebrows. "I still care about you. A lot."

She closed her eyes, resting in his touch, and he cradled her cheek with his palm. "I shouldn't have kissed you the other day. It was too fast, too much . . . and that was right after you told me at the museum not to rush."

"Wasn't your fault." Her words floated out in a whisper, her eyes still closed, her face still heavy in his hand. Pure contentment rested across her face.

He wanted her to feel that safe forever.

"Regardless, I take responsibility for it. I want to do things right. Want you to see that I'm not the immature boy you used to know. I'm different now, different from the guy who hurt you, ran out on you—and hurt your sister."

Her eyes opened then, as if reality had knocked hard on the front door. "Kat." She stared hard into the darkness of the back lot, as if heading into a trance. Or coming out of one.

"Right." He frowned. Not like she had any other sisters. "Kat." Was she okay? "Stella?"

She snapped out of it then, easing away from him on the swing, drawing her legs up to her chest. "Stella, don't do that."

She rested her chin on her knees, her voice tightening. "I'm not doing anything."

"Yes, you are. You're turning invisible." He wanted to shake her out of it. "Quit it."

"We can't do this." Crickets chirped from the trees overhead, arguing their point. Or agreeing with her.

No matter. He was going to argue.

"*Yes*, we can. We just were. Just did." Or almost did, anyway. She'd been so receptive just moments ago. What had changed?

The mention of her sister. He closed his eyes in defeat. Now reality pounded on his door.

She'd already talked to Kat.

"What did she say?" His voice deepened with a mixture of emotions, ones he couldn't quite identify.

Stella inched even further away from him on the swing. "She thinks I'm an idiot."

"Of course she does." He let her go, let her scoot away. He wasn't going to fight a battle before knowing the full terms of war. "She doesn't know me anymore."

"She said she's trying to protect me."

He wanted that job. Not Kat. He wanted to protect Stella, to rescue her, to be a part of her healing. To watch the broken pieces form into something beautiful, as he knew they could with the right timing and prompting. Timing he felt certain God had revealed to him was *now*. "Do you feel like you need protection from me, Stella?"

She shook her head, her voice so quiet he could barely make it out. "No."

Frustration reigned. He tried to dial it back, knowing the anger was simply a projection of his fear. Fear of losing her.

Again.

He waited until he could keep his voice even, his tone level. "Then what's the problem? This is our decision. Not your sister's."

She bit her lower lip, turning her face into her knees. "Not completely."

"How is that even possible? You don't have to answer to anyone but yourself." And God. But he already had that part figured out for the both of them. He'd taken care of that, checked into the cosmic calendar. Darren had all but said so right there in the fire station.

"I can't be the reason my sister doesn't speak to me again, Chase." She craned her head, still resting on her knees, to face him, eyes pleading with him to understand. But he didn't. Couldn't. "I can't be the cause of any more family strife. You have no idea how long it took me to build that back with my sister."

"She's married, Stella. Why is she holding on to this so hard? She can't possibly have feelings for me still."

"It's not that. She and Lucas are stupid-happy together."

"Then why does her opinion matter so much?"

And then it hit him. Like a two-by-four across the forehead. He eased away in the swing, pulling back to look her in the face. "You *are* afraid of healing."

She sat up straight, shoulders square, the swing bouncing off balance. "No, I'm not."

"Yes, you are. Your sister has a problem with us, but it's nothing we couldn't work through if you wanted to badly enough." He stood up, the swing rocking wildly. She put her legs down for balance, gripped the bottom of the wooden slats. "You're afraid of healing."

She was hiding behind her sister. Hiding behind the feud. Dixie was right. Stella was afraid to heal. Because healing meant being put back together, being fused. Fusion hurt. Healing hurt.

She'd gotten lost in her brokenness. The raw edges were familiar. He knew as well as anyone that bad familiar could be a lot more comfortable than the unknown. He was Stella's unknown. He represented her healing.

And she was clinging to the false safety in her brokenness.

"You have no idea what you're talking about. You think you can figure things out just like that." Stella stood up, abandoning the swing altogether. "Did you ever think that maybe you're wrong? That maybe I don't feel all that strongly for you after all and am just trying to let you down easy?"

The words shot into his heart like an arrow hitting its target. But it wasn't a bull's-eye. She was lying.

"I'm calling that bluff." Before she could argue, or even take a breath, he covered the two steps between them and gathered her into his arms, kissing her soundly.

She whimpered once in protest, but before he could let her go, she collapsed into his kiss, her arms tightening around his back, fingers digging into his shoulder blades. She held on as if she'd fall into a million pieces if she let go.

He knew the feeling. He'd do the same.

Their kiss deepened, his arms pulling her so close, so tight, until he felt he almost couldn't breathe. But didn't want to. Didn't have to. He could breathe her in, and that was plenty.

Then her lips found his neck, and a warning alarm lit the haze in his mind. He gripped her by her upper arms and gently held her away from him, pulse racing like a prize thoroughbred. They both fought to catch their breath.

He let her go, reluctantly, and took a step back, already missing the warmth of her hands on his back. "Still want to go with the 'let me down easy' argument?"

She opened her mouth, shut it, opened it again. Then shook

her head, piercing him with her stare. "Thanks for showing me you're different."

His stomach twisted in regret.

Bull's-eye.

seventeen

The Ninth Cameo was almost complete.

Another two weeks, tops, and they'd be ready for a grand opening. Lyle and Howard were painting the theater now, and as soon as the paint dried, she'd be able to hang her tapestries on each side of the stage curtains and start plugging in all the other details that would breathe fresh life into the Cameo.

She could use a dose of that herself.

Fortunately Chase was working somewhere outside of the Cameo today, and she wouldn't run into him. A welcome reprieve, after their last disastrous meeting.

She grabbed a roller and an extra paint tray and set to work in the lobby, rolling a fresh coat of gold over the accent wall behind the refreshment counter. Watching the tired texture get a shiny new layer whispered inspiration into the recesses of her heart.

After dashing the hope right off of Chase last night, she needed inspiration.

But how dare he stand there and affirm that Dixie was right, after he'd just accused her of being creepy? Either God used the unique woman, or He didn't—and who was Chase to get to determine that fact, anyway? He couldn't keep twisting words to mean what he wanted them to.

She reached high and pressed the roller to the wall, trying not to take her aggression and irritation out on the paint job. He'd said he was different, that he wanted to show her he had changed—yet he proved his point by kissing her, using her, just like the others. How could he preach to her that her beauty was inward when he kept resorting to the physical?

Not that it had exactly been one-sided. Her face heated at the memory. He'd called her bluff, all right. After his accusation that Dixie had been onto something about her fears, she'd tried to take the easy way out. And it had backfired right in her face.

Afraid of healing. What did that even mean?

Still, a niggling hint of truth wouldn't quite leave her alone, the sensation that maybe there was something to it after all.

Her roller slowed its rhythm on the wall. What if Dixie was right, though? What if Stella was allowing Kat's hesitations to determine her own life? What if she was essentially hiding behind her family?

Being with Chase would be a risk. It would potentially hurt.

And having him leave her for a *second* time would hurt to the point of no return. Her heart was already so broken that she wondered if healing was even possible. Reliving something like that would shatter her into oblivion. There'd be no coming back from it.

How could she intentionally choose to set herself up for potential disaster? Didn't her heart deserve a break?

She painted faster, covering more of the wall this time as she attempted to channel her energy into something productive. The Cameo was almost complete. After a few more days, a week or two, max, she wouldn't have a reason to see Chase regularly anymore. If he wanted to pursue her after that, try to win her over from her fears, fine. He was welcome to try.

And fail.

But there was something else bothering her. Even more than she feared his attempts, she feared he wouldn't even bother.

"Nice job, Stella!" Cowboy Bob's booming voice filled the lobby. Stella jerked, the roller splattering gold onto the tarp she'd laid on the floor.

"Thanks, Bob."

She turned. The Downtown Director wasn't alone. Chase and Tim stood flanked on each side, like a set of uneven spurs.

"I came to see your progress, and the boys here told me you guys were nearing completion. That's ahead of schedule, I believe." Bob looked around, appreciation lighting his face. "I'm impressed, I must say."

The compliment warmed her all the way through. She was back. She might be alone, and destined to be that way, but her work was proving itself again. Maybe this job would open up new doors for her and her career, after all. She glanced at Chase, who carefully avoided her eyes.

Maybe it *was* time to start looking at jobs out of state again.

"You've all done a fine job so far." Bob rocked back on his heels as he took in the entire lobby.

"You should see the girls' bathroom!" A usual, Tim spoke before completely thinking his sentence through, and blushed at the look Stella shot him.

253

"I'll do that." Bob chuckled. "And I won't ask, son. I won't ask." He turned to Chase. "The committee wants to schedule a big grand opening night, once we get an official completion date on the record."

"Shouldn't be a problem." Chase crossed his arms, nodding slowly, looking so handsome and focused Stella wished she could relive last night's kiss. Just *one* more time before saying good-bye to the idea forever.

But hadn't she just convinced herself that she was offended by his kissing her?

Man. She was starting to get on her own nerves.

"How about August sixteenth?" Bob began typing the date into his iPad. "That work for you?"

The shelter's big sale was scheduled for the night before. But that shouldn't matter. Stella nodded. "Sounds good to me."

Chase nodded, too, not even bothering to check his calendar. He patted Bob on the shoulder. "You'll have to excuse me, Bob. I need to get back to work." He disappeared inside the theater without another glance.

Tim lingered in the lobby with the two of them, frowning after Chase's back. "What's wrong with him?"

"He's just focused. Busy." Stella smiled reassuringly, even though she didn't believe her own words for a minute.

"You better follow that example, son." Bob gestured after Chase. "I bet there'll be pretty girls at the grand opening. You don't want to keep them waiting."

Tim rolled his eyes, then winked at Stella. "I know for sure there'll be at least one there."

"Well played, my boy." Bob laughed and all but shoved Tim

toward the theater. "Get to it, then." He shook his head at Stella after Tim had vanished from sight. "You must have had an interesting time working with this bunch."

"It hasn't been too bad. They're all talk." Some more talk than others. Of course, if Chase had been just talk instead of action, maybe she wouldn't be so torn up right now. Stella forced a smile, turning her attention back to the painting and away from Bob's curious expression. "I'm glad you're pleased with the progress."

"It's more than I could have hoped. And the color scheme . . . well, I'm happy to hear a compromise was reached." He smiled gently, suddenly more father figure than wannabe cowboy. "Funny how things work out sometimes."

Funny? Maybe.

Crazy? Definitely.

She kept painting. Changed the subject. "You going to wear your boots to the grand opening?"

"Just try to keep 'em off me." Bob chuckled. "I think your friend in there would look pretty nice in a pair too. Don't you think?"

Great. Now the Downtown Director was attempting to play matchmaker. Stella shrugged as if she'd never considered the idea of Chase in boots or anything else out of the ordinary.

But he'd totally make an amazing cowboy. The memory of their conversation about the horse statue rose to the forefront of her mind: *I like living on purpose,* he had said. *Living out loud.*

What if she had that kind of courage? What if she put her fears aside and embraced the idea of something intentional? Intentionally scary, but also intentionally amazing. She couldn't deny the connection she and Chase had—and not just physically. Their conversations over the last few months of working at the Cameo just brought back all the good times they'd had years ago before he moved to Texas.

Before life had robbed them of a second chance.

But maybe—in his fiancée's death, in the abandonment of her husband—they were being given a third one.

Chase brought out the real Stella, the Stella she'd thought long buried. Her old sass, her former spunk. What had he called it that day? Moxie. That was it. Chase brought out in her all the things Dillon had tried to smother.

Chase made her want to find her colors again. For the first time in years she didn't want to stay neutral and bland. She *wanted* to shine. Wanted to find a different, deeper kind of beauty that went beyond wardrobes and hairdos and tiaras. Wanted to embrace her true self. And feel safe within it.

Within him.

Hope built a slow crescendo in her heart. Was there a chance she could get Kat to relieve her of her promise? She hadn't been ready before. She still needed to heal. Dixie helped her see that. So did her mom, for that matter. And Chase.

They said it took a village to raise a child. And maybe so. But she'd swear all day long it also took a village to recover from divorce.

Chase was right. Dixie was right. She was afraid of healing. But maybe admitting that was the first step toward recovery.

"Sorry to interrupt whatever big daydream you've got going there, miss, but I'm going to head back to the office now, get this date on the calendar all official-like." Bob grinned and nodded at her. "I'll see you at the Grand Opening, if not before."

She snapped out of her trance. "Yes, sir." She waved absently. Her mind raced as Bob headed toward the exit.

"And Stella?" Bob turned before slipping out the lobby door and tipped his cowboy hat at her. "You be sure to bring yourself a date that night. You hear?"

Oh, she would. She definitely would.

Just needed to find out what size boots he wore.

ఴఴ

It seemed like all Chase did lately was either catch Stella Varland or apologize to her.

Sometimes both at the same time.

Chase watched as Howard finished cutting in the back wall of the theater. He was torn between heading back into the lobby to confront Stella about last night, or just picking up a paintbrush and letting it all go.

Letting her go.

The thought ripped his heart into shreds, and he couldn't bear it. Not again. It'd been torture to leave her the first time. If he hadn't been trying to do what he could to save Stella's relationship with Kat, he would never have bailed for Texas in the first place. He'd been scared—of his own feelings for Stella, of the way he'd handled Kat's heart. It'd been too much. He freaked and took the coward's way out.

He had vanished, just as Stella accused him.

He had known then, without a doubt, that his continued presence in Bayou Bend would only continue to cause a rift between them. In their entire family.

Maybe Stella was onto something. Maybe *he* was the one in denial. The issue, although years old, had been one of apparently epic proportions.

And from his experience, issues with women didn't tend to shrink over the years. If anything, they expanded.

Maybe after the Cameo was completed, it would be time for him to move again. Not back to Houston. But maybe find a fresh start somewhere else. His mom would kill him for getting her hopes up, but he couldn't go backward. And he couldn't really stay here, either, if he wanted to move forward. Not with his feelings for Stella as deep as they were, not with the walls between them as solid as they were.

A light hand tapped on his shoulder, and he jumped.

Stella.

"You were right." The words rushed out in a heap, jumbling and tangling in the space between them. "I was wrong, and Dixie was right."

Wait, who? Him or Dixie? Oh wait, they'd said the same thing. He tried to focus, but her eyes shone with such depth and grace he couldn't think straight. A swipe of gold paint shimmered on her left cheekbone. He made a mental note to check the quality of the paint job in the lobby.

Just in case.

He tugged her away from the back wall, away from Howard and toward a little bit of privacy. "Go on." Then he crossed his arms over his chest so he wouldn't give in to the temptation to pull her into a hug.

"I was hiding. Hiding behind Kat, and the past, and everything else I could find in order not to risk my heart again." She pressed both hands against her chest, over her dark T-shirt also speckled with gold paint. "I didn't think I had enough of a heart left to give."

She had no idea how big that broken heart really was. How fragile and perfect it was. How much he longed to protect it, guard it, love it. Love her.

He was up for it.

But he'd clearly misunderstood God's timing. Darren had been wrong, or, most likely, he'd read Darren's advice wrong. Rushed ahead, as he always did, and messed it up. Would he ever learn?

Apparently they both had demons to wrestle.

"I just wanted to say I'm sorry. And last night . . ." She pressed her fingers briefly against her lips, and his gaze followed. He swallowed hard, looked away.

She continued. "I wasn't offended by your kiss. It was wrong of me to say so when clearly—clearly I wasn't."

Clearly. Yeah. There'd been that. He shifted his weight, unsure of what to say, wanting to say so much but finding it completely pointless because they'd looped around this way before. Maybe not to the letter, maybe not in the exact same circumstance, but this back and forth was too familiar. One of them was always getting their courage up to approach the other, and the other was always shooting it down for various reasons.

If it was too soon to stir up or awaken love, then it was just too soon. It was never going to work. They couldn't force it.

A fact they both needed to realize and accept.

"I'm glad to hear this. Really." He clenched his arms harder against the urge to unfold and embrace her. "But it doesn't matter, Stella."

She frowned, confusion puckering her brow. "What do you mean?"

"It matters, of course. I mean, for you. For your healing. It's good for you." He shook his head, the pain of denying her burning a hole through his heart. "But this still isn't right."

"Because of Kat?"

"That. And other things." Like the rest of her family, a bullet he kept putting off having to dodge. Claire Varland would be even harder to convince than Kat. And did he or Stella have what it took to fight that war?

He thought so. Or he used to. But now he was just so tired of the uncertain, the unknown, the wondering. He wasn't sure he could fight anymore. He just wanted to go home.

And he didn't have anywhere to go.

"Kat is still an issue." Stella nodded, though the light in her eyes had dimmed. "I wasn't trying to say anything had changed. Other than I see what you mean, and . . . thank you. Thank you for making me see the truth about myself."

No way. That hadn't been all she was wanting with this conversation. But she'd realized that was all she was going to get, and was slipping quickly into self-defense mode. Survival measures. He could read her exactly.

He knew, because that's what he would have done in her shoes.

"I'm glad to hear it."

She waited, shifting her weight from one foot to another, as if hoping he'd say something else. But what else was there to say? They'd done this dance enough times now. It was time for the music to end before they were tortured any further.

He'd stepped on her toes enough.

"Okay, so . . ." Her voice wandered, then she cleared her throat. Determination lit her eyes. "Friends?"

There was the final death blow. He nodded slowly, forcing a smile he didn't feel. "Of course. Friends."

She took a step back, awkward, unsure. He hated this. Hated all of it.

But loved her enough to quit putting them through it.

Despite her new revelation, she wasn't going to change her mind about them if Kat didn't. And there was no way Kat Varland—make that Kat Brannen—was ever going to have any opinion of Chase Taylor other than completely negative.

The Varland women all wore stubbornness like a tiara.

Stella just somehow made hers look good.

"Guess I'll get back to my wall, then." She looked lost, whereas moments before, she'd seemed so confident.

He shook off the guilt. He was doing her a favor, doing both of their hearts a service. "I'm sure you're doing a good job." He'd go double check after she left.

"Let me know if you need anything else." Now she was stilted, as if they were partners. Or worse, like they were employee-boss.

He nodded stiffly. "Will do." He turned back to watch Howard finish painting, debating once again on going home for the day or grabbing a brush and jumping in. He couldn't stand by idly, not while Stella was in the next room, working on making more things beautiful.

That's it. He had to paint.

He took three quick steps forward, then stopped as two arms launched themselves around his torso. What?

He looked down at the two thin, gold-speckled arms, and

felt a chunk of his defense melt away. "Stella." He pried them off, turned, but she stayed close and burrowed back in before he could block her.

"You owe me a hug." She whispered the words into his shoulder, and he hesitated, knowing the feel of her in his arms was going to be his undoing. But then she snuggled closer, and he was toast.

He wrapped his arms around her, held her tight. Breathed in her scent, memorized it. Memorized her.

Tried to remember exactly what he was staying strong for, again.

Then she was gone.

Back to the lobby. Back to work. Back to reality.

While he clung for a moment longer to the past.

❧

If she had to paint Chase Taylor into some form of art, she'd choose abstract. He was all over the place. Bright here, sullen there. A blur of shiny and shadow and shapes all mixed into one mesmerizing and disturbing work.

Which was more than she could say for her mosaic tile project. She had all but given up on it. Still, something kept her drawn to it, kept her reaching for redemption in the darkness. She couldn't see what this thing was yet, but something told her it was going to *be* a thing, and the artist in her couldn't ignore that drive. She had to find out what.

Even if it killed her.

She rearranged the pieces on the canvas again, wishing she wasn't so distracted. But Chase had been one giant puzzle earlier, one she couldn't quite work out. She thought he'd be happy to hear her revelation about herself, to think she was on the right track toward healing. But he'd almost just seemed to tolerate the news, rather than revel in it. Did he not understand she was going to try to talk to Kat again, and try to smooth the way for her and Chase to be together?

The familiar wave of doubts began its slow assault.

Maybe he had changed his mind about her. Wasn't that what everyone did eventually?

No. She rearranged the random shards on her canvas, fighting back the shadowy lies. She was on her way to healing now, and that started with the truth. She wouldn't be afraid anymore—not afraid of the brokenness, and not afraid of the healing.

Dixie's words rang in her mind from the grave site that day, fighting back the lies like sunshine burning off a fog. Stella breathed a prayer of gratitude and focused once again on the pieces before her. But her internal monologue wouldn't turn off. Now Dixie's words were running together with Chase's.

Don't be afraid of the rain. I'm more for stomping in the puddles than dancing in 'em.

She listened absently as she worked, mixing up all the broken pieces like a puzzle. At least the words were truth, this time, and not going to destroy her or derail her.

God tells us to come to Him with faith like a child. I figure that means with our storms too.

If it's going to rain anyway . . . might as well make something out of it.

She picked up the curved piece, dotted with rhinestones, remembering how Dixie had handed it to her after digging it out of the trash bag. As if she'd come for that express purpose, and then left.

She fitted the piece on the canvas, then tilted her head and gasped.

She quickly moved a few more pieces, trading sharp edges for blunt, rounding this edge, pointing this one into an angle.

Until the broken shapes before her resembled an almost perfect umbrella—an upside-down umbrella.

Instead of hiding under umbrellas, we should stomp in the puddles.

She stared in disbelief at the project before her, so caught off guard by the transformation that she felt as if she'd had nothing to do with it. Here was living proof. Beauty from the broken.

She'd made something beautiful. Out of the fragments of what others deemed refuse. Trash. A waste.

She adjusted the curved rhinestone stick—the handle of the umbrella—and smiled. She'd done it.

And if she could do something like this with literal pieces of junk . . . what could God do in her heart?

Suddenly she knew the answer to her own question, as if God had revealed it just to her.

Nothing was ever too broken to be healed.

She laughed, long and loud and surprised, her voice echoing in the small room until the entire space seemed to overflow with joy. Hope. Potential.

Beauty.

Tears welled up in her eyes, and Dixie's words from the afternoon at the graveyard suddenly struck loud and clear.

Told you you needed an umbrella.

eighteen

The next two weeks flew by in a blur of touch-up paint, fabric glue, and Dustbusters. Just when they deemed the Cameo perfect, another detail would pop up to tend to.

Finally, on the night of the shelter's big fund-raiser, Stella put down her duster and grabbed Chase's arm. He had hung, rehung, and straightened the same picture in the lobby at least four times. "You do realize at some point, we just have to stop."

"I know." Chase glanced around the finished lobby. There had to be at least one more thing that needed tweaking before the Grand Opening the next night. But Stella was right. They just had to stop and be done.

"Besides, I have something to show you." She pulled her phone from her pocket and began scrolling through her photos.

He packed his tools into the toolbox and snapped the lid shut. "What's that?" He'd been surprised, but somehow, he and Stella had managed to find a rhythm over the last two weeks, a rhythm of friendship they both could live with that didn't lead to too much awkwardness.

He still wanted more. And wanted to believe she felt the same.

But he remained convinced friendship was the only real option. Until he could pack up and head out again, anyway. He wouldn't vanish on Stella again, not completely. No way would he be responsible for doing that to her mending heart.

There'd been a change in Stella over the last two weeks. A light inside her that hadn't fully existed before, a security and confidence he hadn't seen since she'd been on stage. Except now it was stronger, somehow. Deeper.

Stella Varland was healing.

And it had nothing to do with Chase Taylor.

"I finally figured it out." She held her phone against her chest so he couldn't see it yet, a shy smile creeping up her face. "I wanted to show you, because, well—you're the only one who knows my secret."

He knew a lot of her secrets.

"Remember all the pieces I've been collecting from the Cameo?"

"Right. The mosaic tile project." She had voiced her frustration over it more than once, and he had gladly listened—though he rarely chose to bring up the sore subject after the ordeal of him accidentally stumbling across her art room. He knew not to push.

"I finished it."

"What?" A genuine happiness rose in Chase's chest. He reached for the phone, grinning. "Let me see! When? What is it?" He couldn't wait.

"The other night. When it finally came together, I just knew . . . well. I just knew. You'll see."

"Then let me see, already."

But she held it out of reach again, teasing, and he pinned one arm against her side in order to grab for the phone once again. She cackled, laughing. Nervous? Still, she trusted him with her secret. Just as she trusted him with her designs for the Cameo. As she'd trusted him with her heart.

Her kisses.

He inhaled slowly, turning off that train of thought. He wanted to support her. As a *friend*. He could do this.

She held up the phone. "Remember, no one knows about this." She waited for his nod before gradually turning it around. "Ta-da."

An umbrella. An upside-down umbrella.

Their conversation that night in the rain rushed back to him, and his smile turned to laughter. "Tiara. I am *so* proud of you."

Tears welled in her eyes, and she surrendered the phone as he held it up closer, examining every detail. "Is it glued? Or just chilling on the canvas?"

"It's done. I framed it last night, though that part isn't in the picture."

He scrolled his fingers across the screen to widen the shot. "I remember that piece."

"The handle?"

He nodded. "The one Dixie gave you."

"She spoke of umbrellas to me twice before you did." Stella shook her head. "I should have been listening sooner."

"Nah. I think the timing was just as it should be."

She caught his gaze, held it. "I hope so."

They stared at each other, then he pulled her into a one-armed hug. A "friend" hug. Or so he rationalized. The truth was, he couldn't stand not touching her, and this was the only way he could justify it.

After a moment they pulled apart and started gathering their cleaning supplies. He'd sent Lyle and Tim home hours earlier, after they'd cracked one joke too many about maid services. Howard had also left a little while ago, to get the rest of what he was bringing to the shelter for the sale that night.

"I'm coming this evening, by the way. I couldn't remember if I had mentioned it." Chase picked up his toolbox, double-checking to make sure he'd snapped the top lids containing all the screws and nails.

"You are?" Stella tucked the duster she'd been using into a tote bag and slung it over her shoulder. "Interested in buying some pageant dresses?"

"Very funny." He wasn't quite that desperate yet for a tangible memento of Stella, but at this rate, the day might be coming. "I promised Howard I'd come check out that rocking horse of his."

Stella nodded her approval. Not that he'd been seeking it. Just a pleasant bonus. "Did you ever give him that stain?"

"Yep. He said it made all the difference."

"I bet someone pays good money for it. It's unique."

Like Howard. Like Dixie.

They were growing on him. All of them were. He'd miss them if he left Bayou Bend.

If he ever decided, that is. He kept delaying making that decision. Partially because of dashing his mom's hopes, and mostly because he wasn't sure if he had what it took to walk out of Stella Varland's life for a second time.

He shook off the heaviness. Those were decisions for later.

Right now, they should just be basking in the relief of a project completed.

Chase checked to make sure he had his keys as they headed out of the lobby. He paused to lock the doors behind him. "Moment of truth. Forget anything? Last chance before the grand opening tomorrow."

Actually, it wasn't. They could run up there during the day if they needed to. They'd have to get there early to prepare, anyway, make sure the movie screen worked. The Downtown Development Committee was supposed to be choosing a classic film to show on the scroll-down screen during the program. They'd also be serving free popcorn and giving away sodas. Stella had insisted on Scotch-guarding all the newly upholstered theater seats after she'd heard about the free drinks.

"No, I think that's all. I believe this old place is ready to breathe again." Stella adjusted the bag on her shoulder. "I can't think of anything that could make it better."

Neither could he. He locked the doors, then stopped short. Looked at Stella's retreating back as she headed to her car. And got a genius idea.

Actually, he *could* think of one thing.

⸏⸏⸏

The shelter fund-raiser was in full swing, residents laughing, patrons shopping, and jukebox blaring when Stella arrived a few minutes after six o'clock. She quickly found Kat near the front kitchen, serving cupcakes, and grabbed one from the cooling rack on the stove. "Need any help back here?"

Her sister deposited another tray of strawberry cakes onto the serving platter on the counter, and four pairs of waiting hands immediately snatched them up. "Nope. Looks like we have a winner." She laughed, reaching back to adjust the ties on her apron.

Stella turned her sister around and retied the bow for her. "Nothing new there. Everyone loves your cupcakes."

"I'm offering these basic ones as refreshments for the party. My fairytale collections over there are part of the sale." Kat pointed to a rectangular display she must have brought with her, since it wasn't typically there. Inside sparkled all of her princess cakes, glittery and tempting beneath the glass.

"Good idea. Those will definitely sell like . . ." Stella's voice trailed off.

"Hotcakes?" Kat grinned. "Yeah. I was waiting for that pun. Saw it coming a mile away."

"I couldn't resist." She craned her head to see toward the back of the shelter, where the tables were lined up with all the products to sell. "Have any of my dresses sold yet?"

Kat shrugged. "I've been up here the whole time. Go check it out and see. I know Howard's rocking horse has been fought over at least twice. They had a bidding war going a minute ago."

That was great news—and so encouraging for Howard. Stella slipped back around the counter, excused herself through the throng of people in line waiting for cupcakes, and headed toward the back.

And nearly collided with Chase as he whisked in the front door.

She pulled up short and laughed, her hand landing on Chase's arm just as her eyes locked with Kat's. Her sister's eyes narrowed and Stella guiltily removed her hand.

Then remembered, Chase was her friend. *Her* friend.

But that didn't mean she had to flaunt it in front of her sister. "Let's go check out Howard's bidding war."

"Sweet. I just might participate." Chase grinned, straining to see over the crowd as they made their way toward the back.

A wave of admiration over Chase's support of her homeless friends nearly knocked Stella off balance. A few weeks ago, he'd thought they were strange, weird . . . creepy. Now, he was truly invested in their well–being, in their lives, their work.

Well, he still thought they were a *little* creepy, but in a different way than originally intended.

She'd take it.

Stella held on to his arm, loosely, so as not to get lost in the crowd—or so she told herself, anyway. Grateful for the packed room and the excuse to hold on to Chase, she maneuvered with him through the people until they could see the action up front.

"Forty-five dollars! Do I hear fifty?" To Stella's surprise, subdued, suit-clad Nancy Martin had taken the role of auctioneer upon herself, working the crowd like a pro.

She pointed to someone in the crowd who raised a hand. "Fifty dollars! Who will pay fifty-five for this beautiful hard-carved horse?"

Howard stood to one side of the man beside the rocking horse, his head turning back and forth between the bidding crowd and Nancy as if he were watching a Ping-Pong tournament.

"Fifty-five dollars!" Nancy pointed to someone else, fist pumping in excitement. "All right! From the woman in that lovely blue dress." She was working it now, clearly having missed her calling in life. "Who else wants to bid on this wonderful piece? Do I hear sixty? Sixty bucks?"

"I bid one hundred dollars." A confident voice rang through the crowd. The group parted as a short woman with dark hair made her way toward Howard and the rocking horse.

"Dixie?" Stella gasped.

Beside her, Chase lowered to whisper into her ear. "I have to admit, I didn't see that one coming."

How in the world? She watched as Dixie held up a hundred-dollar bill, smiled at Howard, and reached down to pat the horse's glued-on yarn mane. She turned as if waiting for the crowd to argue or outbid.

No one did.

"Any more bids?" Nancy urged. "Going once, going twice—sold, for one hundred dollars."

Suddenly, all the rumors about Dixie being homeless on purpose rose to the surface. There was a story there, and Stella wondered if she'd ever get it in its entirety. If Dixie even fully knew the story herself.

Or maybe Dixie knew a whole lot more than Stella—or anyone else, for that matter—realized.

"Stella, I'm glad you're here." Nancy, abandoning her role as auctioneer, grasped Stella's arm in her manicured hand. "Can you work one of the sales tables for a bit? We're swamped—which is a good problem. But one of my volunteers went home sick and there's no one taking offers at the kitchenware table."

"Sure."

She looked at Chase, who nodded for her to go on. "I'm going to go chat with Howard."

Stella followed Nancy to the workstation she'd indicated, and began taking bids and working the makeshift register. Most of the shoppers knew the sale was a fund-raiser for a good cause, and they were content to pay the asking price on the labels Kat had carefully prepared. Others were still determined to get a deal, but Stella fought them back up to near sticker price most of the time.

After a half hour had flown by, Stella looked up. The crowd had thinned slightly but still mingled around the product tables. She hadn't seen Chase in all that time. Hopefully he and Howard had had a good conversation.

But he wasn't her priority. Chase could entertain—and take care of—himself.

It had just been nice to be able to pretend they were together. Aware of where the other was at all times.

Again, it was the little things about being part of a couple that tripped her up the most.

Kat suddenly appeared in front of her table. "Time to go."

"What do you mean? Is my shift over?" Stella checked for her watch, then remembered she wasn't wearing one. She grabbed for her phone instead. "Nancy didn't specify how long I needed to stay."

"No, it's time to go. *Now.*" Kat's eyes widened and she pressed a hand against her bulging stomach. "To the hospital."

"Oh. Oh!" Stella shoved into action. Where were her keys? She felt in her back pocket. Nothing. She'd left her purse locked in the car so she wouldn't have to keep up with it all—and she bet her keys were still in her purse. Front left pocket. She groaned.

"Where are your keys?" She ushered Kat toward the front door, guiding her through the still mingling crowd. "I'll text Nancy and tell her what happened. She can help guard and sell your cupcakes."

"I don't have my keys. Lucas dropped me off on his way to

Tyler's. They were having dinner with Tyler's parents. You remember him, right? The kid on his team a few years ago, with the alcoholic father? He's like a nephew to Lucas." Kat sucked in a long breath and squeezed her eyes shut as a contraction rendered her momentarily speechless. "His dad is sort of coming around, and has gotten interested in church."

"Right. Um . . . that's great news, Kat. You can tell me this later, though." Stella reached toward her sister, unsure if she should touch her for support or steer clear. "You know. When you're not having a baby."

"Good idea." Kat gripped the handle of the front door, then let out a quick sigh once the contraction fully passed. "We'll have to take your car."

Uh-oh. "There's just one problem with that . . ." Stella patted her empty pockets and held up both hands. "I locked my keys in my car. And just realized it."

"Stella!" Kat's lecture was interrupted by another contraction. "I swear if I have this baby in a homeless shelter, Stella Varland, I'll—"

"I'll just text Lucas." Stella fumbled for her phone, almost dropping it in her panic.

"Ladies, let's go. I've already told Nancy what's happening." Chase appeared, smooth as molasses, and ushered both of them outside. "I'm parked to the right." He offered Kat his arm and she didn't even argue, just leaned heavily against him as another contraction racked her body.

He opened the back door of the truck and helped Kat inside. "Sit in the back with her."

His calm, authoritative approach calmed them both. Stella slid obediently into the back of the truck, grabbing Kat's hand. She squeezed hard until the contraction passed.

Chase cranked the engine. "Won't be long. I promise."

"Call Lucas." Kat squeezed out the words. Then shot her sister a look. "Don't you dare tell him where I am."

"He won't care. You're having a baby, Kat!" Stella called Lucas, left a voicemail, and then sent an emergency text. "He'll answer in a minute. You know he will."

"I don't know. Tyler's parents can get pretty intense." True. Lucas had always been a father figure to Tyler—Stella even remembered that much. He'd always felt extra responsibility to the boy, even keeping up with him after he graduated. So Kat was right. It might be a minute.

Stella looked back at the phone and began dialing. "I'll call Mom."

Her sister winced, and Stella wasn't sure if it was because of another contraction or if it was the thought of having to deal with their mom while under duress.

"You okay back there?" Chase made eye contact briefly with Stella in the rearview mirror before glancing at Kat.

"Doing great." Kat nodded, breathing sharply through her nose and mouth. "But feel free to speed."

"Already on it." Chase looked back at the road. They were at the hospital within minutes. He pulled up to the Emergency Room, hazards lights still flashing, and helped Kat out of the truck. Then he reached up to assist Stella.

This time, she accepted his help. "Thank you." She lingered in his grip a moment longer than necessary. Then she rushed after her waddling sister.

❧❧❧

He'd just driven his ex-girlfriend to the hospital. To have a baby.

While his wannabe girlfriend—her *sister*—rode along.

How did Stella keep getting him into these soap-opera-worthy situations?

Chase ran his fingers over his hair, shifting in the uncomfortable waiting room chair. The metal armrest dug into his side. He shifted his weight again. Nope. Not any better. How could anyone stand these things?

They had been back there at least half an hour. He was surprised Stella hadn't come out with an update. He wasn't entirely familiar with the process of having babies, but he knew enough to know Kat hadn't been about to give birth in his truck. There was still time to go—so where was Stella?

And why hadn't she texted him the status yet? Were they getting Kat checked in and settled? She'd have to change. And there was probably an IV to run, on top of many other things.

Still . . .

He finally stood up and began pacing the empty room, poking his head around the corner to check down the long hall toward the front desk occasionally for any sign of Lucas. Last he'd heard, the guy still hadn't responded to the texts or calls both girls had sent. He better hurry it up—Chase was familiar with Kat's temper, and wouldn't want to be on the receiving end of it in a circumstance like this.

A familiar blonde form strode toward the desk, high heels clacking against the tile floor and a giant purse flapping against her hip. A woman on a mission.

Claire Varland.

Chase swallowed. Nowhere to run, nowhere to hide . . .

The nurse behind the desk directed her toward him with a quick gesture. Claire looked up, and her eagle-sharp gaze landed directly on him.

Her eyebrows shot straight up to her coiffed hairline. "Chase?"

"Evening, Mrs. Varland." He wouldn't call her Claire. Not to her face, anyway. It was hard enough to even think of her that way. The lady demanded respect and propriety.

Not to mention stark-white fear.

He had been younger then, of course. But some things didn't change.

She approached him, studying him like a specimen under a microscope, and he tried not to shift uncomfortably under the scrutiny.

He fought for something neutral to say. "Congratulations on becoming a grandmother."

"Almost." She lifted her chin. "I'm assuming I'm not too late?" She looked down the hall of the maternity ward.

"I don't think so."

"Good." She settled into one of the stiff chairs, crossing her legs. "Where's Lucas?"

"Not here yet."

"Well, why are *you* here?"

He continued to pace, watching for Lucas. "I drove the girls."

Her eyebrows lifted again, this time without the anvil of judgment weighing them down. "I see." The surprise, though, was evident. Very evident.

He wanted to explain, but didn't want to throw Stella under

the irresponsibility bus by blaming the car key situation on her. "We were all at the homeless shelter's fund-raiser, and—it's a long story."

"Apparently." She tilted her head back, her blonde hair never moving from its perfect position on her head. "You have a lot of those, don't you?"

Okay. That was it. He was done with the snide comments, the snarky, underhanded sly remarks. It was getting ridiculous. "Mrs. Varland, I realize I hurt your daughters. Both of them. And I'm not a parent, but I can only imagine how that must feel. To see your kids heartbroken." He took the chair next to her, ignored her shock at his directness, and leaned in close. "But I beg you to let this water under the bridge stay under the bridge already."

"Don't be silly, Chase." She laughed, a nervous edge to her voice, and he almost fell out of his chair. He, making Claire Varland nervous?

Maybe, like Stella, she wasn't used to anyone calling her out on her bluffs.

She smoothed her skirt over her knees. "I have no interest in stirring up any old water."

"Good." He relaxed—as much as he could in that terrible chair—and let out a relieved sigh. "Then we're on the same page."

"Well, I highly doubt that."

He groaned.

Fortunately, any further conversation was interrupted by the joint arrival of both Lucas and Mr. Varland.

Make that *Pastor* Varland. He stood up again, reached to shake hands. Pretended to ignore the surprise on both men's faces.

The routine of the night, apparently.

ceee

"I can't believe you left Chase out there all alone. You know Mom is on her way, if not already here." Kat crunched another ice chip and returned the cup to her bedside tray.

"It's good for him." Stella grinned from the plastic green couch beside the window. "Besides, I'm not going to leave you."

"If my husband doesn't answer the phone soon, I swear . . ." Kat threatened to throw her cell across the room. Her blood pressure monitor beeped as it began to take another automatic reading from her arm.

Stella quickly grabbed her sister's cell for safekeeping and tucked it beside her, then turned down the volume on the wall-mounted TV so she'd be sure to hear the phone ring. "He'll be here. Calm down."

Kat's contractions had slowed now that she was in bed and had her feet propped up. But they'd already administered the epidural, given she was dilated to a five. The nurses were predicting two hours or less, at her current rate of progress.

Two hours, and she'd be an aunt.

Two hours, and her sister would be a mom.

It was a lot to absorb.

"I didn't think you'd be all that concerned about Chase anyway." Stella looked around, trying not to redecorate the room in her mind, but totally unable to prevent it. Just as Chase had predicted that day . . .

The salmon wallpaper would be the first thing to go. No, wait. Make that the gaudy, flaked gold lamp on the bedside table.

Kat crunched another ice chip. "It was really good of him, taking care of us like that."

"Taking care of you, you mean." Stella shot her a pointed look.

Kat sighed. Rolled her eyes. Then finally relinquished. "Yeah. Me."

"It was nice, wasn't it?" She didn't want to push, but oh she hoped. How she hoped.

"Stella, I owe you an apology." Kat rubbed her stomach, wincing as another contraction lit up the monitors. She'd explained last time the lines on the graphs had jumped high on the screen that she couldn't exactly feel the pain of the contraction, but she still felt the pressure. Like a rubber band tightening around her waist and then releasing. "I didn't mean to be so harsh about Chase. He proved tonight he's a good man. A decent man, anyway." She wrinkled her nose. "I guess with more time he can prove himself good."

"More time?" Stella's heart quickened. Good thing she wasn't hooked up to a BP machine herself at the moment. Her pulse barreled straight out of control. "Meaning, you'll give him a chance to prove it?"

"It's your life, little sister." Kat shifted uncomfortably on the bed, the taut hospital gown making her belly appear even larger. "I just want you happy. As happy as me and Lucas." She narrowed her eyes as the lines on the contraction monitor leapt off the top of the screen. "That is, as happy as we'll be after I kill him for not being here."

Stella's heart twisted in sympathy. If she were in Kat's shoes—or, well, make that gown, since she was barefooted—she'd probably be freaking out too. Still . . .

"He'll be here." Lucas was the most responsible man Stella knew. He wouldn't ignore his phone for long, especially knowing how close Kat was to her due date.

Well, she was almost three weeks out still, technically, but from the size of her belly, Stella had been pretty certain all along the doctors had guessed that one wrong.

The door opened with a quick snap and Mom dashed into the room. "I can't believe you girls didn't tell me where to come."

"I texted you!" Stella held up Kat's phone for proof, then looked at it again in a double take. "Oops. Bad reception. It never sent."

"Bad reception? What if Lucas tried to call?" Kat reached for her phone then, despite being all the way across the room from it.

"Hang on just a minute." Mom held up both hands. "Lucas is here. He's with your dad in the waiting room." She paused. "With Chase."

Well, that wasn't an awkward scenario. Stella winced. "Is he okay?"

"He's nervous. He's about to become a father, after all."

She meant Chase, but she let that one go. Kat waved her arms from the bed. "Um, hello. Lady giving birth, here. Why is my husband not in this room?"

"They only allow so many visitors at a time." Mom swept her hair back. "I wanted to see my baby first. He'll come back here and stay, and then I'd have missed my chance."

"You can take my spot, Mom." Stella stood, already sore from her hour on the uncomfortable couch, and rubbed her lower back. "I'll trade with Lucas."

Kat held up a hand. "No, I don't want you to go. I'm not done yet. And we have plenty of time before anything really starts to happen." Kat set her cup of ice on the bedside table and winced again as another contraction lit up the monitors. "Okay, maybe not. I'll talk quickly."

Stella sat back down on the edge of the couch, her mother joining her on the other side and moving aside the TV remote. "This place is terrible. You should get hired here." Mom bumped Stella's leg, as if she expected her to get up and go place an interior design bid immediately at the front desk.

Kat ignored her. "Stella, I'm serious about what I said about Chase."

"Wait. What about Chase?" *Now* Mom was more interested in the conversation than in the wallpaper.

Kat ignored her. "This pregnancy has taught me a lot about control—and how I don't have much."

Stella nodded. She could see that, if only in her sister's unpredictable mood swings and food cravings. That'd be enough for any sane person to deal with. Control was just an illusion—an illusion that pickle chips dipped in peanut butter could never really satisfy.

"I had to realize God is the only one really in control. And the sooner I let go, the better off I was. I wanted a healthy baby so badly, but I couldn't make that happen. Only He could." Kat pointed toward heaven, then rubbed her hands over her stomach. "And so far, everything's turned out just fine."

It didn't always. Stella knew that firsthand. Sometimes you could pray your heart out for days, weeks, months . . . and seemingly get no response.

But then in hindsight, hadn't God answered those prayers too? All those nights on her knees, pleading for her marriage?

God hadn't said no. Dillon had.

But God said "Even though."

Even though she was divorced, she was free. *Even though* she was struggling to make ends meet, they were meeting—and she was getting to do jobs she loved. *Even though* she had no idea what her future held, He did—and His Word promised there would be a purpose for all the pain. *Even though* there were storms, there were plenty of puddles to stomp.

Even though she'd been broken—she was healing.

And it was beautiful.

"Thanks, sis." Stella blinked back tears, wondering if pregnancy hormones were contagious. She'd cried more in the last six months with her sister than she had in the entire last decade.

"You do what you want to do with Chase. I'll support you either way." Kat lifted both hands in the air. "It's your life, your decision. Your love story."

"Love story? With Chase Taylor?" Mom finally clued in on the depth of the conversation and sighed with resignation. "Is that really an option?"

"Mom." Kat's voice held a growl of pre-Mama-bear warning, well-meaning though misdirected. Stella didn't need defending.

But she'd take it, regardless. "She's right, Mom. It's my choice. And Chase's." She hesitated. "You and Dad raised me well. I'm not one to typically make the same mistakes twice."

"So then why are you considering going back to him?" Suddenly Mom looked tired, so tired. Not nearly perfect and flawless; just a regular mom, in a hospital room, with *her* baby who was about to *have* a baby.

"Because he's not a mistake."

Mom met her eyes then, and Stella held her stare, letting her search out the truth as she'd taught both of her daughters to do. Finally, she released Stella's gaze and nodded with a sigh. "I trust you." She looked at Kat, including her in the discussion. "Both of you."

"It's okay not to be perfect, Mom." Kat's soft admission rang through the room. "None of us is."

"What do you mean?" She brushed at her skirt.

"That. Right there. You're wearing a skirt to the hospital and worried about lint. Really?" Kat grinned. "Do you ever just relax, Mom? Or go somewhere without makeup?"

Her mother's expression radiated such pure horror Stella couldn't help but laugh.

"One thing at a time," she mouthed to her sister.

Kat nodded back with a grin, then gestured for their mom to hand her the remote control. "Someone go get my husband now, please."

"I will." Gladly. And that meant she could see Chase at the same time. Sweet relief, downright joy, flooded Stella's soul. It might not change anything on Chase's side that she had her family's approval of their relationship now, but . . . it might.

And that was a risk she was more than happy to take.

She was halfway to the door when Kat gasped. "Wait a minute. Is this live?" She cranked up the volume on the TV as Stella turned.

And saw the homeless shelter downtown engulfed in flames.

nineteen

Chase moved through the thick crowd standing outside the charred remains of the homeless shelter, and searched the sea of firemen's faces for Ethan. His cousin had been on the scene as part of the backup unit they'd brought in, after realizing how quickly the flames had spread.

His grip tightened around Stella's waist, unwilling to let her go in the crowd and unwilling to leave her in case she had a panic attack. Her distress was real.

The entire drive from the hospital, she kept wailing that it was all her fault, despite the news reports claiming the fire department had yet to determine the actual cause of the flames.

"They said on the TV that no one was hurt, Stella. That's the important thing." He'd said it over and over until they'd parked his truck a block from the shelter and jogged toward the throng milling around.

"Ethan!" He finally spotted his cousin in the crowd, waved him over. His cousin's gear was covered in soot. "What's the latest, man?"

Ethan tucked his helmet under his arm, keeping one eye on the smoke billowing as he talked. "Everyone got out. No one was injured." He shook his head. "It's like a miracle. A fire this size, and a crowd this big . . ."

"See." Chase squeezed Stella's shoulder. "Everyone is okay." He could even see Dixie and Howard off to the side, huddled in a group including Nancy and a few other residents he recognized. Dixie's rocking horse rocked gently at her feet. The other residents appeared to have grabbed some of the donation boxes, but judging by the sparse piles, they hadn't been able to get everything out.

Darren joined them, and Chase performed a quick round of introductions, most of which he was sure soared straight over Stella's head. She was totally zoned out.

He turned back to Ethan, the flashing red lights of the nearby ambulance casting dark shadows across his cousin's face. "Any word yet on the cause?"

"They're leaning toward faulty wiring." Ethan clapped dust and ash off the thick fireproof sleeves of his bunker gear. "This building is ancient."

"Which is why they were about to rebuild it." Stella closed her eyes with apparent grief. "They were having a fund-raiser here tonight for that very cause."

Ethan winced. "Ah, man. I hate to hear that. Some people just can't catch a break."

Darren held up one hand. "Sometimes it seems that way. That doesn't mean God doesn't see this. And doesn't mean He won't provide another way."

"Another way to what?" Stella gestured wildly toward the

building. "There's nothing left to expand on. Now they'll need even more money than they would have before."

"What about insurance?" Chase eased Stella's hands down after one of her dramatic motions almost clocked Darren in the cheek. "Since it was a fire, they should be able to get a decent claim." There would probably be a lengthy investigation to rule out fraud first, but delayed payment was better than nothing.

"They don't have insurance."

Oh.

Stella's voice was choked with tears now, her eyes blinking rapidly as she watched the smoke spilling from the frame of the devastated building. "The city stopped paying that investment a long time ago, and Nancy couldn't afford it on her own. They have nothing now." Tears slipped down her cheeks. "Those who already had next to nothing now really have nowhere to go." She hiccupped. "And it's all my fault."

"Stella." He pulled her close, away from the crowd, as Darren shot them both a concerned look. "You've got to quit assuming blame for this fire until they can figure out what happened. Do you want to get accused of arson?"

"No, but it's all part of that same incident from before. With the sprinkler system." Stella struggled to draw a full breath, the air catching in her lungs and heaving her chest in sporadic shudders. "It has to be. What are the odds?"

"You don't know that." He rubbed her arms in an attempt to soothe her, wishing he could shove the truth through her skull. "Listen, you've got to calm down or the paramedics are going to have to work on you next."

"How can I calm down? I did this to them." Stella was shaking now, her breath whistling between her teeth. "I shut down the shelter *again*, this time for good!"

"Stella. Listen to me." Chase grabbed her face and held her cheeks firmly between both hands. But her gaze still wouldn't land directly on him. "This wasn't your fault. Old buildings burn down. It happens."

But no. She was losing it, he was losing her. "Stella. Snap out of it."

"May I?" Darren stepped forward, seeking permission with his eyes. "I'm worried about her going into some kind of shock."

"She gets panic attacks." Chase whispered, unsure Stella would notice, even if she heard him.

Darren accepted the information with a nod, and Chase stepped back, hands off, letting Darren take over. Good luck.

Darren gently touched Stella's arm, urging her farther away from the crowd pressing in like ants to a picnic. Chase followed, but hung a heartbeat behind. "Stella, was it?"

She nodded, eyes large and wide, flitting here and there and landing on everything going on around them.

He smiled patiently. "Stella, can you look me in the eyes for a minute?"

Again, good luck.

She tried. Blinked. Shook her head. Almost made it.

"What's your middle name?"

She thought hard. "Michelle."

Darren grinned. "That's pretty."

She relaxed, her shoulders visibly growing less tense. Chase stepped closer, rested his hand on her back, felt the knots ease. He applied rhythmic, circular pressure on the worst ones as Darren continued to talk to her in quiet, even tones. Simple questions. Where she lived. What she liked most about her job.

Which reminded him of the surprise he still needed to pull off for the next night. Hopefully it would be a good thing, something to snap Stella out of this guilty trance she'd fallen into. He'd never seen anyone take something as vague as a fire so personally. He felt bad for the residents, too, but instead of slipping into panic mode, he was brainstorming ideas as to how to help.

In fact, maybe that's what she needed to do. Refocus.

He tuned back into her conversation with Darren just in time to realize Darren was on the same track. "I tell my guys at the station that it's not healthy to assume responsibility for something that wasn't your fault. When you go that route, then you're going to start dealing with misplaced guilt and a host of other issues."

Exactly. Not good.

"So let's switch tactics here, Stella." Darren's voice even calmed down the bit of anxiety roiling in Chase's stomach. How did the man do that? "How can you help make a difference for the residents *now*? Today?"

She fidgeted a little, shoving her hands in her pockets, then pulling them back out to pick at her nails. Still signs of suppressing panic. "I don't know. I have a tiny little apartment. Nowhere for them to go."

Darren nodded. "Where *would* be big enough for the residents to go?"

And just like that, Stella was back, an idea lighting up her eyes as she whipped around and grabbed Chase's arm. "Hey, what about the Cameo? It could house some of the residents temporarily. The lobby is big enough for cots."

Now she was thinking. Chase agreed, promised he'd find out about it, check with Bob. He'd know who to contact for permission.

Darren pressed her further. "What else can you do, Stella? Practically speaking."

"We can pick up some breakfast in the morning, since we'll be killing time before the grand opening of the theater." She looked over her shoulder at the regular residents milling about Nancy. "And we should invite them all to the party. There'll be free popcorn and drinks there already, which will help too."

"You feel better?" Darren patted her arm. "Nothing wrong with needing a little help easing away from the edge."

"That was a big help. Thank you." Stella surprised him with a quick hug before Darren excused himself to go minister to some of the residents.

Stella wrapped herself in Chase's embrace next. "I am *so* sorry about that."

"Don't be sorry. That was a victory."

She pulled back, stared into his eyes. "What do you mean? I just almost lost it over something I basically invented in my own head." She shook her head, huffed out a sigh. "So ridiculous."

"You don't see it, do you?" He used her favorite line on her, and grinned. "You went through everything this evening—your sister going into labor, losing your keys, the hospital visit, the fire, the misplaced guilt . . . everything—without a full-out panic attack."

She looked around, almost in awe, as if realizing for the first time he was right. "True." She smirked. "I'm still conscious."

He pulled her into another hug—just as a portion of the shelter's roof collapsed.

She winced as fresh ash and soot rained down around them,

but he didn't loosen his grip. After a moment, she relaxed completely back into his embrace. "This wasn't my fault."

"Good girl." He held her tight, despite the memory of her family's disapproval fresh in his mind from the waiting room just hours before. "You're learning."

Unfortunately, he didn't think he was.

~

In all the excitement and horror of the fire the evening before, Stella never got a chance to tell Chase about her conversation with her sister and her mom at the hospital.

Hopefully tonight would be a night to remember, in a way much more positive than last night's version. At least the regulars from the shelter had agreed to come to the Cameo for the grand opening celebration that evening. They'd get free air conditioning and free food, which was a much better gig than sleeping on the streets. Maybe Chase would have found out by now about temporary housing at the theater.

She needed to get going, needed to check on all those things before the party started. Needed to tell Chase her good news.

Hopefully he'd agree with her on that. But if not, at least she knew she had done all she could. The investigators had found the cause of the fire—the ancient water heater in the back of the facility. If the heater could have just hung on a few more weeks, they'd have started construction and replaced the thing with a new one. It could have been avoided.

But the timing was out of her control, and she was learning to let go of the things she couldn't handle herself.

And embrace the ones she could.

That made her think of Chase, of the warmth of his hugs. If she hurried, she might have time to talk with him before the start of the show. At least that way she wouldn't be a wreck all during the movie.

She quickly opened her jewelry box for the first time in ages and removed a large pair of dangly silver hoop earrings. Then she tugged her favorite ring, her birthstone, onto her right ring finger. It felt so foreign. When was the last time she'd worn jewelry?

On her divorce court date, maybe.

She checked her reflection briefly in the mirror. Approached it slowly, like a beast. Touched her makeup bag. Snatched her hand back. Then touched it again.

Maybe just a little. She was wearing a dress, after all. A sleeve-less turquoise sheath the exact color of the fabric samples for the Ninth Cameo. And heels.

She couldn't wear heels without a touch of makeup.

She dabbed on a bit of concealer, amazed at how her eyes immediately lit. Then a few brushes of a neutral powder, just enough to cover the slightly uneven tones around her nose, followed by several swipes of blush. Subtle. Glowing. Nothing too intense.

But her eyes . . . they begged for a bit of attention.

She studied her eye shadow palette. A smoky gray, maybe? It was nighttime, after all, and a big event. She'd worked hard for this.

She'd earned it.

She created a subtle smoky eye with two different shadows and a nearly-black eyeliner, followed with a few strokes of the mascara brush. Her favorite lip-balm and lip-gloss combo was still in her purse. She pulled it out of the side pocket and dabbed the peachy shade over her lips.

She stared at the mirror in shock—and happiness. It was . . . Stella. The old Stella.

But not exactly. Not the made-up plastic Barbie doll she had once seen in the three-way pageant mirror. Not the one whose life centered around dresses and pageants and tiaras. This was someone else. Not the old Stella, but a new one.

She felt beautiful.

She felt safe.

And she couldn't wait to see Chase. Then she grinned.

Scratch that.

She couldn't wait for Chase to see *her*.

ↄℓℓℴ

The Downtown Development Committee had chosen *Breakfast at Tiffany's* as the theater's debut film. Nothing said "vintage" or "classic" better than Audrey Hepburn.

Stella hesitated outside the double doors of the Cameo, held open by two men in tuxedos. Tuxedos? Wow. The Downtown Development Committee had gone all out to make the evening special.

She took a deep breath, smiled at the men, and strode into the brightly lit lobby.

Straight into a bygone Hollywood era. People in ball gowns and cocktail dresses and skinny jeans, sipping champagne from crystal flutes and carrying around red-and-white striped cartons of popcorn. Milling about, pointing out the decorations, the ceiling tiles, the new floor. Noticing the very details she and Chase spent hours perfecting.

Amazing.

She just hoped the shelter's residents didn't feel out of place in the middle of all this unexpected glamour.

"Surprise!" Cowboy Bob was at her side immediately, looking nice in a dark navy suit. He still wore his trademark boots, and she remembered too late she'd wanted to try to convince Chase to wear some too. But that was when she thought the night would be much more casual, much less . . . magical. Hollywood magical.

"What is all this?" She took the flute glass a server handed her, but turned down the popcorn. Not yet. Not until she talked to Chase.

"We figured you guys worked so hard, we'd fancy up the event a little." Bob grinned, obviously proud of himself, then did a double take. "Wow, Miss Stella, you're looking really lovely tonight."

She brushed off the compliment. It wasn't the one she wanted. "Thank you."

Bob turned back to the crowd, waving at someone he knew across the room. "I knew you'd appreciate the extravagance, and well, Chase didn't mind. I told him about it last week, but he said to let it be a surprise to you."

And what a surprise it was. There was even a string quartet in the far corner of the lobby, filling the place with peaceful classical music.

Chase so owed her a dance after all this was done.

"He asked me about putting some cots in here temporarily, to let the residents of the shelter have somewhere to sleep for a bit."

Stella nodded, turning hopeful eyes up at Bob. "And?" He had to say yes. If he didn't . . .

"I don't see any harm in it, if you don't think they'll mess up the place."

"Of course not. They're very careful. We'd have the same rules here as we do at the shelter. And I bet Nancy would come stay with them." In fact, she'd even be willing to come stay herself. Those residents—Dixie, Howard, and the whole gang—had sneaked into her heart. One crazy story at a time, one cupcake at a time.

"That's what Chase said you'd say." Bob chuckled. "Sounds like a plan, then."

She suddenly wanted to see Chase so badly it hurt. "Where is he? Has he gotten here yet?"

And then there he was, halfway across the room, wearing a sharp black suit with a turquoise tie, popping bright against the white of his dress shirt.

Had he matched the Cameo's color scheme on purpose, as she had? Or was it just another case of great minds thinking alike? Her heartbeat accelerated as he strode toward her, his eyes reflecting the same emotions roiling through her stomach. Fear. Joy. Hope. Anxiety.

He reached her side, slipped his arm around her in a hug. His eyes looked her up and down in wonder. "Wow. You look . . . amazing."

His compliment warmed her, all the way to the tip of her toes peeking out from her silver heeled sandals.

Warmed her. But didn't complete her.

She smiled with relief. Mission accomplished.

She was free.

She looked him in the eye. "So do you."

"Thank you." He was still hugging her. She didn't mind in the least. "I have a surprise for you."

"More than all of this?" How could there be more? This was amazing. Already, it was the perfect night, and the movie hadn't even started yet.

"Yep, more than all of this. Just one more thing, actually." Chase's grin was contagious. He held out his hand, and she slipped hers into his palm. "Follow me, please."

Gladly. Anywhere, if he asked.

"I have to talk to you too. Before the movie, if we can." He was walking fast, and she struggled to keep the pace in her heels.

"Sure. Whatever you want." He grinned at her as he led the way to the back corner of the lobby, where a small crowd gathered around a portion of the wall. She couldn't remember what usually hung in that spot, and she craned her head to see around the cluster of heads in front of it. "What is that?"

Chase waited, still smiling, squeezing her hand. "You'll see."

She waited, not as patiently as Chase, and then the crowd parted as several people slowly moved away from the object of interest. She heard murmurs as they passed.

So interesting.

I wonder what the story is behind that piece.

It's so beautiful.

Why couldn't she remember what was hung in that spot? A mirror, maybe? No. Surely not.

And then she saw it.

An upside-down umbrella.

Broken bits made into a whole.

Her umbrella.

Her breath caught in her throat. The room thickened, tightened. She clutched Chase's arm. "How did—why is—"

"Surprise!" Chase said, as if her world wasn't spiraling down around her. "It's your mosaic tile project."

"I know." Her voice came out in a rasp, and she cleared her throat, then shoved back a sip of the champagne she suddenly remembered she was holding. "Why—how?"

"You said you'd already had it framed, so I thought it the perfect place to debut. The grand opening of the Cameo." Chase pulled her toward the picture, and she struggled, attempting to walk backward away from it as he tugged her forward. "Look, I even put a plaque under it, explaining where all the pieces came from."

He had named it too. PUDDLE STOMPER by Stella Varland.

She couldn't move. Couldn't breathe.

His eyes grew more concerned the longer her silence lasted. He cleared his throat. "I know it's a shock. I hope you're not mad."

Mad? She couldn't even breathe enough air to get to mad. Mad was so far out of reach. Mad would be a calming relief. She clenched and unclenched her fists as more people passed by, commenting about the design.

That's different.

Pretty cool, I guess.

Kind of random.

Isn't all art random, though?

They were already criticizing. Already judging.

The room dipped. Spun.

"You broke into my house?" She asked the first question she

could grab, the biggest one that made any sense at all. The worst betrayal.

"No!" Chase frowned, casting a quick look around to see if anyone had heard as he pulled her farther from the throng of people, right up against the frame. "Don't be crazy. I used your extra key."

"My key!" Her voice rose louder than she meant for it to. "I never told you where my extra key was."

"Sorry, I forgot to tell you. You have a key on top—"

"I know where my spare key is." She was downright hissing now, like a snake. Like a poisonous snake, out of control, unable to predict where it might strike next. "How dare you? I trusted you."

He had betrayed her. Had gone into her home without her permission and taken the most private of her accomplishments. The best part of her.

And bared it for all to see.

Chase's face fell. "Stella, I'm sorry. I didn't think. I mean, I didn't intend—"

No. He was lying. "How could you *not* mean this? You knew that project was a secret. *My* secret." It was like her divorce all over again. The lack of trust. The betrayal of what was sacred. The invasion of her privacy and her home.

She pressed her fingers against her eyes, trying to stop the pounding in her head, the voices in her heart.

Her hands came away smeared with makeup.

She stared at the stain. At the umbrella portrait. At her heels.

What was she doing? She wasn't safe. Who was she kidding?

Puddle Stomper. What an illusion.

She grabbed for the frame, but he'd hung it well. It wouldn't budge. "Stella, be careful. Don't—" Chase tried to pull her away, pull her into a hug, but she pushed him away.

"Let go of me." She wrenched her arm free, even though he'd barely even touched her. "Don't even try to fix this. You can't." She felt the tears coming, knew her embarrassment level was about to jump from a three to about a twelve on a scale of ten.

"I've got to go." Yes. She *had* to go. Now. Before she heard what anyone else said about her work. Before the panic took over.

Before she fainted in Chase's arms for the fourth time.

twenty

He was an idiot.

He should have known Stella would react that way. She'd made such progress over the last several weeks, but she wasn't completely healed. No one was. He should have known she'd feel violated.

And then he realized—here he was judging Stella's progress, while his own had grown more than a little stagnant. Wasn't he supposed to be working on *him*? On not rushing ahead and moving too fast and missing the important things along the way? Important things like details about the woman he loved.

Details that weren't even secret.

He *had* betrayed her. She wasn't ready for her art to go public, might not ever be, and that wasn't his choice. It was hers.

He'd rushed and overstepped. Ruined it.

Again.

He stood in front of the umbrella and hated himself.

"Is she okay?" Dixie strolled up to him, an unfamiliar man in a suit and one of those fancy French hats—a beret—at her side.

He was too worked up to even care why her date had a beret. It was Dixie. Anything was normal, while at the same time, nothing was normal. "No. And it's my fault."

"I told her she needed an umbrella."

"Yes, you did." Chase smiled despite himself. "She heard you."

"She heard Him." Dixie pointed to the ceiling and Chase nodded.

"No argument here."

"But where is she now?"

"Upset."

Dixie frowned. "Ladies' room upset, or parking lot to get a cab upset?"

More like, flee her small town and move to another city upset. But Chase had no idea what she'd actually do. "I'm really not sure, Dixie."

Dixie frowned harder.

He pulled out his phone, started typing Stella a text. "I'll ask her but I doubt she'll respond to me."

"She won't. She's too upset."

Well if Dixie knew that, why had she asked?

"I wanted her to meet my friend." She pointed to the man in the beret, who extended his hand to Chase. "Jonas Prince."

He shook it warily. "Nice to meet you."

"You too. I'm an art broker in California. And I'm really interested in this umbrella piece." His eyes roamed the umbrella with appreciation, studying it intently as if searching for hidden meaning. "Do you happen to know if it's for sale?"

Dixie beamed with pride. "My friend."

Chase's jaw dropped. "Um . . ." Why was an art broker at a theater grand opening in Bayou Bend?

"I invited him. My friend." Dixie winked, as if that cleared up everything.

And for her, it might.

"I'd really like to meet the artist, if she's around tonight." Jonas scrawled a figure on a business card and handed it to Chase. "That's the amount I'm willing to offer. Please, text or call me after the movie if you can find her."

Chase's eyes registered on the monetary figure in black ink, and he swallowed.

Oh, he'd find her all right.

He shot off another desperate text message as Dixie and Jonas filed into the theater with the rest of the crowd, then realized he'd have to do this the old-fashioned way.

On foot.

He tucked the business card safely in his jacket pocket, and made his way to the infamous ladies' room. He asked a teenager coming out if she could verify if Stella was inside. She wasn't.

Well, he knew she wasn't in the men's room.

He poked his head inside the back of the theater, but she wouldn't have gone there to hide or cry if she knew the crowd would be filing in any minute.

He headed for the front doors, slipped outside into the warm evening air.

Saw a flash of turquoise sitting on the curb.

"You're going to wrinkle your dress." He sank down onto the sidewalk beside her. She had driven here. Why hadn't she left?

Maybe she wanted to be found.

He touched the business card in his pocket, then waited. Not yet. "What were you going to talk to me about before the show, Stella?"

Her voice was as listless as her form, her legs stretched in front of her. Shoes off and resting beside her on the concrete. "Doesn't matter now."

"Why not? What changed?"

She snapped her head around to stare at him in disbelief. "Are you kidding me?"

There was the spark he'd been trying to ignite. He sat back, waiting for Stella to do her thing. To vent, to process. To come back to the same fact that he kept coming back to.

It was time. Their time.

"You betrayed me."

"But only with good intentions."

She opened her mouth, then snapped it shut. "What does that even mean?"

"It means I didn't mean to hurt you. Yes, I went behind your back. Yes, I technically stole your art. But I know how good that piece is, Stella, what it means. What it could mean to another hurting person here at the theater tonight—to one of the residents at the shelter who doesn't have anywhere to go later." He gestured behind them to the lobby doors. "Everyone is dealing with rain in some form or another. Why shouldn't they be taught how to be puddle stompers too?"

She licked her lips, glossy tonight, and he wondered briefly if they tasted the color they looked. Like fresh peaches. "I didn't think of it that way."

"It's selfish to have a gift and withhold it."

"Are you calling me selfish?"

He shrugged. "Not yet. But up until now, I'd have called you afraid." He paused. "I don't think you're afraid anymore, Stella. I think you're just hiding because you're used to it."

She took the remark well, nodding slowly as she stared into space. Nodding agreement? Or nodding to some unspoken agreement in her own head that would come back to bite him?

He never could tell anymore.

"Afraid of the healing, you mean."

"That's one way to put it." He shifted his position on the curb, nudged her shoulder with his. "This is for you." He handed her the card.

She read the name and the amount, and blinked. "I don't understand."

"Your friend Dixie is apparently best buds with some art broker in California. He wants to buy your umbrella mosaic."

"For that much money?" Stella's eyes bugged. "Is he crazy?"

"Who knows? He's friends with Dixie." He grinned.

But Stella was still too busy freaking out to notice. "He has to be crazy. It isn't worth that. It's just a bunch of broken pieces."

"You're still not looking at the whole." He gently trapped her chin between his fingers, tugged her face toward his. Looked into her eyes. "Look at the whole thing, Stella. I am." He reached up with his thumb and grazed it over her lips. "And it's not broken anymore."

She pulled away before he could consider planting a kiss on those lips and getting an answer to his question about peaches. "If he really means it . . . if he's serious about that much cash . . . I still don't know. That's *my* picture. It's sentimental." She looked at Chase as if he could make the call for her. "But that much money could really help the shelter right now."

It could, indeed. Go a really long way, actually.

"It's your call, Tiara." Chase stood up, reached down, and pulled her to his feet. "What's it going to be?"

❧

The movie was going to end way too soon, much sooner than Stella was prepared for. Not that she'd ever feel fully prepared to give an art dealer a response about so much money. For a piece of her own heart. It felt like a dream.

But if this was a dream, then the shelter's fire was a definite nightmare.

And she was the only one right now who could help.

"More champagne?"

Stella shook her head at the well-dressed server, her eyes glued to the double doors of the lobby. Chase had texted the man as requested, and they waited now for him to join them by the umbrella.

She sagged against the wall, straightened her dress, then sagged again. Tonight hadn't gone nearly the way she'd planned. By now, she was supposed to be snuggled in the theater with Chase, holding hands, sharing popcorn, and dreaming about the future.

Not trying to figure out what to tell a West Coast art dealer about a secret art project that should have never left the light of her apartment.

"Ah, there she is." The art dealer—Chase had told her his name was Jonas—was by her side in moments. "The genius herself."

Genius? Hardly. She shook his hand, allowed the kiss he planted on the back of it, and looked to Chase for help. He smoothly stepped in, asked Jonas what they thought about the movie so far.

Stella looked at Dixie, standing serenely by Jonas, and wondered how in the world she was going to make this decision.

"My friend." Dixie pointed to Jonas and grinned.

"He's very nice."

"And very talented." Dixie pointed at Stella. "That's why I brought him."

She balked. "For me?"

"To meet you. To see your talent."

But how did Dixie even know—well, she'd been the one to give her the umbrella handle piece in the first place. Maybe Dixie knew a lot more than Stella thought she did.

"I know rain, my dear." When she whispered, she seemed normal—downright regal, even. And for once, she wasn't wearing her trademark blazer. "And this umbrella needs to be seen. Too many people are afraid of rain."

"What was your rain, Dixie?" Stella twisted the ring around on her finger, half expecting Dixie to cop out of the question with some crazy, irrelevant remark.

But she didn't.

"I lost my daughter. My only daughter." Her eyes grew remorseful. "It's been so long. But after that . . . I didn't want the life I had anymore. It was scary. Too many unknowns."

Stella nodded, her throat tightening. She knew that feeling. She cast a look at Chase and Jonas, still in negotiations over her art.

And she still had no idea what she was going to do.

"I decided to embrace my worst fear head-on."

"What was that?" With Dixie, there was no telling.

"To live a life of the unexpected." She spread her hands, pulled out the empty pockets of her worn tunic dress. "No money. No home. Just me and God. God and me."

"And what did God do with your unexpected, Dixie?" She didn't doubt He honored such a sacrifice in a big way. Maybe that was why Dixie heard Him so clearly.

"Found my husband again."

Stella shook her head. "What? Again?" Dixie was married?

"We divorced. Before our daughter was born." Dixie rubbed her bare left ring finger. "He didn't know about her. He left."

Dixie had been left too. Wow. "But we found each other again."

Stella frowned in confusion. Surely not Jonas . . . Her eyes flew open. Howard.

Dixie grinned as if she'd heard Stella's thoughts. "Howard."

Talk about Alice in Wonderland and rabbit holes. Nothing made sense. But somehow, at the same time, it all began to be more clear than ever before. "But you're not married again."

"Not legally. Not yet." Dixie pointed to the heavens. "He told us to wait. To date. To fall in love again."

Stella blew out a slow breath, wondering how on earth she was going to absorb all of that at one time. Chase caught her eye from several steps away, still deep in conversation with Jonas, and he held her gaze for a minute before he winked.

Her stomach fluttered, tickled. Like it always did when she was with Chase. She might still be mad at him, but he was right. He'd done this for her.

And look at what jewels had come from the discovery.

Then an image popped to mind, a flashback of another evening with Chase, spent on a bench at the bayou, making up stories about tree bark and umbrellas. "Dixie, did you and Howard ever carve—"

She was already nodding.

Of course she was.

Stella looked at her portrait on the wall. Looked at all the various umbrella pieces, then at the umbrella as a whole.

She couldn't sell it. It was hers. It was Dixie's. It was Chase's.

It was the entire town's.

It was for anyone who ever feared the rain. Who needed to be taught the storm was just an opportunity to play in a different way. To stomp in puddles and splash and own the rain rather than let the rain own them.

To embrace the trials of life, because those very storms they ran from were what finally led to healing.

Total healing.

"My answer is no." Her voice rang solidly across the lobby, effectively cutting off Jonas's rambling conversation with Chase.

Jonas was at her side in an instant. "Then you must agree to commission several other pieces for me. I have many mosaic tile ideas, all right up your ally." He kept scribbling on another business card, his accent thickening in his excitement. "I have an idea for this one about a tree. And another about a—"

"She'll call you. Don't worry." Chase cut Jonas off, handed Stella the card, and offered his hand. "We appreciate your business, sir."

"So we have a deal?" He looked with anticipation back and forth between Chase and Stella.

Chase showed Stella the figures on the card, and she gasped.

Then nodded. "Yes, sir. We sure do." She could keep her umbrella portrait and be able to help rebuild the shelter. It almost seemed too good be true.

"I want to see the end of the movie." Dixie began to tug Jonas away. After quick good-byes, Stella breathed a grateful prayer of thanks to God for allowing Dixie to come into her life.

Crazy? Maybe. But she walked with God a lot closer than most.

Stella slowly turned to face Chase. "I owe you a thank you." She wanted to avert her eyes until she knew his reaction, but she fought the instinct. She was done hiding.

His smile was more than enough reassurance. "You don't owe me a thing."

"Well . . . *you* might owe *me* a dance." The quartet was playing again in the corner, gearing up for the movie that was going to let out any minute. "That's what I thought earlier, anyway."

"Earlier, you mean, before I ruined your night?" Chase pulled her gently into his arms, gripped her waist lightly in his hands. Turned her to the music.

"Pretty sure you didn't ruin it. I almost did. But you—you made it better." She danced in a little closer to him, wrapped her arms around his waist. "Perfect, really."

"I embarrassed you. Made you face your biggest fear. Had you sitting outside in a cocktail dress crying on a curb." Chase winced. "That was perfection?"

"It ended here, didn't it?"

"That it did." Chase wrapped her up tighter, and she almost burst with everything she wanted to tell him. Kat's approval of their being together. Howard and Dixie. Dixie's former lifestyle. Who knew?

God knew.

God knew all along. Knew how He was going to take the most broken of things and turn it all into something beautiful.

And then teach her how to do the same.

Teach her how to love the broken pieces. How to mend them.

"I'm still not whole." She whispered that truth to Chase, who had started humming softly in her ear.

"That's okay, Tiara. Not many of us are." He dipped her backward, then pulled her up until their faces were inches apart.

"I might still have some rough edges." More than a few, probably. But she was getting there.

"I love the broken parts of you. They're my favorite." He turned her again, pulled her in closer as the music rose in crescendo. "Want to know a secret?"

She nodded, pressing her cheek against his, reveling in the rough stubble he never could quite seem to shave off.

He lowered his voice to a whisper. "The broken bits are what make you the most beautiful."

And then he kissed her. Beneath an upside-down umbrella. Ready to catch all her rain. All of their blessings.

Because, as it turned out, most of the time—they were one and the same.

epilogue

"Dude. I'm telling you, it's shocking how many Baby's First Christmas bibs can actually exist in one child's dresser drawer." Lucas's voice held as much awe as someone who was standing before the Eiffel Tower for the first time, or maybe the Grand Canyon.

Stella snorted back a laugh at the conversation between Chase and Lucas as she switched three-month-old Ryan to her other shoulder. "Guys. Come on. At least Kat threw out all the pink ones."

"That's what he thinks, anyway," Kat mumbled under her breath, bumping Stella's arm with the bulging diaper bag as they walked.

Lucas might not believe how overboard his wife could go with the holiday clothing. Stella was shocked at how much stuff it took to go anywhere with a baby in general.

Like for their group field trip to the art gallery in East Texas, where Jonas had hung her latest mosaic tile project for sale. The bag Kat carried, full of wet wipes and extra clothes and containers of formula, weighed more than the baby on Stella's shoulder—even in his full diaper. Stinky diaper.

Ew. She wrinkled her nose and handed Ryan back to his mom. "Your turn, Mama. Do your thing."

Kat winked. "Watch this." She cleared her throat, pouring honey into a voice that was about three shades of Claire Varland. "Hey, super-husband?"

"She's not even trying to be subtle anymore, is she?" Chase fell back from the bantering new parents to join Stella's side.

"Nope. She'll play that 'I already put in my nine months of time' card for as long as he lets her." Stella watched her sister hand over the baby to Lucas, who resisted, then relented at the kiss she planted on his cheek. They ended up heading to the restroom for diaper duty together.

She couldn't look away from the happy little family as they disappeared around the corner, her heart full to bursting with gratitude that they'd come. All together, all willing to put aside the past for the hope of the future, for appreciation of the present. Chase and Lucas were even slowly becoming friends.

Chase followed her gaze to where Kat and Lucas had vanished. "That could be us soon, you know."

She winced. "Not too soon." She wanted a baby. Maybe two.

But she wanted Chase to herself for a little while first.

"Right. Not too soon," he agreed as he wrapped his arm around Stella's waist and guided her once again toward her project hanging under a spotlight—this one a sprawling oak tree with initials carved into the thick trunk. Dixie and Howard's tree. "And that is, of course, assuming you can even quit being a famous artist long enough to have a baby." He nudged her playfully.

She held up her left hand, allowing her diamond engagement ring to catch the light and cast snippets of tiny rainbows across the wall. "Did I ever tell you I'm a fantastic multitasker?" She craned her neck to accept the kiss she knew he'd be offering.

She wasn't disappointed.

"Hey, no making out in front of the new display," Lucas hollered from across the gallery as he and Kat returned from the restroom, baby Ryan in tow.

"Oops." Chase dragged Stella away from her art and toward the fountain in the center of the room instead. "This better?" He planted another kiss on her, this one slow and lingering and enough to make Stella wish they hadn't set their wedding date for January.

"Much better," she whispered, her voice intentionally husky, and loved the glimmer that flashed in Chase's eyes.

"Hey now. You better watch it, Tiara." His grip around her waist tightened. "There's more where that came from."

"Is that a threat—or a promise?" She grinned up at him.

He leaned down and pressed his forehead against hers, a soft growling sound emitting from the back of his throat. "You make me crazy, woman."

She blinked innocently. "Now *that* I believe."

"Me too." Kat sidled up to them, lowering Ryan into the stroller they'd brought but so far hadn't used. "In fact, you're both a little crazy."

Crazy in love. Which totally worked. Stella slid her hand into Chase's, loving the way he automatically threaded their fingers and held tight. Always reading her needs. Always there to catch her.

But not so close that she couldn't falter a little on her own first.

"Not sure if we said this twenty times on the drive over, but just in case—we're really proud of you, Stella." Lucas gestured to the mosaic tile project hanging on the wall and shook his head. "It's still unbelievable."

No kidding. It all still felt like a dream. And the fact that Jonas had commissioned two more pieces from her between now and Valentine's Day. She'd be busy before *and* after her wedding.

Chase's grip tightened on her hand, and she squeezed back, the butterflies in her stomach soaring into overdrive. Not *too* busy though.

"Thank you." She smiled her appreciation at her brother-in-law, grateful for her family and wishing not for the first time that Aunt Mags were here to see her success. She and Kat had both finally achieved their dreams—as untraditional as the method might have been, here they were. With thriving careers and supportive men. With wedding plans and babies and a friendship between the two of them that went far beyond sisterhood.

Not to mention the shelter that had been rebuilt with the proceeds from her first commissioned piece. And she was getting weekly offers for interior design projects, mostly from new clients who saw her work at the Cameo on her website.

Unbelievable, for sure.

They stood silently, the four of them—well, five, counting Ryan—before the tiled oak tree, the massive limbs spreading wide as droplets of blue fell from the cloud-dotted sky.

Stella leaned into Chase's side, smiling as Ryan softly cooed baby talk from the stroller.

The blessings were showering down.

She might never need an umbrella again.

Acknowledgments

$\mathcal{I}$ can't even begin to express how much help I needed during the crafting of this novel. The entire completion of this book was a literal miracle, and I'm forever grateful to the following people:

My super-talented editor, Becky Philpott—you pushed me, and I flew. Thank you, thank you, thank you.

My amazing agents, Tamela Hancock Murray and Steve Laube—I know when you say you'll pray for me, you really do. So thankful for the guidance and wisdom I receive from you both!

My marketing and editorial teams at HarperCollins. My, what big hearts you have! ☺ I just love working with you ladies!

Garry Thompson—thanks for letting me pick your brain for all things construction related. But most of all, thanks for being a great "uncle" to my sweet daughter. I couldn't do this single-mom thing without you and Julie!

Cat—your friendship is such a unique gift! Thanks for cheering me on to the finish line, and for rescuing me. I still have that Coke can.

My parents—I couldn't ask for a better support system or for a better Nana and Papa to our sweet Bunny. Love you!

Audrey—my Little Miss, my Bunnypop, my heartbeat, the Rory to my Loralei. You don't even blink an eye at the phrase "Mama's on deadline" anymore. Let's go to Build-A-Bear.

Jesus—when my heart cracked, broke, and shattered, You carefully saved every single piece. I'm a work in progress, but the mosaic masterpiece is coming. I'm Yours. I love You.

Discussion Questions

1. Stella thought time had healed her after her divorce, but she didn't realize until her interactions with Chase how much healing she still had left to do. Can you relate to this? Why do you think people who walk through life-changing or traumatic circumstances often stuff down the issues needing to be addressed in their hearts?

2. Having finally grown close to Kat, Stella is afraid to do anything with Chase that might push her sister away. Have you ever had to give something up that you wanted, even temporarily, because of love for someone else?

3. Stella's identity was based in her appearance. So when she realized even her beauty wasn't enough to save her marriage, she lost all confidence in herself and forgot who she really was. Have you ever struggled with self-image? Why do you think this is such a common issue for women today?

4. Stella's relationship with her mother was strained the majority of her life because of miscommunication, and because of her mother's perfectionist tendencies—not realizing that she inherited a lot of those same faults herself. What personality

traits have been passed down in your family that you see as challenges to overcome? Why is it so important to communicate well within your family unit and not assume the worst?

5. Stella lost her husband by his choice to divorce, while Chase lost his fiancée to death, which was outside of his control. Do you think the losses and pain are comparable, despite the different circumstances? What unique struggles accompany each?

6. After her divorce, Stella's counselor suggested she get involved with a charity to get her focus off her problems. Have you ever volunteered at a homeless shelter or for another good cause? If so, did you experience that similar perspective shift?

7. Stella's passion for art became her therapy. But despite her talent, she was afraid to let anyone know her secret. She didn't want to be exposed because that meant potential rejection again. Have you ever kept a secret or skill hidden away out of fear of rejection or failure?

8. Stella was drawn to mosaic tiles because of the hope of being able to create something beautiful from something broken. What is your favorite form of art?

9. After her divorce, Stella occasionally experienced panic attacks when she felt trapped or anxious, or when the stress and pain from memories began to build. Have you ever struggled with panic attacks? How did you find relief?

10. After his fiancée's death, Chase was determined to live life full-speed and not miss a thing. He never took time to slow down and appreciate what he had before him. Do you or does someone you know struggle with going-going-going? What are the benefits to taking a breath and pausing to be in the moment where you are?

An Excerpt from All's Fair in
and Cupcakes by Betsy St. Am

One

There was more to life than vanilla buttercream. Or at least, Kat Varland used to believe so.

Once upon a time, she created magic with flour and sugar and eggs. With cinnamon and nutmeg and vanilla. Every measured cup was instinct, every whisked ingredient inspiration. Baking held promise, potential. Power.

Now she could make the simple cupcakes filling the Sweetie Pies shop display in her sleep—in fact, one morning after she'd been up late experimenting with new recipes, she very nearly had. But Sweetie Pies had a reputation, and the owner, her aunt Maggie Mayfield, kept that even more sparkling than the tiny sugar crystals adorning the otherwise plain desserts. *Fancy* didn't have a home at Sweetie Pies, and neither did *gourmet*. Or, as Aunt Maggie usually put it, *weird*.

The display lights caught the clear sprinkles and the miniature cakes seemed to wink, as if knowing Kat could do so much more.

were just begging her to try. Who was satisfied with
ity, anyway?

't.

or to the shop swung open, letting in a burst of crisp
. Kat straightened on instinct, like a child caught day-
in school. The bell on the knob tinkled as a smattering
n leaves followed Aunt Maggie inside, skittering across the
d-white checkerboard floor. Little did they know they'd be
ut within the hour—or else.

'm back, finally." Her aunt attempted a smile as she bus-
behind the counter to join Kat, but the lines around her eyes
eared to be etched deeper than usual, sabotaging her effort.
uesday afternoon already. Did I miss anything Saturday? My,
at I hate being sick." She tied her trademark white ruffled apron
round her round waist, but it didn't fit nearly as snugly as it used to.
She glanced around the spotless work area. "Where's Amy?" Then
she must have caught sight of the leaves in her peripheral vision,
because she frowned and marched toward the storage room door
before Kat could catch up—figuratively or literally.

"Amy left early to study for her test since business was a little
slow." Not that it was ever technically busy, but at least having
Amy's part-time, high school help allowed Kat some days off and
picked up the slack when Maggie was sick. Which was more and
more frequent these days.

Kat sidestepped to make it to the storage room first, unwilling
to let her aunt, who clearly didn't feel much better than she had
last weekend, do more labor than necessary. Maggie was her mom's
much older sister in the first place, and now that she'd been sick so
often, Kat wanted to protect her strength even more than usual.

"I'll handle the leaves, Aunt Maggie."

Her aunt didn't argue, which proved how poorly she must still
be feeling. Once again, Kat fought a burst of guilt from her internal, ongoing frustration over her aunt's baking restrictions. Maggie

owned the shop—not Kat. It was her choice what products they sold, and if Maggie liked vanilla, strawberry, and chocolate, then vanilla, strawberry, and chocolate it was.

Even if Kat had just perfected a raspberry lemonade torte recipe that could very likely bring world peace.

She grabbed the broom and began to sweep the leaves back to their rightful place outside as Maggie opened the register and riffled through receipts. "Don't worry, you didn't miss much Saturday. We had the usual stream of customers, is all."

Kat could predict them like clockwork. Right on schedule, Heidi Mann had shown up for the single chocolate cupcake she routinely bought each Saturday as a reward for making it through another week of teaching preschoolers. And then there was the group of stay-athome moms, including Kat's friend, Rachel Cole. As usual, they wanted to distract their husbands with chocolate cupcakes so they wouldn't notice the piles of laundry they hadn't been able to get to all week. There was Mrs. Lucille, Kat's father's secretary at the Bayou Bend Church of Grace where he pastored, who needed her weekend indulgence. And of course, Kat's best friend, Coach Lucas Brannen, with his standing order of two dozen strawberry cupcakes for his high school football team's weekend practice. If Kat had been given free cupcakes every weekend in high school, she might have gone out for a team too.

Most of the other Bayou Bend regulars seemed to suddenly realize the shop would be closed for two days and had to rush in for their favorites before they missed their chance.

But Kat knew the business could be so much more than what appealed to the regulars. She had so many ideas for marketing that got lost in the oppressing aura of routine at Sweetie Pies. Ideas that could expand Maggie's business, allow Kat to bake the recipes of her heart, draw in customers from surrounding counties—the works.

But not with strawberry, chocolate, and vanilla.

Kat lowered her voice, nearly muttering to herself. "Nope.

Didn't miss much at all." She swept harder, as if attempting to scrub the black off the black tiles. As if effort and hard work made a difference. As if one could create color from darkness.

"That's nice, hon." Maggie didn't seem to be listening anymore, immersed in the contents of the register from that day's sales. But Kat knew she didn't really care about profits. As long as she kept her shop in beloved Bayou Bend, Louisiana, and made enough to cover her bills, Maggie was content. No, she probably just didn't want to think about the doctor's appointment she'd had that morning, and if she wasn't telling, Kat wasn't asking.

She'd learned two things since coming to bake for her aunt almost five years ago. One—less is more, unless sugar is involved, and then you should be exact. And two—privacy equals respect. If you don't allow someone their privacy, you don't respect them. That perhaps explained why Kat was twenty-six years old and still in the exact same spot in life since graduating college with her bachelor's degree in Business. No one asked her what she wanted.

Her ex-boyfriend, Chase, surely hadn't asked when he suddenly decided he preferred blondes.

But that was a lifetime ago.

She worked a rhythm with the broom, watching the leaves swirl back into the late afternoon sun, wishing she could capture their exact color in her piping bag. She could make an autumn harvest cupcake, maybe apple and cinnamon with an apricot icing and a sugared date on top, or a caramel apple cupcake with generous dustings of brown sugar and—

"Hey, watch out!"

The warning came a split second before she swept straight into a jean-clad leg. The stick of the broom bounced off the victim's shin, and bristles coated the unsuspecting navy-and-gray athletic shoes with clods of dirt and dust. Very familiar athletic shoes. She couldn't hide her smile as she lifted her gaze to meet Lucas's. "Hey, your shoes are dirty."

"I guess that's what I get for keeping the boys late at practice." His eyes, the color of the cocoa she mixed into the chocolate cake batter every morning, warmed, and she knew he didn't really care. Lucas wore those shoes to every team practice, and they'd long since seen better days. His gaze darted over her head toward her aunt, and he leaned in and lowered his voice. "Do you have any of the good stuff in the shop today?"

A red flush heated Kat's neck, and she pretended to smack him with the broom. "Hush. My aunt will hear you."

"Good. Then maybe she'll realize there are some people in Bayou Bend who enjoy *weird* cupcakes." He winked, his broad shoulders filling the door frame of the shop.

"Not weird. Gourmet." The retort flew off her lips before she could process that he was teasing. How many times had she held that reply in around her aunt, wishing she could just speak her heart?

She glanced over her shoulder, but Aunt Maggie must have gone into the kitchen. Come to think of it, Kat probably did have some rejected recipes in her file at home that could only be defined as weird. But how did you know unless you tried? That was the best part of baking—getting to experiment and figure it out as you went. If it didn't work, you just poured out the batter and started over.

There was always a second chance.

Lucas must have taken her sudden silence for insult. "I'm teasing, Kat. I would never speak ill of Maggie. The town loves her."

Rightly so. She was a wonderful woman—just not a visionary. "I know. She's . . . vanilla. A staple. Classic." Sort of like everyone else in her family in Bayou Bend. Between her father's pastoring, her mother's committee heading, her aunt's cupcake shop, and her younger sister's pageant wins, Kat was the only expendable one in the family.

Figured her family, who had options, didn't even want out of Bayou Bend, while she remained stuck. Permanently.

"Nice observation." Lucas crossed his arms over his chest, the sleeves of his dark gray T-shirt pulling across his biceps as he studied her. He leaned against the door frame. "So what flavor are you?"

Her breath hitched in her throat as she met his steady gaze. She knew right away what Lucas's flavor would be—dark chocolate with cherry ganache filling. A deep, bittersweet taste that lingered long after it was gone.

But no—she didn't know her own.

She drew a tight breath, eager to break the unintentionally heavy turn of the conversation. "Hey, I'm so busy baking for you on the side . . . I don't have time for taste tests."

Lucas might be her best friend, but he didn't need her dumping her self-analyzing psychobabble on him. After all, he came for cupcakes. She should save the rest of her drama for Rachel. Somehow, even while knee-deep in PTA forms and stacks of baby onesies to monogram, her friend always found the right thing to say when Lucas couldn't.

Or when the topic was *about* Lucas, which had been happening way more than it should lately.

Kat gestured with the broom inside the shop, ignoring how sweaty her palms suddenly felt against the handle. "You coming in, or are you just going to stand here and let more leaves inside?"

Lucas stepped fully inside the shop and the door swung shut. "Actually, the guys were especially hungry Saturday, so I didn't get my strawberry cupcake then. Going to need a replacement."

"You should have told me. I'd have snuck you one at church on Sunday." It wouldn't be the first time she'd passed him a bag of homemade treats after the morning welcome or in the parking lot. Lucas was a great sport about tasting her experiments. Only once in the two years she'd started daring to bake her own recipes had he spit one back into his hand.

Apparently licorice and Greek olives didn't go together after all.

"I should have. I think I was still in denial that I'm this addicted." Lucas rubbed his jaw, his five o'clock shadow scratching under his fingers. His eyes roved over the display behind her, though Kat wasn't sure what he was expecting to see. It hadn't changed in the decades since her aunt had opened Sweetie Pies. "Too bad you don't have any of those raspberry things you made me try last week. That one had medicinal qualities—should be a prescription for a bad day."

"You're corny." She swatted at him, but the compliment attempted to fill the nooks and crannies inside—the hollow spots that still whispered fear into her heart. At least if nothing else, she knew Lucas loved her creations—all of them, exactly for what they were. Not only the simple cupcakes filling the racks inside Sweetie Pies, but the ones she baked from her heart. Of Lucas, she was certain.

It was the rest of the town that had her guessing.

"Not corny. Cheesy." Lucas grinned, then his expression sobered. "Seriously, Kat, my mission is to make you less humble. You're good."

She clutched the broom like a life preserver, simultaneously wishing his words didn't carry so much weight and wishing he would keep speaking them forever. "Good, huh?" She swallowed, her throat dry. She wanted to think so. But she wanted so much more than good. She wanted great.

She wanted to be seen.

"Very good. You just need to believe it already."

He reached out and ruffled her hair, and the feeling of fullness leaked away at the brotherly gesture. The best friend line blurred more often than she cared to admit, but Lucas was good about yanking her back from the edge of that particular precipice when she veered too close. Even if it stung—and even if he was unaware how often she teetered.

Hopefully, he'd stay that way.

She moved to put the counter between them, pausing to lean the broom against the far corner of the wall. Under the framed photo of her sister, Stella, from last year's win, tiara perched snugly atop a mass of perfect curls. Blonde curls.

But Chase wasn't Stella's fault.

No, putting all her hopes and dreams into a very flawed man was completely her own fault—though maybe she wouldn't have done so if she'd imagined she'd ever have a chance of more than a friendship with Lucas.

With a resigned breath, she took her place behind the cupcake counter. "So what'll it be?" She tugged on a clear glove and let her hand hover above the trays of desserts. "Oh, strawberry, right?"

She knew what she'd choose.

But dark chocolate cupcakes with cherry ganache filling were definitely *not* on the menu.

❦

For someone used to calling plays for a living, he sure was seeing a lot of penalty flags.

He'd actually ruffled her hair. Good grief, it was a shock he hadn't gone ahead and slapped her on the shoulder or called her "buddy." Lucas wrinkled the white pastry bag in his hand and tried to keep his expression neutral as he waited for Kat to close out the register so he could walk her home. He'd apparently spent way too much time on the field with his football players and not enough time dating.

Though he certainly spent more time than he should imagining what it'd be like dating Kat.

Talented, beautiful, completely oblivious Kat.

Lucas pulled his cupcake from the bag and took a bite, less from impatience and more from needing to mask the flood of embarrassment over his fumble. He'd just placed a bid on Roger Johnson's old farmhouse on Highway 169 and the accompanying ten acres of land—land he pictured strolling with Kat. Curling up under the live oak that spread its massive limbs halfway to heaven and back. Tossing a football to their children over the wheat-colored fields every autumn. Maybe planting their own pumpkin patch.

He wasn't going to see his dream come true by ruffling a woman's hair. Kat Varland needed a hero, and heroes didn't act like immature high school boys every time they came around. What was wrong with him?

He couldn't help watching her work behind the counter. Hmm. Maybe he was addicted to more than the cupcakes.

"All done." She shut the register drawer with a solid click, reminding Lucas it was time to stop staring at those shiny brown strands of hair still tousled from his idiocy. "Let me just check on Aunt Maggie and see if she wants me to take the deposit tonight or if it's okay to wait until tomorrow." She disappeared into the back, where Maggie's office was tucked off the corner of the small but efficient industrial kitchen.

As the swinging door shut behind her, Lucas dropped the uneaten half of his cupcake back into its sack and folded the bag closed. The strawberry cakes were great, but man, Kat could do better. *Did* better, in fact, every time she went home, put her hair up, and baked to a background of Sinatra. How many times had he watched her do just that over the years, while he sat on the walnut bar stool and offered suggestions, prompting her to take it to another level?

Somewhere along the way, one batch of cupcakes along the way, he'd tripped right over the label of Best Friends they'd worn the majority of their teen years and landed upside down on the field of Love.

And suddenly, he had zero plays to call.

"Ready?" She pushed back into the front of the shop, shouldering the strap of her oversize turquoise bag. He'd teased her last year about the size of her previous purple one until she bought the bigger turquoise just on principle. He wisely kept his mouth shut after that, in case he pushed her into toting around an actual suitcase for a purse. He knew when to prod and when to shut up, when to encourage her to take it one step further and when to dial it back. No one knew Kat better than him.

Some days he wondered if he knew her better than she did.

"Lucas? You ready?" The pinch of her brow reminded him she'd already asked that question once. Ready? Well, no. But *yes*—the main problem being he had no idea if she was.

He straightened his shoulders. "I'm always ready." His trademark retort rolled easily off his lips, bringing a smile and erasing the confusion that lingered on her expression. He offered his arm. "To the bank?" He hoped not. He hoped he could walk her straight home and she'd invite him in and they'd cook stir-fry or something else delicious.

"No, I'll take the deposit tomorrow. They're about to close, and Maggie said it wasn't worth the rush."

Win. He struggled to hide his victory smile as she came around the counter and linked her arm through his, exactly the same as they'd done a hundred times over the years. But nothing with Kat was the same anymore. It was exhilarating and frustrating all at the same time.

She craned her neck to peer up at him, her wide blue eyes inquisitive. "I have some stir-fry at the house. Want to stay for dinner?"

Another win. "Only if you promise to make dessert."

She tried to plant her free hand on her hip, but the giant purse got in the way and nearly swung her off balance. She lifted her chin, apparently in an attempt at indignation instead. "Hey, now. I'm not cooking dinner *and* dessert after baking cupcakes here all day."

He tugged her toward the door, laughing. "Then I'll handle the stir-fry. You just do what you do best."

Her responding smile made him want to offer to do the dishes too. "Nice play, Coach."

She had no idea.

The story continues in *All's Fair in Love and Cupcakes* by Betsy St. Amant.

About the Author

Betsy St. Amant lives in Louisiana with her young daughter and has a heart for sharing the amazing news of God's grace through her novels. A freelance journalist, Betsy is a member of American Christian Fiction Writers. When she's not reading, writing, or singing along to a Disney soundtrack with her daughter, Betsy enjoys inspirational speaking and teaching on the craft of writing.

⁂

Visit her website at www.betsystamant.com
Facebook: BetsySt.Amant
Twitter: @betsystamant